BA

Stella Gibbons was bo
went to the North London Collegiate School
and studied journalism at University College,
London. She then spent ten years working for
various newspapers, including the *Evening
Standard*. Stella Gibbons is the author of twenty-
five novels, three volumes of short stories and
four volumes of poetry. Her first publication
was a book of poems, *The Mountain Beast*
(1930), and her first novel *Cold Comfort Farm*
(1932) won the Femina Vie Heureuse Prize in
1933. Amongst her works are *Christmas at Cold
Comfort Farm* (1940), *Westwood* (1946),
*Conference at Cold Comfort Farm* (1959) and
*Starlight* (1967). She was elected a Fellow of the
Royal Society of Literature in 1950. In 1933 she
married the actor and singer Allan Webb. They
had one daughter. Stella Gibbons died in 1989.

ALSO BY STELLA GIBBONS

STELLA GIBBONS

# Bassett

VINTAGE BOOKS
London

Published by Vintage 2011

2 4 6 8 10 9 7 5 3 1

First published in Great Britain by Longmans, Green & Co. Ltd in 1934

Vintage
Random House, 20 Vauxhall Bridge Road,
London SW1V 2SA

www.vintage-classics.info

Addresses for companies within The Random House Group
Limited can be found at: www.randomhouse.co.uk/offices.htm

The Random House Group Limited Reg. No. 954009

A CIP catalogue record for this book
is available from the British Library

ISBN 9780099529378

The Random House Group Limited supports The Forest Stewardship
Council (FSC®), the leading international forest certification organisation.
Our books carrying the FSC label are printed on FSC® certified paper.
FSC is the only forest certification scheme endorsed by the leading
environmental organisations, including Greenpeace. Our
paper procurement policy can be found at
www.randomhouse.co.uk/environment

MIX
Paper from
responsible sources
FSC® C018072

Printed and bound in Great Britain by Clays Ltd, St Ives PLC

TO
AUNTIE RU

## NOTE

I OBTAINED the information about badger-watching from Mr. Arthur R. Thompson's charming and informative *Nature by Night*, a model for books of its kind.

No persons or institutions mentioned in this book are intended to represent existing persons or institutions.

" I never mean to marry ; it is so disagreeable."
(THE HEIR OF REDCLYFFE.)

" But still, you will be an old maid—and that's so dreadful ! "
(EMMA.)

PART I

# CHAPTER I

THERE is a simplicity which comes from living too much in the world, as well as a simplicity which comes from living out of the world.

Miss Hilda Baker was neither a wise nor a sophisticated woman, although she had earned her living for twenty-one years in the office of a small firm that sold paper patterns in the West End of London, and had bought her clothes at the big stores, and spent some of her three pounds fifteen shillings a week in visits to famous London theatres.

Museums and galleries, dens and historic haunts of peace lay all about Miss Baker, yet she lived as narrowly as a mouse in its hole; and went backwards and forwards between her lodgings and the offices in Reubens House, Strand, for twenty-one years without much change being made in her dark ordinary face.

She dressed neatly and badly in ugly little hats and ugly little necklaces. She took great interest in her clothes, saying that in business it was a good investment to be smart, and that a woman owed it to herself to look nice; each season she planned the wardrobe that she would buy, and never bought it but much enjoyed the planning.

Nor had Miss Baker wistful secret longings for beauty and love and for a richer, wider life. She had never walked in a beautiful garden that was not a public garden nor kissed a man on the mouth with all her heart.

3

She never thought about God and she was vague about the facts of sex and reproduction. She lived in one room, for she was an orphan ; and she had few friends.

Sensitive and intelligent people will refuse to believe that Miss Baker could be happy. However, Miss Baker was happy.

She had managed to save one hundred and eighty pounds in twenty-one years out of a salary which had risen from eight shillings a week (her parents had been living in those days) to three pounds and fifteen shillings a week. Then, when she was thirty-eight, an uncle who was a grocer died and left her two hundred pounds, and she at once put it into her Savings Bank account and it rather worried her because she did not know what to do with it.

Three hundred and eighty pounds seemed an enormous sum of money to Miss Baker (and indeed, it is quite a large sum, if one stops thinking snobbishly about money, and realises for what a long time such a sum would keep one in roof and food).

" It quite worries me," said Miss Baker to her friend Miss Worrall, the head pattern-cutter, as they sat one Saturday afternoon, a few weeks after Christmas, in the Charing Cross Lyons' Corner House, after having been to see Ronald Colman at the Tivoli. " It's a lot of money, three hundred and eighty pounds is. I feel I ought to be doing something with it, somehow."

" It wouldn't worry me," said Miss Worrall, who was very envious of Miss Baker's three hundred and eighty pounds and thought that Miss Baker was not properly grateful about it. " I think it's lovely. Why, just think, Hilda, if you were to be sacked to-morrow, you could live on it for months."

" I'm afraid of it Dribbling Away," said Miss Baker

ominously. "You know. A bit here and a bit there and before you know where it is, it's all gone and nothing to show for it. Like it is sometimes when you go out shopping."

"You might go abroad," suggested Miss Worrall.

"I've been. With one of those Lunn's tours. Eight years ago. You remember. I can't say I liked it much, either. Geneva was all right, but the other places looked so foreign. There wasn't anything to do except look at things. I wasn't sorry to get home. East, west, home's best. Besides, Lily, if I went abroad I should lose my job. Jobs aren't so easy to get, nowadays."

"They might keep it open for you. You've been there longer than anyone."

"Oh yeah?" said Miss Baker, putting a penny under her plate for the waitress. Miss Worrall put twopence. She earned four pounds fifteen a week; and graded her charities accordingly.

"Well . . . they might. You never know."

"Yes, I do know. They wouldn't. Besides, I don't want to go abroad. Wasting a lot of money on looking at things."

"You might buy a little car."

"I can't drive one. No idea how they work."

"If it was me, I should buy clothes," said Miss Worrall, in a soft, gloatingly voluptuous voice. Miss Worrall already wore more clothes, and beads too, than one would have thought it possible to arrange on one smallish woman, but this did not prevent her from wanting to buy more. "Lily has a lovely taste in clothes, but a bit too dressy for me," Miss Baker would say of her friend.

"Oh, well . . . I must think it over, that's all," said Miss Baker. They parted without having decided what

was to be done with the blessed money : Miss Baker
darted into the Tube which took her back to Camden
Town and Miss Worrall went back to Catford, where
she lived with an old mother with whom she quarrelled
and argued from morning till night.

Miss Baker continued to think it over for the next
few days.

What went on in Miss Baker's head, however, can
hardly be described as thinking. A series of exclamations
which took the form of " Oo, that's an idea ! " and,
" Ooo, I could never stand that," went in at one end of
her mind and out at the other, but she decided nothing.
She kept on thinking over the blessed money until it
was a regular nuisance : and she stood in a draught which
whined through the hot cutting-room, and that gave
her neuralgia : at least, she said it was neuralgia, but
Miss Worrall (who liked exciting and disagreeable things
to happen) said that it was probably a decayed tooth right
up at the back of her head, and that she ought to go to
the dentist and let him see to it ; he would probably say
that it had to come out. Miss Worrall hoped that he
would, though of course she did not say that she hoped
he would.

So one evening Miss Baker asked if she might go
home an hour earlier because she had to go and see
the dentist, and having got permission, off she went.

She was not feeling at all cheerful.

It was partly because her face ached, and partly because
she felt she ought to do something about that blessed
money, and she could not make up her mind what :
and partly because it was a nasty evening : so black, so
despairingly sunk in winter that all the shop windows
and streets seemed lit up in defiance of the night, as
though the sun had gone for good, and the world was

to be artificially lit for evermore. Also, it had been raining all day; and that made umbrellas and heavy coats smell stuffy and horrid, and everybody pushed snarlingly for the buses and tubes.

" Glad to get home, and no error," thought Miss Baker crossly, hanging from the roof of the carriage.

Her dentist lived in Camden Town, on a corner quite close to her lodgings : she got there punctually, and sat in the waiting-room with one or two other cross and frightened people, waiting her turn and looking at the jokes in *The Humorist*. There was a copy of a sixpenny paper called *Town and Country* on the table with the others, and Miss Baker picked it up, hoping that there might be a tale in it. She always enjoyed a tale.

There was no tale; but there was, among other features, a column entitled " The Helping Hand."

Underneath this heading there were given details about partnerships, described by a lady who signed herself " Phœbe," and who conducted this column from the safe retreat of an obscure side-street in Holborn. She it was who put, by letter, untrained but willing spinsters in touch with energetic gentlewomen with some capital; and set them off on a glorious career of breeding chickens in St. Ives or running an arts and crafts shop in Newcastle-on-Tyne. Nor did she ever hear (except sometimes indirectly and long years afterwards) whether the partnership had been a success, or whether the ladies had slit each other's throats within the first half-hour of meeting. She sowed ruin and rapture among the readers of *Town and Country*, but herself remained (perhaps wisely) invisible and anonymous.

Miss Baker read " The Helping Hand " with her mind running vaguely on that blessed money; a partnership of some kind had been one of the things she had thought she might do with it.

None of them sounded interesting until she came to No. 7, which said :

> " A reader who owns a large furnished house near Reading would like to meet with another lady, with some capital, with the object of turning the house into a guest house.  My reader assures me that the house is within easy reach of Reading by bus and suggests that some of the students at Reading University might be glad of the chance to live in beautiful country outside the town.  The house has a large garden.  If any reader is interested will she please write to Box E. A. P., care of this office, and I shall be delighted to forward letters to my reader living near Reading."

Miss Baker, at the end of her reading, raised her head and threw a bold and steady stare round the waiting-room.  Several people were looking at her, in the hopeless way people do look at other people in dentists' waiting-rooms, but she did not mind a bit. She tore out the paragraph, folded it up and put it in her bag, and replaced the copy of *Town and Country* on the table.

Everybody felt shocked, but nobody had the spirit even to raise their eyebrows, and Miss Baker's turn being next, she was shortly borne away by the dentist's maid and seen no more that night.

But when she got home (for there was no more the matter with her tooth than neuralgia, which she had caught from standing in that draught) she wrote to the lady who lived just outside Reading.

It was all done on the spur of the moment.  Something seemed to come over her, as she said to Miss Worrall afterwards.  It had to be.

She told the lady living near Reading that she had some money but she did not say how much. She said that she liked the idea of the large garden and the students. She added that her mother had kept a boarding-house in Wandsworth for·thirty years, and suggested that it might be her mother coming out in her, and left the other lady to make all plans.

After the letter was written and posted, she felt more comfortable in her mind : she had begun to do something about that blessed money.

"There'll be lots of others writing. There always are, for those things," said Miss Worrall, on being told about it. "You'll never hear from her, don't you fret your fat."

"Hundreds of other people haven't got three hundred and eighty pounds (well, it's really three hundred and seventy nine and sixteen shillings, now, I took out four shillings when I was a bit short at the end of last week) to invest," said Miss Baker. "I bet you I hear from her."

And so she did, a week later, on another dark evening when she had hurried home to nurse her neuralgia, which refused to go away.

The letter came by the nine o'clock post. Miss Baker, sitting over her little gas fire mending her stockings, heard the postman's knock and went down into the hall to see if there was anything for her.

One letter lay on the mat, looking very white in the dimness of the narrow hall, and Miss Baker picked it up and saw that it was, indeed, for her.

"Ah, 'e don't forget you. One of the faithful kind, 'e is," said her landlord Mr. Peeley, who.had come up from the depths to see if there was anything for him. "When's it going to be ?" Mr. Peeley had made this joke for fifteen years, this being the length of time that

Miss Baker had lived in Mr. and Mrs. Peeley's house.
Miss Baker replied that it would be either the fifth of
November or the first of April next year, and went
upstairs with her letter to her room.

She stood under the faintly popping gas, and looked
at the envelope for a little while, before she opened it.
It was a thin grey envelope, addressed in a thin grey
writing.

The postmark was " Bassett."

She had never heard of such a place : but as she did
not know the writing, she concluded that it must be
from the lady near Reading, and opened it with a feeling
of excitement.

> " The Tower,
> > Crane Hill,
> > > Bassett, Bucks.

DEAR MISS BAKER,

After much *earnest* thought I have decided that
yours is the most *suitable* letter I have received as a
result of the notice which appeared in *Town and Country*.
*I am sure that the house could be made a success.* It is not
damp. Some of the letters were *most unsuitable*. There
was one from a Mr. Arthur Craft. Frequent buses,
but rather a *long walk* to them ! ! ! It is so difficult, in
these days, to know what to do for the best. Mr.
Craft suggested a *Club*. I have a geyser and there are
beautiful views. Perhaps we could lay out the tennis
court again in the field behind the house. We are six miles
from the station, but the buses run past the bottom of
the hill. I thought that we might take Indians (not
Negroes of course) as guests. Is afternoon tea included
do you know ? I believe not. Perhaps you will let
me know what you think. Or perhaps it would be
better if you came down one Saturday. It is easier to
go to Reading and take the bus. I could meet you,
if we decided to meet in Town, at half. past three in
the Clock Department. Perhaps you would suggest
a day, if Saturday doesn't suit you. (This Saturday

is no good for me I am afraid, as I have my W.I.) But
of course, they close on Saturday afternoons. Will
you let me know, by return if possible, whether you
will meet me as arranged.

Yours faithfully,

ELEANOR AMY PADSOE.

P.S.—It is on clay soil, but some of it is on chalk.
*Very healthy ! ! ! "*

Miss Baker read this three times, in some bewilderment.
If a person had earned their living in London for
twenty-one years, they acquire a kind of rat-like neatness
of behaviour. They can skip quickly from place to place,
pop in and out of tea shops, board buses and make
sharp little plans which are carried out rat! tat! as
deftly as an automatic ticket machine pops out a ticket
at Leicester Square tube station. The more obscure and
ordinary the person, the more necessary it is that they
should acquire this rat-like deftness. They may be
simple as daisies mentally, but physically they are deft
as rats, flicking themselves neatly in and out of their
London holes.

Miss Baker was like this. So she was much taken
aback by Miss Padsoe's letter, and muttered to herself
that she could not make head or tail of it. A dark
thought flitted across her mind. Was Miss Padsoe all
there ?

" Anyway, I'd better go down on Sunday and chance
it," she decided, wondering what Miss Padsoe's W.I.
was. " If she's out, she's out, that's all. It won't do
any harm to go, and it will make a nice change for me."

So she took out a writing-pad, and wrote firmly to
Miss Padsoe, announcing that she would come down to
see her next Sunday morning, but that Miss Padsoe was
not to bother about giving her any lunch, because she

would have a big breakfast and would not want any.
(She said this for manners' sake but did not really mean
it.) They would talk over everything when they met.
She stamped the letter (Miss Baker was one of the people
who always have stamps) and popped out to post it.

The night was colder than it had been when she came
home at half-past six. A pure cold smell was wandering
through the London streets, drifting between the smell
of smoke and wet stones ; it was the smell of the snow
that was on its way from the steppes of Russia. The
papers promised England a snowy week-end.

Miss Baker posted her letter, and popped home to
bed in her narrow creaking bedstead. She had arranged
four old cushions on top of the mattress to make it
softer, but they did not : and when she put out the gas,
the street lamp's light fell on her wall through the
curtains with a disturbing glare. But she was used to
these things, nor did the melancholy clanging of the
distant trams keep her awake.

In Buckinghamshire the leaves slowly whitened with
rime under the moonless sky. The wet pavements of
London frosted over. The snow was coming.

# CHAPTER II

She caught a train on Sunday morning, which got into Reading just before eleven. The snow had come, and the fog too : and the streets in London were masked with greasy yellow paste, and gritty layers of dirty white lay along ledges and sloping roofs.

There was the same sight in Reading, as Miss Baker came out of the station into the Sunday hush ; greasy, mean streets, dirty snow. The loudest sound was the bells pealing for church. This sound is only melancholy when it is heard at six o'clock on a winter's evening ; when it is heard on a Sunday morning, across the snowy roofs of an unfamiliar town, it is a pleasant sound, making quietness more quiet. Miss Baker was quite enjoying it, in spite of her neuralgia.

" Can I get a bus to Bassett ? " asked Miss Baker of a taxi-driver who was standing outside the station admiring a gorgeous, enormous, bright-blue sports car which was parked beside his own taxi.

The driver looked at Miss Baker.

" No buses to Bassett on Sundays," said the driver with relish. He saw that Miss Baker was no good for a fare, in her worn coat with ratty fur on its collar and her pot of a hat, but there was no reason why he should pretend to be sorry that no buses ran to Bassett on Sunday.

" Oh," said Miss Baker. " That's cheerful, I must say. Then how do I get there ? "

"Taxi," said the taxi-driver.

"I see," said Miss Baker. The worst had come. She would either have to take a taxi out to this Bassett, or else go home again and come on a Saturday. It was true that she had fifteen shillings in her bag, and three hundred and eighty pounds in the bank, but one hundred and eighty pounds of that money was there chiefly because she had known when not to take taxis. Why! she had only been in a taxi four times in all her life. And country taxis were not like town taxis. They were more of a Car, as you might say. They usually had a Fixed Rate. She ought to have found out about the buses before she came, but she had taken it for granted that there would be Sunday buses to Bassett. There were Sunday buses in London.

"Bassett's a out-of-the-way place," embroidered the driver, reading her soul. "Right up in the 'ills. Good ten miles away, it is. Difficult place to find, too."

"Could one walk there?" asked Miss Baker with dignity.

The taxi-driver smiled a large, patronizing, masculine smile.

"Not in this weather you couldn't. Why . . . there's drifts up in them woods . . . dozens of feet deep, they are. 'Ard going in this weather."

He made the beechwoods of Buckinghamshire sound as perilous as the Everglades : and so they might have been for all Miss Baker knew. To what kind of a place had she come that had snowdrifts dozens of feet deep, places right up in the hills, and no buses on Sunday ?

She said no more for a second or two. She was trying to summon courage to ask the taxi-driver how much he would charge to drive her out to this Bassett. It would probably be an awful lot. It would probably be ten shillings.

In the pause a young man had come out of the station carrying a suitcase, and followed by a girl and a porter wheeling a little trunk on a truck. The young man began to heave the case into the gorgeous car, while the girl stood silently watching him, close to the open door.

" You won't take the trunk, sir ? " asked the porter.

" Why not ? There's plenty of room for it . . . only for god's sake don't scratch my beautiful new leather," said the young man ; and the porter, much shocked but admiring the wild ways of the rich, packed the little trunk into the back seat of the car.

" How much is the fare to Bassett, then ? " asked Miss Baker severely, at last.

The taxi-driver drew himself up. Now he would show pot-hat just where she got off. She annoyed him . . . standin' there with her teeth stickin' out.

" Twenty-five shillin's return," lied the taxi-driver, loudly and cruelly.

" That seems a lot," said Miss Baker, who was now furious. She was sure it could not be as much as that. It was not in nature to believe that such a fare existed.

" Not for that journey, it isn't," said the taxi-driver, also becoming suddenly furious. " It's cheap, lady, that's what it is. Twenty miles there and back, in this weather."

The young man had overheard all this. He had waved the silent girl into the seat next that of the driver, and was just going to climb in beside her, but now he looked across at Miss Baker and the taxi-driver, and then came over to them, saying agreeably :

" Can I give you a lift ? I'm going into Bassett."

" Oh, I say ! Well, that *is* kind of you," cried Miss

Baker. " But are you sure it's really all right ? Not takin' you out of your way or anything ? "

" No, it's quite all right. I live there. In you get . . . do you mind sitting with the trunk ? I think there's room for both of you."

Miss Baker cried that she did not mind at all, and that it was ever so kind of him ; and then she stowed herself away beside the little trunk, and pulled up her coat collar to keep the cold wind away from her neuralgia, and off they went.

Now Miss Baker really began to enjoy herself. If there was anything she did like, it was a bit of luxury and comfort. Her life was an affair of twopences and ninepences, baked beans on toast and thrice-mended shoes, thrice-breathed air and fifth-hand opinions. The price of this great humming car would have kept anyone in baked beans on toast (had anyone so wished to be kept) for life.

They went over a bridge where the grey river slid between fragile leafless willows, and soon they were out in the country. None of the three said a word. The young man never talked while he was driving, the girl was naturally a silent girl, and Miss Baker was too busy trying to breathe through half an inch of imitation beaver fur. She was feeling so pleased at having got the better of that taxi-driver that she had forgotten to wonder how she would get back from Bassett to Reading.

Once the young man glanced round at her, and smiled ; a beautiful, mocking yet kind smile that was also a little wistful. It is difficult to get all these qualities into one smile if you try to do it, but the young man's nature was a complex one and it managed the smile for him without difficulty.

" Cold ? " he asked.

Miss Baker thanked him ever so, and said that she was not. She screamed at him that it was pretty country and must be lovely in the summer. The girl did not look round. " Stuck up," thought Miss Baker.

In addition to that rat-like deftness of behaviour which we have already talked about, persons who earn their livings in large cities by perching precariously on the ends of little jobs, like birds on a bough, acquire a bird-like suspiciousness of everybody. They are always desperately afraid of being cheated, mocked at, and snubbed. Miss Baker was not afraid of being mocked at, because she had no sense of humour, but she was very suspicious indeed of being cheated and snubbed. An attempt had already been made to cheat her. An attempt was now being made to snub her. She took stock of the silent girl's hat and back, and decided that her mackintosh was one of the fifteen and elevenpenny kind, and her hat one of the eight and elevenpenny kind. What right, then, had such a hat and such a mackintosh to snub anybody ?

All she could see of the girl, as she turned sometimes to look out of the window into the snowy depths of the silent woods, was a pale curve of plump cheek and an upward curl of short dark eyelash.

" Nearly there now," said the young man cheerfully. " Not cold, are you, Miss Catton ? "

" No, thank you," replied Miss Catton.

(" She's too fat," thought Miss Baker. " Not the type I admire. Wonder who she is. Not his style at all, I should have thought. She's poor. He's rich. Must be something in it.")

The car seemed to have come a long way from Reading, flying along narrow roads between tall beeches, occasion-

ally crossing main roads on which the snow was·threaded
with car tracks.  Sometimes snow fell from the branches
far down in the heart of the white and silent woods, and
Miss Baker saw the released branch sway back into place.
There was no other movement in the woods ;  everything
was solemn, silent, far away.

Miss Baker was not at all sure that she liked it.  What
would it be like to live in such a quiet place ?  Oh well,
nothing was settled yet, and she need not stay if she did
not want to ;  she had a good job, as jobs go, and money
in the Savings Bank.

"Any particular part of Bassett do you want ? " asked
the young man.  The car was climbing the steepest hill
it had yet attempted.

"Well, if it won't take you out of your way too much,
I really wanted The Tower, Crane Hill.  Miss Padsoe's
house.  But please don't trouble if it's out of your way.
I can easily Ask," and Miss Baker glanced all round into
the silent woods, as though they were full of convenient
peasants whom she might Ask.

"No bother.  It's just at the top.  This is Crane Hill.
I'll drop you just at the gates, shall I ? "

"Thanks ever so, if you will."

·  The top of the hill was crowned by another wood,
but before the car reached this, the young man stopped
it in front of a pair of closed white wooden gates.  On
them was painted " The Tower."

It was very quiet when the young man had shut off
the engine of the car.  The three sat still for a few
seconds, listening to the silence, with their breath
going up into the frosty air.  It was certainly very quiet
indeed.  "Exquisitely quiet," thought the young man,
who loved music better than anything in the world,
and, next to it, silence.

"Enough to give you the creeps," thought Miss Baker, beginning to disentangle herself from the inside of the car.

"They're rich," thought the silent girl. "Much, much richer than I thought they'd be. I'm not going to like it."

"Here you are," said the young man, opening the door of the car for Miss Baker. "You'll be all right now, won't you? Good-bye."

"Good-bye, and thanks *ever* so. I don't know *what* I should have done if you hadn't been so kind."

The car moved on, and just as it left Miss Baker, the girl looked round and gave her a brief and nervous smile.

Miss Baker did not return the smile.

"Afraid of crackin' her face, I should think," muttered Miss Baker.

There she was, left outside The Tower, seemingly alone in the middle of snow-buried Buckinghamshire. She looked over the white gate into a drive that curved away between snow-covered hedges of laurel and rhododendron. It was a shadowy drive, even on this clear grey day filled with light thrown up from the snow; tall firs and beeches made it shadowy. The house could not be seen. The evergreen bushes and the still, thick trees shut it off completely from the road. On the opposite side of the road to the gate was a screen of trees, through which, far off, more snowy hills could be seen.

Miss Baker's neuralgia had started again and she was feeling hungry. Addressing herself as Hilda my girl, Miss Baker remarked that this would not do, and stepped briskly up to the gates.

They parted at her touch, and she stepped through them.

The shadow of the old firs fell on her; it was very cold in their shade. Suddenly, high overhead in the tower that gave the house its name a light, high-pitched bell quickly struck twelve. The sound made the firs, the motionless snow-burdened laurels, the quiet air, seem lonelier.

The short drive ended in a screen of firs, and there was the house. She looked across a large lawn, covered with untrodden snow. On the opposite shore of this lake of snow stood the large house of red brick, a round tower at one end. Beds full of withered plants lay under the low windows facing the lawn and on the same side of the house as the tower, and just beneath it there was a small conservatory: Miss Baker could see the long fingers of palms spread against the frosty glass.

She found the front door at the side of the house, set in a deep gloomy porch over which grew snow-covered ivy.

There was not a sound; the large house might have been full of dead people and Miss Baker, being a Cockney, had not noticed a track of footprints in the snow, leading away from the house down the drive. They were long, narrow, elegant prints; they proved that a lady had left the house earlier that morning, and had not yet returned.

Miss Baker pulled an iron bell-handle.

It came rushing out to an alarming length in her hand, but she did not hear it ringing inside the house. She stood there waiting, with her collar pulled up about her neuralgic jaw, and her plain sallow face pinched with cold, feeling cross but not nervous: it needs imagination to make a person nervous, and that Miss Baker had not got.

"They don't hurry themselves, I must say," she

muttered after waiting two minutes; and she pulled again.

It was unfortunate, for even as the bell slid back she heard firm steps crossing a stone floor, and a blurred figure appeared behind the birds and leaves on the stained glass panels.

The figure paused. It seemed to be peering at Miss Baker before opening the door, and Miss Baker, having no friends who lived in great clean houses with maids to open the door, did not realise what a very queer thing this was for a parlourmaid to do. It seemed quite ordinary to her. It was what she would have done, if she had lived in the depths of the lonely country and someone had come on a dull snowy morning and loudly pulled the front-door bell. You never know, these days.

# CHAPTER III

WHEN at last the door was opened it was done so very slowly, as though the figure peering through the dull reds and blues of the stained glass were reluctant to make the movement. Miss Baker looked up into the cold suspicious face of a handsome girl in cap and apron, framed in the dark crack between open door and door-frame. It was a pity she was so much taller than Miss Baker. Miss Baker at once became furious—at this, at the slow opening of the door, at the girl's suspicious stare.

"Good morning. I've come to see Miss Padsoe. She's expecting me. I wrote to her Friday, to say I'd come to-day. I'm Miss Hilda Baker. Is Miss Padsoe in?"

There was a pause.

"No," said the girl at last. "Miss Padsoe is at church. I don't think she was expectin' you. She never said so."

She had not moved the door a fraction. A whiff of roasting meat suddenly drifted out to Miss Baker from the darkness of the hall, and reminded her that she was hungry. She became more furious still. Her face went dark and wrinkled, like a marmoset's in a rage.

"She's expecting me all right. I'll come in and wait," she said firmly, and put one ill-shod foot on to the doorstep.

. The girl was forced to move back because she did not want Miss Baker on the top of her, but she did it

22

very slowly and she never took her stare off Miss Baker's
face.

" It's very funny.   She never *said* anythin' about anyone comin'."

" P'raps she did, only you forgot," said Miss Baker
tartly, still advancing remorselessly, yet so slowly that
no onlooker could have sworn to it that she was advancing at all ; and at last the girl was forced to stand sullenly
aside and let her come into the high, dark, quiet hall.
An old clock ticked loudly in a corner, but otherwise
there was silence.   All the doors opening into the hall
were closed, and it was unpleasantly cold.

" How long will Miss Padsoe be ? "

" I couldn't say."

The girl had the most disagreeable of all voices except
a downright wicked one ;  the gross vowels of the peasant
overlaid by the whine of the mean streets in a large
country town.   Miss Baker merely thought she sounded
saucy.   She had no room in her life for sauce ;  she was
always on the lookout for it, she tracked it down like
a trapper in the ways and back-answers of Muriel, the
little errand girl at the office ;  she could smell it a mile
off, and she smelt it now.

" Well, it doesn't matter.   I'll wait," she snapped,
and looked round expectantly.   She was not going to
wait in this icy hall.

The next instant she was being shown into the most
beautiful room she had ever seen.

She did not know that she was walking into a perfect
specimen of an Edwardian drawing-room, which at
once reflected and embalmed, like a mirror and a crystal
in one, the happy thoughtlessness of an era gone for ever.
Yet so it was.   No period is so lost as the Edwardian.
The state of society that made it possible is more dead

B

than the prehistoric ferns pressed into streaks of coal :
that exquisite silliness summed up in the name " Dolly "
can never return.

Miss Baker was so impressed by the size and beauty
of the room that she was quite awed.  She sat on the
edge of a chesterfield covered in faded rose brocade, with
her feet looking very plain indeed on a white bearskin
rug, and stared up at the girl, who stared back, with
less confidence.  A lady would have said " That will
do."  Miss Baker did not know what to say, so she just
stared.

It seemed to her that she and the girl just stared for
an exceedingly long time.  It made her go quite hot,
it was so queer.  The room was so quiet, and the beautiful
snowy landscape framed between the rose brocade
curtains at the windows made it seem quieter still, and
the narrow, dusty green leaves of the palms in their pots
looked curiously neglected and forgotten.

Miss Baker was not used to sitting in silence with
another person : she had never done such a thing in her
life, and she and Miss Worrall would have felt what they
would have described as " funny " had a silence fallen
between them for longer than five seconds during one
of their visits to the Corner House.

But at last, with a flouncing, bustling movement, the parlourmaid turned and went out of the
room.

Miss Baker was glad.  Now she could have a good
stare round.  She would have had a good stare had
anyone been there, but it would have been difficult to
do so while talking, and she could have a really good
one while she was alone.

She sat quite still, but her eyes moved rapidly in her
face like busy little beetles, running over the large gilt

harp that stood by the piano, the broad wreaths of pale
flowers on a carpet the colour of a giraffe's belly, the
white wallpaper covered with alternate dull and shining
stripes, the festoons of pale blue and rose-coloured
flowers which decorated the wallpaper just below the
ceiling.

The walls were covered with watercolour landscapes
in wide gilt frames, with painted fans, with tiny beaded
shoes, with mandolins and guitars caught up by faded
yellow ribbons. A procession of silver elephants, the
biggest as large as a tea-cup, marched across the mantel-
piece. A procession of tiny brown jugs, the biggest as
large as a bumble bee, marched just behind them, in
front of the clock on which writhed gilt figures engaged
in sacrificing somebody.

It was a room whose furnishings should have been
completed by the sound of sweet silly voices, the
crackle of a fire and the tinkle of a piano and the
smell of freshly made tea. But all was chill, airless and
silent.

A large painting of a pretty young woman in a white
evening dress, with a rose in her bosom and one in her
hair, hung over the mantelpiece.

"Her younger sister. Dead or married," thought
Miss Baker, when the beetles in the course of their
tour came to the pretty young woman.

She was shocked to notice that the procession of
elephants badly needed a polish. The little jugs
did, too. The whole room was not exactly dusty,
but it would have been, had it been a room in
London.

Miss Baker suddenly shivered, and then muttered to
herself that a goose was walking over her grave. She
seemed to have been there a very long time.

Suddenly, high overhead and sounding muffled and far away, the same light bell struck the half-hour.   Miss Baker was startled to see a figure pass the window ;  and a moment later the door of the drawing-room opened and in fluttered a lady.

# CHAPTER IV

At the first glance Miss Baker and Miss Padsoe took at one another, three difficulties arose.

To begin with, they disliked one another immediately. Miss Baker thought Miss Padsoe looked as balmy as her letters, if not balmier; and Miss Padsoe who had been vaguely hoping that Miss Baker was not going to look like *her* letters, found that she did. A dreadful little woman, thought Miss Padsoe, clenching the fists inside her worn gloves and thinking desperately with one side of her mind that she *could not* make proposals about money to this person, while the other side was skirring vaguely off in thoughts about God making everything all right for her some day and what she would like to put into the garden for next summer.

The second difficulty was the fact that if this interview had been taking place thirty years ago, Miss Padsoe would have been interviewing Miss Baker as a prospective house-parlourmaid, and Miss Baker would have been m'ming her. The War, a bared sword, lay between 1903 and 1933, but Miss Padsoe had never quite taken in the War, somehow. She missed the m'ming. ·

The third difficulty was that neither Miss Baker nor Miss Padsoe knew anything about money at all (thanks to their respective menfolk, who had regarded money and sex as the two great unmentionables which could not be discussed in front of ladies) and each was passionately determined not to be cheated by the other.

Neither had any idea about money in her head. " Let
*her* mention it first " was the prowling, cautious
thought of each.

Miss Baker had a fourth difficulty of her own ; she
suddenly found that she had never seriously thought of
going into partnership with Miss Padsoe at all, and
woke up with a bang, as it were, to find herself in a
bit of a hole.

Miss Padsoe was all vague smiles. She hid her
determination not to be cheated, her shame, her dislike,
except for the steady, bright, peering looks she gave
Miss Baker every now and again. She did not know she
gave them : but people were beginning to comment on
those sudden, wild stares. They had grown more
frequent, people said, in the last two years. They were,
in truth, given by Miss Padsoe's frightened mind,
suddenly scrutinizing reality through her two eyes. But
there was no doubt they made her look very queer
indeed.

" Oh, how do you do, Miss Baker. I'm so sorry. It's
the walk up the hill, you know. Always a little difficult
in the winter, and then I walked with Mrs. Schofield . . .
her rheumatism. I do hope you haven't been waiting
very long ? Such a cold day—but *really* rather pleasant,
don't you think ? I like a bite in the air. And then
the Vicar wanted to speak to me about dates
clashing for the girls' entertainment and the W.I.
dramatic " (a flash of recognition on Miss Baker's face,
and she nodded vigorously and smiled. There it was
again . . . but what *could* it be ? Something churchy,
no doubt, if the Vicar was mixed up in it) " and that,
of course. . . . It all takes time. I do hope you found
your way safely ? We are *very* cut off in winter. Quite
a little colony, I always say. And Mrs. Schofield has

had such an interesting letter from her son in Persia.
(Persian oil, you know.) "

Suddenly Miss Padsoe ceased her flow of words and
stopped fluttering about the room. She paused right in
front of Miss Baker and fixed her with a very intent,
considering sort of smile, with her head slightly on one
side and her blue eyes bright as stars in her thin faded
face. Yet somehow the smile and the eyes did not seem
really to see Miss Baker at all, and for a second Miss
Baker felt quite queer. The dark thought that she had
had on first reading Miss Padsoe's letter, flitted again
across her mind.

Miss Padsoe was shockingly thin. Her clothes were
like no clothes Miss Baker had seen for years, except in
old photographs of past Ascots, reprinted in the *Daily
Mirror* on Gold Cup Day. Then there was the light
film of dust on the procession of marching elephants,
and the slow suspicious way in which that servant had
opened the front door and stared at her.

It was certainly a funny sort of house. She would
think a very long time before she parted with any of
her three hundred and eighty pounds.

And yet . . . there was something about Miss Padsoe.
She was getting on in years, yet she put Miss Baker in
mind of a little kiddie. Miss Baker wondered furiously
if anyone were giving Miss Padsoe any sauce. Was anyone cheating her or snubbing her ? What about that Mrs.
Schofield ? Miss Baker knew how ready people were to
cheat and sauce and snub . . . none better. It was
true that people were frequently surprised when you
flew out at them and accused them of sauce, cheating
and snubs. They said the thought had never entered
their heads. But that was only their artfulness. You
never knew, these days. You had to keep your eyes open.

She did not quite know how to reply to Miss Padsoe, so she said (her voice quite hoarse from disuse):

"I'm all right, thanks. I've only been waiting half an hour. A young fellow gave me a lift from Reading in his car. Lovely big blue one. A regular monster."

"Oh, that would be Mr. Shelling. He goes into town every day on business. There are no buses on Sunday, of course. Such a nuisance. We thought of a round robin. . . . Will you come upstairs? I think lunch . . ." A shadow came down over her face, but it passed.

At the mention of lunch Miss Baker's spirits rose. She trotted upstairs after Miss Padsoe into an enormous dusty bedroom full of texts and cold north light, and combed her hair in front of a dusty mirror and longed to stoop and pick threads off the carpet and set about her with a broom. Miss Padsoe hung up her outdoor clothes in a wardrobe as big as a cottage, showed Miss Baker into a vast dusty bathroom with ill-cleaned taps, and finally sat down opposite her at the head of a table twelve feet long in a dark, heavily furnished room over-looking the garden. Even the snowlight did not fling any radiance into that room, and its cheer was not increased by a number of portraits (" mostly old colonels, and looking as cross as two sticks," thought Miss Baker) which hung on the walls.

Miss Baker did not get enough lunch. Two plates came up, with a tiny slice of burnt beef on each, one small potato and a dab of cold cabbage. No bread was handed. The silver, which Miss Baker did not know was Georgian and beautiful, needed cleaning. "The follow" (as Miss Baker and her brother used, when they were small, to call pudding) was a flavourless lemon jelly. No cheese, and no biscuits. And they drank icy water poured from a jug which Miss Baker did not know was of Waterford glass, and she would not have cared if she had.

The sullen parlourmaid waited on them : and towards the end of the jelly Miss Padsoe, who seemed to have been trying to make up her mind about something for the past few minutes, swallowed resolutely, and turning to the girl, said :

" Winifred, may we have a small fire in the drawing-room before cook goes out this afternoon, please ? Only if there's time before she goes out. . . ."

" I will ask cook, m'm. She may have gone out already."

Miss Baker had no idea how people who lived in houses the size of The Tower spoke to their servants, nor how the servants were supposed to reply, but she did know Sauce when she heard it, and she heard Sauce in the girl's answer. She became furious. She forgot she was still hungry, and that she and Miss Padsoe had been having the queerest and most unsatisfactory sort of conversation, in which Miss Baker stated facts and opinions in brief sentences and her hostess answered with another set of entirely different facts and opinions in very long rambling ones. She forgot that neither guest houses nor money had been mentioned, and that she was worried about how she could get home that evening.

The instant the parlourmaid's round bottom had bustled itself out of the room she leaned eagerly forward across the table and hissed hoarsely :

" I say ! You shouldn't let her, you know. She'll only take advantage. You ought to tell her off."

A dreadful blush rushed up from Miss Padsoe's neck to her thin cheeks and bony forehead, and burned there as though she had been dipped in fire. She lowered her eyelids and moved her thin lips convulsively, but she did not reply, and Miss Baker, with unusual delicacy, felt that perhaps she was Butting In, so she said no more. She remembered that people in books often changed the subject by asking the embarrassed person if they had been to any plays lately, or else by admiring the view. Somehow, she was sure Miss Padsoe had not been to any plays lately, so she decided on the view.

"Lovely view you've got here," she said loudly, looking out of the window. "Must be ever so pretty in the summer."

"Oh . . . oh, yes. It's delightful in the summer," said Miss Padsoe eagerly. "We have a lime avenue, you know. One can make tea. Or the French do, I am told. Such a quaint idea, don't you think? *Tea* made of *limes*. Bassett is down there, quite in the hollow. You cannot see the village at all from here. The limes are a screen, too. A perfect screen. I have often thought one might start a little business, you know. (Of course, quite privately.) Selling the lime tea in bottles. Or perhaps it does not keep. . . . The French are so much better at these things than we are. . . ."

"I was wondering where Bassett was," said Miss Baker, quite relieved to find Miss Padsoe could give a straight reply to a straight remark. She was beginning to doubt it. "Is it a pretty place?"

"Oh, very. The church has double gables on the tower. Very rare, you know. Then there is the inn. Mr. Stokes keeps it. It is quite historic, and has a lovely garden. Of course, we are about twenty minutes from the village. All downhill . . . or uphill, of course, if you happen to be coming from the village."

She rose, and led the way into the drawing-room.

No fire had been lit. The room was chill as a tomb :
Miss Baker's fingers were blue and Miss Padsoe's cheeks
were violet with the cold, but as she saw the black grate
they burned again with the painful flush.

However, she said nothing. They sat down side by
side on the faded rosy sofa, and Miss Baker looked at
the gilt clock and saw it was a quarter to two, and
not a word said yet about money or guest houses ; and
outside, although the afternoon was still young, the
snow-mantled countryside had begun to assume an air
of quiet, an unchanging greyness, that meant dusk
would be here in a little more than an hour ; and how
in the name of all that was maddening was she going
to get back to Reading ?

No gently bred person, Miss Padsoe was thinking
despairingly, ought to be brought to this pass. I can't
begin to talk about it. It's her money. I've hardly
anything. It's like begging. I can't bear to think of
other people, strangers, coming to live in the house.
And she looked wildly round the room, seeing it as it
was thirty years ago, with young men and women
grouped laughing round the piano. Things are just
getting worse and worse. I'm frightened. Things were
all right, only lonely, and suddenly I found they were
dreadful. I don't believe the summer will ever come
again. That's silly, of course. I feel faint : it must be
the cold. I can't ask her. I can't.

So there they both sat, dumb and uncomfortable.

But at last Miss Baker's common sense came to the
rescue. She decided it was no use the two of us sittin'
here lookin' as though we were stuffed owls, and she
said boldly :

" I think this house could be made into a very nice
boarding-house, if it was brightened up a bit."

Miss Padsoe, though the blush returned, at once brightened up a bit herself.

"Oh . . . oh, do you? Oh, I am so glad. Now what do you think about the Hindus? Of course, I would not for one *instant dream* of admitting negroes. My dear father, I am afraid, would have disapproved terribly even of the Hindus. But after all, Hindus are *not* like negroes, are they? A higher type. My cousin, Emily Parkinstone, who did a good deal of missionary work, always said so. *Quite* different. And we need not *see* them except at meals. And of course so many of them are good at tennis, too. That would be a great advantage, of course."

"Why?" asked Miss Baker, quite stunned by this sudden invasion of Hindus.

"Well . . . if we decide to re-do the tennis court at the back of the house. It would be such an attraction, don't you think? And the bathroom, of course . . . yes. There would be *much* to do. When could you come?"

And she fixed suddenly upon Miss Baker another of those intent, disconcerting stares which seemed an attempt to gather her wits in from wool-gathering, and yet seemed to see nothing at all.

Miss Baker quite jumped in her seat. This was going a bit too fast; it was worse than the Hindus.

"Well . . . to tell you the truth, I hadn't quite made up my mind to come yet, at all," said Miss Baker awkwardly. "After all . . . it's a big step to take, isn't it? I mean, once it's done, it's done. I thought I'd like to see the house and talk things over a bit first, and think them over too, come to that. For instance, I don't quite know if I like the idea of those Hindus. I can't abide blacks."

"Oh . . . but we need not have them. It was only a suggestion. They seem so much easier to *get* than white people. I suppose it's because there are so many of them in India. *Millions*, I believe . . . and of course some of them *must* come over here, and what seems a *little* to them there seems a *great* many to us . . . but we need not have them, if you would rather not."

Her face had been dashed, on hearing Miss Baker's cautious speech, from an almost childish brightness and hope to extreme disappointment. Her lips moved uncertainly. Miss Baker could not be quite sure, for the light was fading, whether there were tears in her eyes but she rather thought that there were.

This was dreadful. The woman must be balmy. It was not like talking to a grown-up person at all; it was like talking to a great silly kid. And here it was, getting on for three o'clock, and getting darker every minute, and she was surer every minute that she did not want to be Miss Padsoe's partner, and how on earth was she to get back to Reading? And she was starving hungry; might not have had any lunch at all.

It was all maddening, simply maddening. And the most maddening thing about it all was that she simply could not help feeling sorry for Miss Padsoe, great softie though she might be, alone in her large dusty house with that rude cat of a servant. She felt that she could not desert Miss Padsoe, now that matters had gone so far. If she did, Miss Padsoe would simply be cheated and sauced right out of existence.

Miss Baker looked desperately out of the window at the slowly darkening landscape.

"Is there a bus I can pick up anywhere near here that'll take me into Reading?" she asked bluntly, trying not to notice Miss Padsoe's quivering face. "I'm afraid

I must be getting along. You know how it is, don't you ? I've got to be at work at half-past nine to-morrow, and it'll take me a good three hours gettin' home to London."

" There is no bus to *Reading* on Sunday," said Miss Padsoe carefully. " There is a bus to *High Wycombe*, which leaves Fan's Green at half-past four. I am afraid it means a little *walk*, over the fields, you know. So tiresome. But you will be in *good* time if you leave here at a quarter-past three. I always do."

" Where's High Wycombe, then ? Can I get a train there to London ? " demanded Miss Baker ruthlessly, remorselessly, still refusing to see Miss Padsoe's silly, sad, disappointed face.

" Oh yes, *plenty*," cried Miss Padsoe eagerly. " I am not sure of the *times*, but I am sure that there are *plenty*."

Miss Baker did not for one second believe that there were plenty of trains from this High Wycombe. There might not even be a bus from this Fan's Green or wherever it was ; Miss Padsoe was not the kind of person who gave one confidence in her statements about trains and buses. However, there was no one else to ask unless she got hold of that rude cat of a servant and asked her, so she would just have to chance it.

" P'raps you could put me on my way," she said. " I think I ought to be getting off soon. It's getting dark and I don't want to lose meself." She gave a high mirthless titter ; she was too cross to laugh good-naturedly.

" Oh, but I will come with you as far as Fan's Green. Of course. I shall be glad of the walk. And then the way over the fields is rather rough. The snow. . . . Even on *ordinary* days it is rough. I do not feel the cold."

Miss Padsoe had got up while she was speaking, as

though she were ready to be off that minute, so Miss
Baker had to get up too, and follow her hostess upstairs.
She supposed they were not going to have any tea. How
she did long for a good strong cup of hot tea with thin
bread and butter and a thick wedge of Dundee cake ; her
mouth was watering as she put on her hat in front of
the glass. Miss Padsoe had snapped on the electric
light, which was shadeless, and filled the room with a
cold, desolate glare, and made the windows suddenly
blue with evening. Miss Padsoe looked very fragile
and old, more like a scare-the-birds than a woman as
she carefully wrapped a mothy old bit of fur round her
thin neck, and Miss Baker wondered if she ought to
come out in this bitter cold, and said as much.

" Oh, but of course. . . . I do not mind at all. I
love a bite in the air."

Just as well you do, thought Miss Baker, for it's about
all you do get to bite here, I'll bet my bottom dollar.
She wondered what had become of the rest of that joint
she had smelt cooking. No doubt the rude cat and cook
had done themselves proud on it. Trust them.

Downstairs they went, quietly as a couple of ghosts,
across the hall, and out through the dark porch into
the cold quiet air of the early evening.

And the moment the heavy door had closed after
them and the shadow of the house was left behind, and
they came out beside the open lawn covered with snow,
Miss Baker felt better. It was not so dark as she had
thought ; it was quite a nice afternoon, and there was
plenty of time to catch the bus after all, and if she didn't
buy herself the largest steak and chips at Paddington
Refreshment Room that could be had, her name was not
Hilda Baker. The very thought of it made her feel
better still.

Miss Padsoe seemed to be feeling better, too. It somewhat disconcerted Miss Baker to walk beside a lady who walked so fast that she was almost running, and whose lips moved silently as though she were carrying on a conversation with herself, but at least she had stopped looking as though she were going to cry. In the fading light her face under an awful old toque of black fur looked almost like the face of a young girl; perhaps her light quick movements helped to give her this strange air of youth.

Half-way down the steep snowy hill Miss Padsoe stopped, and gazed away through a screen of beeches on the left.

" There is Bassett," she said. " You can just see the church gables. Double, you know. Very rare."

Miss Baker looked down into the broad, shallow valley.

A village lay screened in leafless elms, whose black boughs were stretched against the rising snowy slopes. Not a light shone from its curtained windows, except one that sparkled strangely like a fairy jewel in a cottage directly opposite the low stone wall of the churchyard. Miss Baker could see the lamp that made this sparkling light behind the curtains, and someone moving about in the low room. A wide, snow-covered road ran between the churchyard wall and a building that Miss Padsoe said was the inn; there was a row of cottages to the right of the church, all dark-windowed, but with plumes of smoke going straight up into the lowering sky. Not a soul was to be seen. The fairy light, the unwavering smoke, and the twin gables of the church tower that were so unusual as to surprise the observer's eye with a sensation almost of their being alive were the only noticeable things that evening in Bassett.

Its miniature beauty and its heavenly solitude were not the kind of qualities that either Miss Baker or Miss Padsoe would have mentioned, though Miss Baker, because it was a country landscape, felt bound to say it was pretty, and did.

We have lived here for nearly a hundred years, thought Miss Padsoe, staring away across the valley with her heart feeling as though it were breaking. My grandfather saw this view, and my father, and my beloved mother. And her face looked more than ever like the face of a haughty, miserable young girl playing at being sixty years old.

She began to move on down the hill, Miss Baker gingerly following, and the woods slowly rose on either hand and hid Bassett.

It was difficult for Miss Baker to believe she had really seen the place : it had slipped away so like a pretty dream. But lord ! it looked lonely ! Miss Baker, then and there, comfortably made up her mind that nothing on earth would persuade her to come and live here, especially when she considered how queer Miss Padsoe was, and how badly those elephants needed a bit of elbow-grease, and what a lot of her money would have to be spent on The Tower to make it a really nice boarding-house. Catch her ! Why, Miss Padsoe would dribble the money away in no time. She looked just the sort. Or she'd invest it in some old speculation and lose it. Still, even if she weren't going to live here, she was glad she had come just for to-day. It made a change. It was all experience.

They were now crossing the road at the bottom of the valley, making for a path that crossed another large hill on the opposite side : it was much darker here because of tall elms lining the road, but Miss Baker, glancing at her companion in response to an indefinable sound from her, could see that she was again on the verge of tears. Gawd stone me up a gum tree! thought Miss Baker, much alarmed and annoyed, What's the matter *now*?

Miss Padsoe was saying, in what Miss Baker called to herself a " put-on voice," " Well, it has been so pleasant to meet you, Miss Baker. I am so sorry we could not have come—have come—have come to some arrangement about the guest house. You see——"

Pause. Gulp. Miss Baker said nothing. She was furious. Just as she had made up her mind nothing could persuade her to go into partnership with Miss Padsoe, here was the wretched woman re-opening the business, instead of just shutting up about it. Making Miss Baker feel as though she had let her down. Not that she had.

" You see, I am rather unfortunately placed, Miss Baker. Of course, I know that in *these* days—*since that dreadful war*—one is really lucky to have a roof over one's head, as they say, is one not? And of course, I am luckier than some. . . . When I think of poor Augusta Warrender . . . so dreadful. All alone in that little room, and no one knowing about her, and she used to be the dearest girl . . . so bright and gay. I am more fortunate than poor Augusta. But somehow there seems *less* to manage on, every quarter, and I sometimes think Winifred and her mother do not manage as well as they might. The bills seem rather *large* for so small an eater as myself. Really, I eat very little. The merest morsel does for me. You see——"

Another pause and gulp. Miss Baker said nothing. She was feeling the snow seep through her shoes, and being furious.

" You see, Miss Baker, I have never been *trained* for any kind of work. For any way in which I could earn my own living, I mean. My dear father wanted his girl at home with him, so of course it was a duty and a pleasure to do what he wished. And then he died . . . and things have been so different, ever . . . ever . . . ever since."

" Haven't you got any relations, then ? " said Miss Baker, when the silence coming after Miss Padsoe's trembling, rapid voice became unbearable.

Miss Padsoe did not reply immediately. Then she said, quickly and very haughtily :

" My two brothers were killed. In the War. I have only a cousin, and her son. . . . They live in Newcastle. I seldom see them. So you see . . ."

The lump in her throat ached as it had once ached when she was seven, and had lost her mother in a crowd at a garden party.

" So you see, it is very necessary for me to find some way of—of—increasing my income."

Miss Baker positively burned to ask her how much a year she had, but did not quite dare. Still she said nothing.

" That was why," gabbled Miss Padsoe, so low and so fast that Miss Baker could scarcely hear, " I hoped we might have been able——"

And then, to her own huge amazement, Miss Baker found herself saying loudly :

" I never said we couldn't, did I ? I only said I wanted a bit of time, to think things over, didn't I ? That's reasonable enough, isn't it ? We may be able to fix up something yet. I daresay we could make it go, between us. Only you'd have to get rid of that Winifred and her mother too, if she's at all like her. I could never get on in the same house, not with those two, I couldn't."

This sentence was all the more amazing because, while she was saying it, Miss Baker was making up her mind even more firmly that a million rampaging wild bulls would not drag her to live at The Tower. Goodness knows what made her say it at all.

For some time Miss Padsòe did not reply. Her silence lasted so long that at last Miss Baker glanced at her, and saw such a troubled, almost frightened face, that she was moved to ask bluntly :

" What's the matter ? Don't you like the idea of them going ? Have they been with you a very long time ? "

" Oh no. Only about two years. They came after my dear Trottie left—that is, Miss Trotman, my father's housekeeper. They are not Bassett people. They come from Reading. Miss Trotman was a Bassett girl : she was with us for nearly thirty years. Winifred and her mother came just after my father died. I was very much distressed at that time, Miss Baker. I am afraid I did not go into the matter of *references* as closely as I should have done. They seemed . . . so efficient. I was very glad to leave the house in their hands. At first, that is. Quite glad. I have never understood much about housekeeping, Miss Baker, and I had always left every-thing to Miss Trotman."

" What did *you* do with yourself all day, then ? "

" Oh," and a pair of large vague eyes were turned to her in a little well-bred surprise. " I read . . . my dear father and I read together. Or I gardened. I did a great deal of gardening, I remember. Papa would sit at the drawing-room window and talk to me while I worked. Then people used to come to tea and to dinner. . . ."

She was silent again for a moment.

"It must be nearly two years," she said, as though she had suddenly realised the fact with surprise, "since I had friends to dinner."

"Why did Miss Trotman leave you, if she was such a treasure?"

"She had to go. To Canada, to look after her brother's children, because her sister-in-law died. Dear Trottie. She only saw *them* once, and she did not approve of them, she said. But I was too unhappy. I never thought about what they were like, inside. Only for the last year, Miss Baker, the housekeeping bills have been so—so *disproportionately* large that I have really begun to wonder. . . ."

"I don't," said Miss Baker. "It's as plain as the nose on my face that they starve you, pinch your money, and sauce you till you daren't say bo to a cat."

"Oh no," said Miss Padsoe faintly.

"Oh *yes*. Now, don't they?"

"It is all meant well . . . really, I do believe it is. They are *very* efficient servants. Rather rude, perhaps, but then dear Trottie . . . after all, one expects *really* good servants to be a little *tyrannical*. Trottie often was. Besides, just supposing I *were* to try to get rid of Winifred and her mother?" (and Miss Padsoe's face expressed the liveliest fear and dismay at the prospect, mingled with longing) "how *should* I put it to them? I have *no* real grounds. . . ."

"Tell 'em it's time they made a change," suggested Miss Baker, stumping madly up the hill (they would lose the bus as sure as eggs were eggs). "But there's no hurry for that, is there? Come to that, there's no hurry at all. All you've got to do now is not to *worry* about it. Don't *fuss*. I'll think it over, see, and drop you a p.c. in a day or two." (No, nor wild horses, neither. Nor if it was the last place in the world, she wouldn't come here. But she was sorry for Miss Padsoe : she couldn't help being. Poor old nannygoat, all alone in that great house with not enough to eat).

" Thank you," said Miss Padsoe, humbly.

She did not feel humble. She only wished to get away by herself, lie on her bed, and thump the pillow while she cried.

.     .     .     .     .

And that was how they left it. Miss Baker caught her bus for High Wycombe at a desolate cross roads under a sky that was nearly dark, and left Miss Padsoe to make her way home alone over the snow. Miss Padsoe, though mournful, seemed more cheerful than before Miss Baker had spoken so unexpectedly. She went off looking more like a scare-the-birds than ever : the driver and the conductor of the bus were both laughing at her, and Miss Baker felt she should die of shame, only she was so furious with the driver and conductor for laughing at Miss Padsoe, and with Miss Padsoe for looking so queer that the driver and the conductor had grounds for laughing, that there was not much room for anything but rage.

The steak and chips were quite as good as she had thought they would be. She sat enjoying them in Paddington Refreshment Room at nearly ten o'clock that night, and wondering about the private affairs of the other people in the refreshment room, who all looked excited and mysterious and a bit feverish, as people taking meals in railway refreshment rooms always do

But though she enjoyed her supper, and though she was glad to be back in London, and though she kept on telling herself she would not go and live at Bassett for

all the gold in Africa, and wishing she had Miss Worrall
there, to relate to her the events of the day and to tell
*her* that she would never dream of going to live there—
all the same, she could not get Miss Padsoe out of her
head.

Though she was not imaginative, she wondered what
kind of an evening Miss Padsoe had spent in the beautiful
dusty drawing-room ; and whether, after the faded rosy
curtains had been drawn to shut out the night stretching
away over the lonely fields, Winifred's mother had been
persuaded into lighting a little fire ?

# CHAPTER V

LIKE the Napoleonic wars, the Great War brought to
the surface of the social cauldron a scum of nihilists,
reformers and mere rebels of both sexes, whose views
and conduct were at once sincere and novel, daring and
glitteringly attractive to the young. The few young
people who were, without knowing it, concerned with
fundamentals rather than with superficialities, found
danger in their particular set, and fought it as best they
might. Some of them were defeated and became disciples
of the glittering rebels. Others shied away, alarmed and
bored and amused without quite knowing why they were
so; and escaped.

The Shellings escaped. George Shelling and his sister
Bell, two of the most annoying people in Buckinghamshire, had tried most of the sets. They were young,
wealthy and charming, and people were eager to be
friends with them, partly because they were an ornament
to any party, and partly because George always owned
a large, new, beautiful car in which even rebels would
have liked to ride: and also their house was in
Buckinghamshire, where it was unfortunately the
fashion for the rebels to walk at week-ends.

The rebels would have much enjoyed being asked to
stay for week-ends at Baines House, where the Shellings
lived in sober comfort on the proceeds from a surgical
instrument factory left to George by his late father;

and indeed they were sometimes asked to parties there. George would suddenly "feel like seeing people" and say to Bell that they must have a party; that they lived like hermits, that it was a disgrace the way they lived, that he would like to see Such-and-Such again, who was so amusing.

They then got permission from their mother to have the party, and George fussed over the wine and the food and their old German cook (for twenty years ago there had been a "c" in Shelling) cooked open tarts with plums and spice in them, and George and Bell wrote little notes and telephoned to those members of the particular set which they were at the moment trying out; and the favoured ones came, rather surprised and flattered to find themselves there at all, and the party either "went" or did not "go"; and hopes of a frequent and pleasant intercourse were raised in the bosoms of the guests.

George and Bell then decided that they were all bores, and uncultured bores at that, and they were never asked again.

The brother and sister returned to their hermit-like life, which was as regular as that of any monastery. On alternate days at half-past nine, George drove himself into Reading or up to Town to visit respectively the factory or the London shop, where he worked extremely hard and returned in time for dinner at half-past seven. In the evening Bell played Bach on the piano and George accompanied her on his violin, which he played badly because he was too lazy to practise. Sometimes they learned a song by Hugo Wolf, or lay back in their chairs the whole evening insulting one another and shrieking with laughter.

They seldom passed an evening with their mother,

who had many old friends in the neighbourhood with whom she played bridge ; and they were content to be together in the room which was still called the nursery, and which was furnished in a way that did not express their personalities in the very least. Here their evenings were usually passed.

In the summer they drove out into the woods, taking their supper with them, and in the winter they went frequently up to London to hear concerts. They read much, both loved luxury, and were undecided upon most questions. People fell frequently in love with them, and George wriggled, and Bell floated with grace out of these unfortunate entanglements.

On the snowy Sunday in January on which George had given Miss Baker a lift into Bassett, the Shellings were still recovering from a party given the previous Friday. George referred to it as the Brilliant Young Scientific Set party, and he and Bell had decided, as usual, that the Brilliant Young Scientific Set was a bore ; an even worse bore than the Motor Racing Set, the Good Time Set, the Literary Set, the Freely Loving Set and the Musical Set.

Of course, every guest at the party had not been a Brilliant Young Scientific ; there were one or two Free Lovers and a Motor Racing Set person. The latter had been invited out of spite by Bell, because he bored her by being in love with her, and she hoped the Brilliant Young Scientifics would set upon him, and that he would have a miserable evening.

In this charitable hope she was disappointed. The Brilliant Young Scientifics did not set upon people. Their gospel was kindness. There was room for *everybody* and *everything* except cruelty and ignorance and lies. The motor-racingite was a dear . . . so vital and

amusing. Oh, we needed that kind of vitality. It was
vitality which, properly directed, was to save the world.

This was Bell's first disappointment. Her second
was the failure of the party; it did not go very well,
and this distressed Bell; although she was so easily
bored, she was a sensitive hostess, and liked her guests
to enjoy themselves.

But how could the poor Brilliant Scientifics be
expected to enjoy themselves (as George explained
afterwards to his depressed sister) when they were all
sternly sleeping with one another's husbands and wives
out of a sense of duty, and not because they liked it in
the least, and were therefore secretly extremely miserable?
Jealousy was a hideous thing, a survival from the era of
the cave and the club, and physical jealousy was the
worst kind of jealousy; and the only way to conquer
physical jealousy was by giving your mate complete
physical freedom. And of course you must have it,
too; and you must both slay jealousy, for the good
of Posterity.

So the Brilliant Scientifics did their duty to Posterity;
and every six months or so one of them might be seen
grimly moving into the house of another two, and sleeping with the husband or the wife; and they all forgathered
at breakfast the next morning in the greatest amity and
good-feeling, until such time as passion should have
exhausted itself and duty to Posterity be done. Their
attitude to lust was like their attitude to a bad tooth: if
you had one, have it out, disagreeable for yourself and
painful for your mate though this remedy might be.

This explains why Bell's party was not a success. It
may also explain why so many of the Brilliant Young
Scientifics were crashing bores.

" What do you suppose she will be like? " asked Bell.

George was about to drive into Reading to fetch his
mother's new companion; Mrs. Shelling had a new
companion every year or so. Most of them wore false-
looking hair and were middle-aged, but this Miss Catton
was only twenty-two, and came with a handsome
reference from the wife of a vicar in South Kensington.

"I've told you. A ruddy nuisance. Ma will be
bored with her because she's too young, and she will
expect to go about with us, and then Ma will be livid."

"Well, don't seduce her on the way here." Bell was
idling about the garage watching her brother fussing
with the car. She had an old tweed coat wrapped round
her thin, graceful body, and no hat; her hair was very
long and silky, and of a fine pale-ginger colour; she
wore it in a coronet twice round her head. Her face
was almost chinless but a dazzlingly fair complexion
and huge round eyes of clearest grey made it enchanting.
She was at this time twenty-six years old; her brother
twenty-five.

"Don't seduce her, I said," repeated Bell, catching
hold of the Alsatian's collar; he would follow the car
for miles if he once got out.

George giggled as he drove away. He was kindness
itself to Miss Catton on the journey, as Miss Baker had
seen; and by the time the car had stopped outside
Baines House again, and Bell had come to the open
window and taken Miss Catton's hand with some
charmingly friendly words, the mischief was done;
Miss Catton, though unaltered in body, was ravished in
spirit; she had fallen helplessly in love with the two
of them.

Like many cases of helpless and violent love, hers at
first took the form of dislike and disapproval. She
disapproved of George's easy silence on the drive out

to Bassett; of the size and splendour of his car, of the rather dirty scarf of violet silk twisted inside Bell's old coat, of the general air of having plenty of money and of not being ashamed that they had which floated about the young Shellings like a perfume. In England, people often look slightly ashamed if they have lashings of money. If they do not look ashamed, they must be cads. But the Shellings were not English—they were German, and they were glad they had lots of money, and did not at all mind being thought cads. Nor was Baines House one of those shabbily comfortable houses. It was centrally heated, speckless, furnished by Tottenham Court Road at its best, and run like a first-class hotel. The untidy Bell and the casual George fitted in so ill with the picture that Miss Catton was more puzzled, more subconsciously fascinated, than ever.

When she was alone in her large impersonal bedroom which looked over the front garden, she solemnly peeled off her jumper to give herself a wash before lunch, and decided that she was going to be unhappy here. She, the daughter of a dentist in Islington, was employed as companion to a rich woman with two spoilt, casual children. Of course she would be unhappy. Very unhappy.

And yet—it was all so comfortable and pleasant! She already liked the large airy rooms that smelt of nothing, the big garden, the quiet, the knowledge that somewhere lunch was being prepared, and that she would not be expected to wash up afterwards. It was surprising and disconcerting to find how natural it seemed to be here, and how much she liked being in the houses of the rich.

It was disconcerting because for the last eighteen months Miss Catton had been steadily telling herself that the rich were the foes of the poor, the oppressors, the blood-suckers, and a lot more. If she had believed in God, they would have been Antichrist, but Miss Catton, having emerged at eighteen from a violent attack of Anglo-Catholicism, was now an agnostic (too intelligent, of course, to be an atheist). And it was surprising because young Miss Catton, at twenty-two, was very sure that she had herself well in hand and could control her beliefs. Young Miss Catton was a Communist.

She looked at herself in the glass, sighed and wished that her chest were not so fat, and then went downstairs, as she had been told to do, to the morning-room which opened into the big hall.

George and Bell had gone to put the car away, but Mrs. Shelling was sitting by the fire reading *The Observer* and gently massaging the cat's belly with the toe of her slipper.

" Ach, there you are, Miss Catton," said Mrs. Shelling cheerfully and in exactly the same tone as she had said, " I do not think I shall want you any more for ever, Miss Bates," to Miss Catton's predecessor when she dismissed her. " Those naughty children have gone to the garage, so we introduce ourselves, eh ? Come here. Sit down. It is cold, eh ? Now you wind this wool for me. You sit on the stool. So. Now."

She slipped the wool over Miss Catton's stubby little hands, and began to wind. Her vague gaze slipped, it seemed unseeingly, over Miss Catton's solemn, intent face ; and during a drive which they took after lunch in the car, she spoke scarcely half a dozen sentences to her.

Nevertheless, as George was winding the eight-day clock in the hall about eleven that night, his mother came over to speak to him, on her way up to bed. She spoke in German.

"George, I ask you to do something for me. I do not often ask you, do I ? So you will do it for me, please ? "

George's face took on the expression which can be best translated into words as " Oh, *lord*." He said in English :

" Depends what it is, Ma."

" George, that is a very nice girl. She is too nice to be made miserable. I ask you not to make love to her. She will be very miserable if you do. I ask you, my son. Will you not make love to her, just to please me ? "

George laughed, but there was indignation as well as amusement in the laugh.

" This is the second warning I've had to-day about Miss Catton. Bell was on at me about her before lunch—only she put it more crudely. In fact, she warned me not to seduce her."

" Well, I ask you not to do that, either. Neither to make love to her, nor to betray her. She is too nice."

" Well, I shan't promise anything," said George, who resented this imputation to himself of impulses which no one could be further from feeling. " Anybody would think I was a sort of lecherous demon or something. Not that I should object to a little lechery with the Catton, mind you. I like her chest."

" George, you should not speak to your mother in that way. It is loose and ill-mannered. You are a very naughty boy. So is Bell ; very naughty. You are both naughty children."

" Yes, Ma," said George, who knew that his mother's lectures seldom got any stronger than this. So long as he worked hard, his mother was placid about what he did ; it was most unusual for her to bestir herself on behalf of one of his girls : usually she contemplated their misery unmoved. He looked at her curiously ; at her tower of fine brown hair, her well-corseted Edwardian figure, her handsome face, irrevocably middle-aged. What went on in the skull under the brown tower ? No more, probably, than was apparent.

She put out her cheek, and George gave it a smacking kiss, at the same time rolling his eyes and squeezing her waist, and telling her he was a devil when roused.

They went amiably upstairs together, entwined, and George asked if they could have another party soon, and his mother said yes. But she added, as she opened the door of her room, that he and Bell were both naughty children.

# CHAPTER VI

MISS BAKER was late for work on Monday, so the day began badly. She woke at dawn, and then, made sleepy by a day of country air, fell asleep again and slept right through the noise of the alarm at half-past seven. Her suspender burst, and she tied the elastic into a knot, and it came undone in the Tube and there was a hole in her heel; and she felt that all these things befell because she had gone off to Bassett yesterday instead of staying at home and mending things. Really, Sunday had been more like a nightmare than an ordinary Sunday, and except that the place was so pretty and she could not help still feeling sorry for Miss Padsoe, she wished she had never gone.

Anyway, it was all over and done with, and towards the end of the week she would write to the poor old nannygoat and tell her so.

. "*He's* been askin' for you," said Miss Worrall in a low and significant voice, as she and Miss Baker took their position before a model draped in flimsiest paper which would one day be a key-pattern for an evening dress. "Asked was you in yet. We had to say no."

"I don't see why. You might have said I was washing. What time was this, then?"

"About twenty-five to. How could I? You wouldn't wash as soon as you got here, would you?"

"Did he seem wild?"

C

"No, He never said anything else. Just asked if
you was in, and then went off to his own room."

This incident gave Miss Baker a disagreeable feeling
of apprehension. " *He* " was Mr. Edwards, the manager,
and one of the directors of the firm. He seldom looked
into the pattern-cutting room ; he buzzed through on
the house telephone, or sent up a skinny girl who was
not only his secretary but a runner of errands indoors
and out, if he wanted to speak to Miss Baker or Miss
Worrall.

"Did you oversleep ? " asked Miss Worrall. " (This
godet needs to be a bit fuller. It looks skimpy.) Doris,
are those thirty-sixes finished yet ? You get a move on,
my girl ; we're seventy behind on that coatee. It's
selling like hot cakes."

"I slept right through the alarm. Woke up at
six and went right off again. The lions woke me
up."

A silence fell, charged with meaning. Miss Baker's
last sentence, spoken a little louder than her earlier
ones, had been clearly heard by Miss Worrall, old Miss
Lime who kept an eye on the kids, the kids themselves,
Gertie and Doris, and Muriel the errand-girl.

No one looked at anyone else. No one allowed a
muscle of her face to move. No one accused Miss
Baker of being a liar. Yet the word Liar thundered
through the room.

"Loud as anything," said Miss Baker doggedly.
" They often do wake me up. It's bein' near the Park,
I suppose."

For fifteen years, ever since she moved to Camden
Town from Wandsworth, Miss Baker had announced
at intervals that the roaring of the lions in the Zoological
Gardens woke her at dawn. She said the roaring was

so loud it quite frightened her; it sounded as if it was
in the back garden. Once Miss Worrall had said perhaps
it really was in the back garden, and why spoil the ship
for a ha'porth of tar, and Miss Baker had been furious
and thenceforward had stuck to the lion story as a
matter of principle. She said she s'posed the lions were
fed at dawn or something, and Miss Worrall said
nonsense, you wouldn't catch the keepers getting up at
that time just to feed the lions; and every time they went
to the Zoo together they made up their minds to ask
the keeper in the Lion House if the lions really were
fed at dawn. But somehow, what with the excitement of
being in the Zoo and screaming with laughter at the
animals and nudging each other over the Baboon Hill,
Miss Baker and Miss Worrall always forgot to ask the
keeper about the lions' feeding time, and when they got
outside the Zoo at the end of a hot and exhausting
afternoon, their first act was to look at each other and
exclaim together :

" There ! we never asked about the lions ! "

So the pattern room continued to think Miss Baker
told whoppers.

The house telephone buzzed and Muriel undulated
across to answer it. When she hung up the receiver and
turned round to face the room, her little face was charged
with excitement, wisely veiled by an unnatural
demureness.

" Please, Miss Baker, Mr. Edwards would like to see
you at once."

It was that " at once " which made Miss Baker's
heart turn over inside her. Miss Worrall, kneeling in
front of the dummy, looked up as Miss Baker got to
her feet and whispered, " Cheer up. You'll soon be
dead," with curiosity, sympathy and pleasure at an

exciting and disagreeable event bursting out all over her face like a rash. Miss Baker made a vaguely gallant kind of grimace, and went out of the room.

At least she knew a buzz of comment would not break out the second the door was shut on her; Miss Worrall did not allow gossip about the other people in the room. Miss Worrall and Miss Baker might gossip as they kneeled before the dummies, with their mouths full of pins : no one else might, and the kids were verbally clouted into submission a dozen times a day. Old Miss Lime had private ailments which kept her busy and happy and silent ; and young Muriel was a nobody, a brat, a whipping-boy for the whole room.

So no one looked at anyone else or breathed a word. But everybody had the darkest possible thoughts, mixed with gratitude that it was not them who were going to see Mr. Edwards at once.

Miss Baker was both frightened and furious. If he was going to make a fuss about her being a quarter or an hour late, she would just tell him how many times she had been late in twenty-one years. Forty times, that was all. About twice a year. And what difference did it make to her work, she would like to know, and how would Mr. Edwards know she was late at all, if the whole staff did not have to sign in that time-book every morning, as though they were a lot of Bolshevik slaves or something ?

Boiled up into a comforting state of Dutch courage, she knocked at Mr. Edwards's door; and heard his faint " Come in."

·        ·        ·        ·        ·        ·

Miss Worrall was still kneeling in front of the dummy. when Miss Baker came back into the cutting-room. She

had arranged herself round at the back, so that she could
ask Miss Baker what had happened without Miss Lime,
the kids and young Muriel hearing everything.

Miss Baker came in with a very red face. It was trying
to look as though nothing had happened to its owner,
but in vain. At one glance, the cutting-room Knew.
And a cold wind of apprehension blew through old
Miss Lime, the kids, and young Muriel. They bent
madly over their work, and old Miss Lime, trying to
work twice as fast as usual, stamped six sleeves with
the " collar " marker.

" She's been catching it," thought everybody, feeling
virtuous because it wasn't them.

Miss Baker lowered herself on her trembling legs
and kneeled in front of the dummy. Her heart was still
banging horribly. Her mouth was still dry. Miss
Worrall turned a pair of popping eyes on her, and,
pushing her lips out as far as they would go and screwing
up her eyes in order to make her meaning more crystal-
clear, mouthed the following sentence at her friend :

" W—as he w—ild ? "

" N—o." Miss Baker, also mouthing, turned round,
and, while reaching for the pin-box off the cutting table,
rapidly · glanced round the room. Miss Lime, the
kids, and young Muriel were carefully not looking
at her.

Then did Miss Baker, leaning slightly towards the
expectant Miss Worrall, mouth at her friend the single
frightful word :

" S—ack ! "

" N—o ! " Miss Worrall's eyes flew open like blinds
going up. " Never ! "

Miss Baker nodded, with her mouth pursed up.

" N—ot 'cos y—ou w—ere l—ate ? "

Vigorous shake of the head from Miss Baker.

"N—ot my w—ork at all. Very p—leased. But c—utting d—own st—aff."

"N—o ! "

"M—onth's n—otice."

"N—o ! "

Miss Baker then mouthed that she intended to lunch at twelve, and invited Miss Worrall to lunch with her, in order to talk it over ; and accordingly at twelve they went off to the Charing Cross Lyons' Corner House which is pleasantly empty at that time ; and over two Welsh rarebits, and two weak coffees, they discussed the shattering news.

Miss Baker, of course, was very angry. She talked of suing the firm, of appealing to the other Directors. She was also frightened, but she did not say so to Miss Worrall. She did not even say so to herself. She wished, as people do wish when they have been suddenly and unexpectedly sacked, that she had not bought a new art-silk scarf last Friday, nor spent the fare to Reading.

But you know how it is. The shadow of the Sack drifts near for a second, like a vulture, and you make mad plans never to spend more than tenpence a day on your lunch, and to save and save. And then perhaps the shadow drifts off ; your little robin-note pipes up once more, and you plan your winter outfit, and even buy it.

And then the vulture swoops.

"Well, you'll be all right for a bit anyway. You're luckier than some," said Miss Worrall, who was by now beginning to recollect numerous signs and portents foretelling this event, which she had observed for the last six months. Mr. Edwards had given Miss Baker a Very Straight Look when he passed them that Saturday

on the stairs. Then there had been that warning
about ·not wasting pins. It all went to show, that
was all.

Miss Baker, who had observed no Straight Look and
who had not let the warning about the pins sink into
her consciousness, and did not believe Miss Worrall
had either, became still more furious.

" How do you mean—lucky ? " she snapped. " Funny
idea of luck you've got, I must say. And on a Monday,
too. It isn't natural. Who ever heard of anyone being
sacked on a Monday ? "

" P'raps he meant to on Friday, only he forgot,"
soothed Miss Worrall, who was enjoying all this immensely ; and she felt so stimulated that she ordered a
cream horn.

" Well, you've got a month. Time to look round in.
And all that money in the bank. You'll be all right.
Now if it was me——"

Miss Worrall paused, and plunged her fork into her
cream horn, dramatically musing over what she would
feel like if it were her.

" Well, it isn't you, is it ? It's me. And my money
won't last for ever."

Miss Worrall then reminded Miss Baker that only
last week she had been magnificently toying with the
idea of going to run a boarding-house in Reading, and
asked her if she had ever really meant to do such a
thing ? If she had, now was her chance.

Miss Baker cried out with horror at the very idea.
The morning had been so busy and exciting that she
had not had a chance to tell Miss Worrall about her
visit to Bassett, but she now did so, with one eye on
the clock, for it was ten to one. Miss Worrall shook
her head saying it just went to show you never knew

what people were like who lived in big houses, and fancy those elephants.

" So of course I couldn't *dream* of going now," said Miss Baker. " I need every farthing I can lay my hands on."

She, though desirous, had not ordered a cream horn. Nor had Miss Worrall offered to stand her one. Cream horns cost threepence each.

# CHAPTER VII

So for a month Miss Baker looked for another job, and did not find one.

The same causes which made her, a withering unused little woman who spent her life cutting flimsy paper, unable to get work, made the big lumbermen of the Canadian fir forests, who cut wood and whose bodies were being used to their last ounce, unable to get work either. The trees which ultimately became the paper cut by Miss Baker themselves remained uncut, towering in beauty to heaven, which did not help Miss Baker or the lumbermen at all.

On Miss Worrall's advice she advertised:

> "Expert cutter, twenty one years' experience, seeks post with pattern firm, with view to improving her position. Excellent references."

She put this in *The Times* and one or two trade papers. She did not get one reply. She wrote to every paper pattern firm, large and small, in London, from *Vogue* to *Mab's Fashions*. Everybody was very polite, everybody was very sorry, but no one had a job to give.

All over England, all over the world, doors were slowly closing, the weaker workers were dropping reluctantly from their precarious hold on their unnecessary little jobs, hatches were being battened down, cordons were being tightened. Firm after firm, all over the world, was paring its staff down to the barest bones, ready to

stand taut and dogged against the long, hard, bad times
that were coming. "Things are bad," people said
(most imprudently) in Tubes and clubs and buses, as the
savage days of January flayed England with cold " but
they're going to be worse." And those who had not
yet suffered felt ten times cosier by contrast with everything else.

" Of course, I'm lucky compared with some," admitted
Miss Baker one day in Lyons', towards the end of the
third week of search. " That three hundred and eighty
pounds—I haven't even touched it yet. I could live
for a year on that."

Miss Worrall screamed. " A year ? So I should
bally well hope. Who are you, I should like to know—
Gloria Swanson ? A year ! You could live for three."

For once Miss Baker did not rise. She sat silently
over her Empress pudding, one hand nursing her jaw,
looking moodily at her plate.

. " I wish this neuralgia would go," was all she said.
" I've had it nearly a fortnight. Enough to drive you
mad."

" You ought to go to the dentist again."

Miss Baker shrugged her shoulders. Dentists cost
money.

She was afraid. Her little world, bright and miniature
as one in a glass paper-weight, was blown to smithereens
and the huge cold world-wind, that was making firms
from Manchester to Para slam their doors, was roaring
all about her. For the first time in her life she thought
with gloom of her old age. Until now, it had been a
matter for joking. .

She had not kept her promise to write to Miss Padsoe.
It pleased her to think she was too busy and worried to
attend to Miss Padsoe's affairs. " Let her get on with

it," she thought, getting some of her anxiety and anger off her chest in the thought, venting it on Miss Padsoe. " Other people have got their troubles, as well as her. Silly old nannygoat." She made up her mind, in fact, not to write to Miss Padsoe at all, but just to forget her.

And so far had she put her visit to Bassett out of her mind, so remote did it already seem, that it was not until this, the last day of the third week, that it occurred to her that she might have to write to Miss Padsoe again and re-open the whole matter, simply because there was nothing else in the world for her to do.

Not that she meant to put any money into that house . . . not she. She was quite firm about *that*. But there was only another week of her job, and what would she do when it was over, and she had left, and the pattern room was going on without her. " Not so dusty as jobs go," she and Miss Worrall were wont to say of their job. That meant a lot from two such grudging, suspicious, withering women. It meant they liked their job more than they would ever know. It meant that to be fired from it was like a smack across the mouth.

Already Mr. Peeley had noticed Miss Baker's low spirits, and every time he saw her he said that somebody not a hundred miles away was crossed in love, or asked her if she had lost sixpence ; and she had to fob off his wit with excuses about neuralgia. She was certainly not going to tell the Peeleys she had lost her job, and have to listen to their nosy questions when she came home in the evenings, after spending the day looking for work. Not she.

At first the idea of going to Bassett after all was a joke, put forward in one of her more cheerful moods ; and Miss Worrall laughed when she said it. A few days later, however, Miss Worrall returned to the suggestion, this time seriously.

"Now don't fly down my throat, Hilda," she began promisingly, "but why shouldn't you go down and stay with Miss Padsoe for a bit after you've left, and see if there's anything in that idea of hers? You said you liked the place, now didn't you?"

Miss Worrall was getting tired of the Miss Baker situation. It was losing its horrid novelty, and besides, there was a gorgeous row blowing up between the kids and Miss Lime which promised to develop into a rich, complicated feud, which would spread satisfyingly over many years, and would only deepen and become more interesting as the kids grew up into women with a sense of their own dignity, and Miss Lime's increasing age and infirmities made her more touchy. This was replacing her interest in Miss Baker's woes, and she now wished to be rid of her friend, in order to savour it to the full.

Miss Baker did not fly down her throat. She was too depressed to resent any suggestion, however unpractical, which was made for her welfare. She looked up at Miss Worrall with a lack-lustre eye, and replied that she expected the old geezer had got somebody now, it was nearly a month since she had been down there.

"I bet she hasn't," said Miss Worrall confidently, because that was what she wanted to be the case. "I bet she'd jump at you, if you were to write to her again. You try, and see if she doesn't. You needn't tie yourself down. Don't say anything definite. And whatever you do, Hilda, don't *sign* anything. (You remember my Aunt Nettie? That was a business, if you like!) No, you just write to her, casually like, and say you've been thinking it over, and you've decided you'd like to come to her for a bit, just until you can look round,

like, and decide whether you want to go in with her or
not."

The result of this advice was that Miss Baker did,
that evening, write the following letter to Miss Padsoe.

"DEAR MISS PADSOE,
Please accept my apologies for not having written
to you till now about that little matter we talked about,
you remember. My plans are now somewhat changed,
so who knows perhaps I might some day see my way
clear to doing what we talked about. Of course it
is not a matter we can decide at once as I am sure you
will agree. What I am wondering is, could you see
your way clear to me coming down for a day or two
just to talk matters over? Of course if this puts you out
at all don't let me trouble you. I have plenty of other
plans just now.
                          Yours faithfully,
                                    HILDA BAKER."

Miss Baker had no other plans at all; alas! every
practical plan had been tried, and had failed. But
she was one of that huge group of people which believes
that a person becomes more eager to have you if they
think you are reluctant to come; and she also believed
that, if people knew you were down on your luck,
they stamped on your face. (And, indeed, people often
do.) The thing to do was to give an impression of
dallying, leisured, condescending wealth. Then people
wanted to have you.

There was no reply for five days: and on the Friday
evening of that week—a terrible evening filled with a
screaming icy wind that drove sheets of hail before it—
the unbelievable happened.

She spent an afternoon in the cutting room for the
last time.

For the last time she glanced up at the clock at five

to three, and said to Miss Worrall, " It isn't worth while starting this flounce now. Tea'll be here in a minute " ; and rose from her cramped knees, dusted her skirt, carefully took four tiny pins from her mouth and stuck them into the worn pearl-coloured satin which covered the big cutting-room pincushion.

For the last time Muriel slavishly pulled up the old wooden chair close to the sulky little fire, in Miss Baker's own corner ; and stood on another chair to reach down the round tin which held the biscuits, and which was kept on a high shelf with the old order-books ; and Mrs. Payne, the firm's tea-lady who had come in every afternoon to make tea for the last thirty years, entered with her black japanned tray covered with six big cups, their saucers piled in one corner, and strong red tea slopping over their sides. For the last time she said " Good afternoon, Miss Baker," and passed Miss Baker her cup, after passing Miss Worrall hers ; and Miss Baker, her foot in its square-toed, shabby slipper tapping thoughtfully against the wire fire-guard, took that first blessèd sip of strong, sweet, hot tea, and sighing with content, said to Miss Worrall, " Ah ! I needed that."

For the last time.

She said it over to herself once or twice, but that did not make it seem more real. And no one in the room said a word about it. . Everyone was pretending to know nothing, though everybody knew all about it ; and high up on the shelf where the order-books were, was a cut glass flower vase with a metal rim, bought yesterday by Miss Worrall in her lunch hour for the sum of ten and sixpence, which was the value set by the cutting-room on Miss Hilda Baker, and collected by Miss Worrall without difficulty.

For everybody, even old Miss Lime who did not really (like so many of us) approve of anyone except herself, was sorry Miss Baker was going. Broke the room up somehow, her going like that. Wouldn't be the same, somehow. 'Course she had her faults. Well, we all have, come to that. Still, the cutting room was sorry; and expressed its regret through a cut glass vase with a narrow metal rim.

Miss Baker was silent as she sipped her tea.

Outside it was getting dark. A streep lamp stood opposite the cutting-room window, and into its downward cone of violet light blew great flurries of snow; and then they swirled away into the narrow darkness of Gloucester Street.

She would never see Gloucester Street again from this window. Oh! she had got the pip.

Miss Baker scrunched ginger biscuit between her front teeth, and decided that she would buy a bottle of Phosferine on her way home.

She was wondering, between scrunches and looking out of the window at the snow, what they were going to give her. She knew they had got something for her, because yesterday Miss Worrall had made a lot of feeble excuses in order to avoid lunching with her—excuses which Miss Baker accepted without a single sniff of disbelief, because she knew Miss Worrall was going off to buy the present.

She was afraid it was something small, because nothing big could have been hidden up on the old order-book shelf, which was where it was. Perhaps it was a watch? She checked the straying of her imagination. Catch them giving her a watch! A three and sixpenny fountain pen, more like.

When tea was over, they went back to their jobs.

The room was quiet, except for the rustle of flimsy paper, the regular thud made by old Miss Lime as she stamped sleeves and collars and panels, and an occasional mutter from Miss Worrall or one of the kids.

Miss Baker always remembered that last bit of work she did for Haddon's Paper Patterns. It was an evening coat, and they had a bit of trouble over the big rucked collar; they could not get the collar to ruck properly at the back and achieve the fashionable height at the nape; and they both got so interested in what they were doing that suddenly Miss Worrall exclaimed, "Mercy, Hilda, look at the time. We must leave this over till Monday."

"*You'll* leave it over, you mean." Miss Baker began elaborately to put on her hat and coat. "You might let me know how it works out. I'd be interested."

Miss Worrall (feeling much embarrassed, as indeed they all were) then solemnly climbed up on Miss Baker's special chair and reached down from its place on the shelf with the old order-books a longish parcel wrapped in tissue, with a bulge at either end. ("Trumpet. Silly fools. I won't half tell them off," thought Miss Baker, catching a lightning glimpse of the parcel out of the corner of her eye.)

Miss Worrall carefully brushed the dust from her fingers, and observed to Muriel that sometime someone really ought to dust down those shelves; they were a disgrace. Muriel eagerly agreed.

Miss Worrall then advanced upon Miss Baker, who was busily turning out a few odds and ends from her own private drawer, with her back carefully turned to the rest of the room.

"Miss Baker—Hilda," said Miss Worrall.

Miss Baker, with an elaborate start, turned round.

" That's me," she said, with a bright, toothy smile.

" This is a little gift from all of us, wishing you luck and all the best," gabbled Miss Worrall, thrusting the parcel at Miss Baker. (" Can't be a trumpet. Not bulgy enough," thought Miss Baker, instantaneously as light.)

" Well, that's very nice of you all, I'm sure," she said, while her fingers were busy unwrapping the parcel. " A vase ! Well, I never ! *Isn't* that pretty ? And so useful, too. I always have flowers in my room at home, and this will just do me nicely. Such a pretty shape, too."

" She hates it," thought everybody, deep in their inmost soul. But no one admitted they thought this. Everyone beamed, and Muriel, wriggling on one toe, pointed out in a whisper that the rim round the top was real silver.

" Well, I never ! So I should hope ! As though we should give Miss Baker something that *wasn't*," cried Miss Worrall shrilly, and everybody laughed heartily at such a ridiculous idea.

" It isn't. Mean cats," thought Miss Baker.

" Well, I do appreciate this little gift *very* much," she said, admiringly looking at it while twiddling it in her fingers. " Whenever I put flowers in it, I shall think of you all. There ! that's quite a poetical idea, isn't it ? The flowers will remind me of you. I shall often come in and see you all, I expect. Say *au revoir* but not good-bye, as the song says."

Everyone laughed.

Then there was a pause. Everyone waited for someone else to say something, but no one had anything to say.

" Well, this won't do," said Miss Baker briskly at last. " I must be off. I've got a lot to do to-night.

Good-bye, Miss Lime.   Good-bye, Gertie.   Good-bye,
Doris.   Good-bye, Muriel."

Miss Lime, Gertie and Doris got handshakes, but
Muriel only got a condescending nod : it was all she
deserved, and ever had deserved.   In another five years,
possibly, she might deserve a handshake.   You never
knew.. Gertie and Doris had ;  and they used to be
Muriels once.

"Coming, Lily ? " asked Miss Baker, when Miss
Lime, Doris, Gertie and Muriel had gone clattering
down the stairs on their way out.

Miss Worrall nodded.   Together, as they had gone
for the last ten years, they went down the stairs, and
shivered as they met the rush of icy air when the side
door leading into Grape Street was opened by Miss
Baker.   There was always a draught there, even on
August evenings, so Miss Worrall swore.

"Last time you'll ever open this door.   Queer,
isn't it ? " said Miss Worrall, her instinct for drama
getting the better of her sympathy.

" I'll open it when I come up to see you all, I suppose,
shan't I—unless you're going to lower a rope out of
the window and haul me up like that, or p'raps I've
always got to come up the front stairs," said Miss
Baker, with frightful and withering sarcasm.

" No, Hilda, don't go off the deep end.   You feel
bad, I know you do.   It's only right and natural you
should . . . after twenty-one years.   But your luck
will turn, dear.   I'm sure it will.   Just keep smiling,
and all will come right in the end.   Oh, there's my bus.
Good-bye, Hilda.   Now, *mind* you phone *soon*.   On
Monday, if there's any news.   So long."

And Miss Worrall went flying off into the blizzard,
her necklace, ear-rings, lace collar, cape, rabbity fur

necklet, umbrella, handbag, and the very gauntlets
of her gloves all bouncing and flying as she went, like
little flags on a ship.

" Don't offer to have a coffee with me, will you ? "
called Miss Baker after her, who by this time felt very
bad indeed, and not at all as though she had four hundred
pounds in the Post Office.   She turned and walked down
Gloucester Street towards Leicester Square tube station,
ramming her umbrella into the flat pressing of the storm,
and pinching her withered little lips together so hard
that she looked as though she were making a face.

Really, when Miss Baker was sitting by her gas stove
that night eating a piece of boiled haddock and drinking
her cocoa, she came to the conclusion that to-day had
been one of the nastiest days she had ever had in her life.
What with a very disagreeable ball which had lodged
itself in the middle of her chest about lunch-time and
got worse as the afternoon wore on, and what with being
given that rotten little vase with imitation silver round
the top (and she never bought flowers—never seemed
to think of it, somehow) and what with having no
job and no prospects of one, and what with Lily Worrall
letting her down like that just when she needed a pal,
and what with having to stand all the way home in the
Tube with large wet men covered with melting snow
lurching against her every time the train stopped, and
everybody smoking like chimneys and making her
cough, and what with having driven the big toe of her
right foot slap through her new stockings, guaranteed
for six months or money refunded—Miss Baker felt
entitled to call it a day.

Thoughtfully she stuck out a square little foot,
and toasted it at the stove's fierce heat, waggling her
big toe through the hole in the stocking.

Suddenly the postman's knock echoed through the house.

Miss Baker did not move. To do so would have meant disarranging her plate of haddock, which was on her knees—and hopping over the cocoa tin, the milk jug, her cup, two saucepans, a loaf, a paper of butter, and a copy of *Smart Novels*, which were spread round her in a charmed circle of comfort.

" Let *them* bring it up," she thought darkly.

" Them " were the Peeleys, with whom she was having one of her prolonged and periodical fits of coolness. This time it was about the bolt on the bathroom door. Time and time again, she had asked if it could be repaired. It wasn't safe. It wasn't nice. It wasn't *decent*.

" Some ladies wouldn't mind a nice young man comin' in while they was in the bath," said Mr. Peeley with a wink at Mrs. Peeley, that hawk-like, surprisingly handsome slut, who smoked all day and only left the depths to go to the pictures.

" *Some* wouldn't, no doubt. I would," retorted Miss Baker frigidly.

But Mr. Peeley could never keep it up for long ; he was too fond of his joke. Sure enough, a minute after the sound of the postman's rap she heard him pounding úpstairs from the depths. There was a pause, while he examined the letters. Then she heard him pounding up the second flight, and an instant later a letter came whizzing under her door, right across the oilcloth almost to where she sat. Mr. Peeley, having vigorously executed "We-are-the-boys-that-make-no-noise " with his palms on the panel of her door, went pounding down to the depths again. This was his way of showing that, as far as he was concerned, he

was willing to raise the siege.    Mrs. Peeley did not care.
So long as she could go to the Camden Town Hippo-
drome cinema twice a week and smoke thirty cigarettes
a day, Mrs. Peeley did not care about anything.

Miss Baker, having observed that Mr. Peeley was a
silly old fool, craned across the cocoa tin and picked
up her letter.

It was from Miss Padsoe.

" This light's bad to-night," muttered Miss Baker,
glancing crossly up at the popping gas, and then down
at the grey envelope.    She could hardly read her own
name.

But it was not all the bad light.    The writing was
fainter, more straggling and confused than it had been,
in the letter she had received a month ago.    In two
places in the address mistakes had been made, crossed
out, and the word rewritten.    It looked—though Miss
Baker did not put her impression so clearly into
thoughts—like the writing of a body whose spirit was
failing, sinking, being slowly overpowered in some
exhausting struggle.

When she had unfolded the letter she had to stand
up and hold it close under the light in order to read it
at all.

" Dear Miss Baker,

I am so sorry that I have not replied to your  letter
before now.    I have had a *severe cold,* which has kept
me indoors.    No indeed it cannot be settled in a hurry
and circumstances now make it *more difficult for me
to speak as plainly* as I should *like.*    But if you *care*
to come I will make you welcome while we discuss
matters.    Perhaps you could come on Monday ?    It
is *very* necessary for me, as I believe I told you, to come
to some arrangement about the *house.*    I am afraid you
must be prepared for unpleasantness——" (and here

the writing ran off round the side of the page) " though I will do my best about it all. I have, of course, reconsidered as you suggested, about the coloured element."

And here the letter ended.

It was not signed.

"Well," sighed Miss Baker, after reading it twice, " she sounds balmier than ever, but that bit about going down's clear enough. I'll go. Unpleasantness indeed ! Who from ? That rude cat of a servant ? Let her just try, that's all ! "

And so, having passed Saturday in some badly planned and timorous shopping which she did not much enjoy because she felt that she ought not to have spent the two pounds, seventeen and eightpence halfpenny which she did spend ; and having passed Sunday in packing all her clothes into two leatherette suitcases and saying ' good-bye ' to the astounded and secretly dubious though outwardly impressed Peeleys and bequeathing to them a wooden poker-work instruction to " Work like Helen B. Merry " ; and having sent a chilly, vague postcard to Miss Worrall, with just her new address on it, and procured twenty pounds of her money from the Post Office—Miss Baker caught the 3.30 to Reading on Monday afternoon.

She was borne down into a Buckinghamshire whose roaring woods looked out over shallow floods. Rain streamed into the sodden fields. Foursquare, the clumped beeches stood against the steady pressure of the March wind. The country was drowned, submerged, lost. The sun and flowers had never been.

" Gawd-stone-me-up-a-gum-tree " mused Miss Baker, rubbing the steam off the carriage windows to look out into the flood. " This is going to be a picnic—I don't think."

London dropped away, lost behind sheets of rain.
Tubes, telephones, the low roar of traffic, the pressure
of narrow streets and the lives of millions of other
human beings—these dwindled—became small—flick!
they were gone! The train rushed on; and the quiet
breast of the country received Miss Baker.

# CHAPTER VIII

BUT how could she possibly guess how quiet that breast was at last to be, when what seemed to spring out at her from the country as the train drew into Reading was More Trouble?

For there, standing on the platform under a huge and frightfully old umbrella for which there was no need since the roof of the platform kept off the rain, and staring anxiously at the windows of the slowing train, was Miss Padsoe.

" Something up. Oh lord," thought Miss Baker, darting her head and shoulders into the carriage again and beginning to drag her suitcases down from the rack. " There's no peace for the wicked. She wouldn't be here if there wasn't something the matter."

And she thrust herself half out of the window again, waving vigorously and giving a false, toothy smile, and wishing Miss Padsoe looked a bit smarter. Like a rag-bag, that's what she was, and an old fashioned one at that.

And Miss Padsoe, greeting Miss Baker with a convulsive flutter of her umbrella-less hand and an equally false and toothy smile, found time to wish amid much mental distress that Miss Baker did not look exactly like an under-housemaid.

The train slowed to a stop.

Miss Padsoe came darting unskilfully through the crowd and nearly cannoned off Miss Baker, who, in her

turn, was darting skilfully, battering people's legs with
her suitcases.  Miss Padsoe's smile had now vanished
as though Miss Baker had only imagined it had ever
been there at all.  She looked ill, worried, embarrassed—
and frightened.

" Can't have me.  All her money's gone," thought
Miss Baker.  " Shan't lend her any."

She said loudly and cheerfully :

" Nice weather for ducks, isn't it ?  I'm sure it's
very kind of you to trouble to come and meet me in all
this rain.  Shocking, isn't it ?  Your cold better ?  I
was sorry to hear you'd been queer."

" Oh yes, thank you.  I am *quite* my old self now,"
replied Miss Padsoe, who seemed to be thinking about
something else as she spoke.  Her voice was faint and
hoarse, as though she had not used it for months. She
glanced anxiously from side to side as they made their
way along the platform to the exit, and Miss Baker's
uneasy conviction that there was something up was
disagreeably strengthened by her companion's curious
manner.

" I suppose," said Miss Baker, laughing heartily at
her own suggestion, " that there's plenty of buses to
Bassett *to-day* ?  Don't want to wait about in all this
rain, do we ?  Do your cold a bit of no-good, that would.
Where do the buses start from ? "

" From the Square.  There's one in about half an
hour," said Miss Padsoe, looking down vaguely at Miss
Baker from under the brim of an old greenish-black felt
hat shaped like a pudding basin.  Her grey hair hung
in wet wisps on either side of her hollow, wind-reddened
cheeks.

" Well—how about some coffee ? "

For Miss Baker, whose arms ached and whose feet

were getting wet, had suddenly realised there would probably be no roaring fires, no hot tea, no cake and muffins, at The Tower. Miles of jogging over streaming country in a damp bus, a hideous climb over wet hills, and then probably no fire! Miss Baker began to wish she had not come. Things were awful. If they got worse, she'd go back to London to-morrow.

" Coffee ? "

" Warm us up. Nothing like it. Come on—here's a place," shouted Miss Baker, adopting with Miss Padsoe the methods of those who deal with a foreigner, a child or a deaf lunatic. For she had suddenly decided Miss Padsoe was batty. And she darted at a door with " Mrs. Brown's Parlour " painted over it, slammed down her wet suitcases, wrenched open the door, picked her cases up again, and marched into a warm room smelling pleasantly of cakes, followed by Miss Padsoe, who was blinking.

When they were sitting in a corner by a large fire, with two steaming cups in front of them, Miss Padsoe suddenly picked up her spoon and began to jab nervously with it at the bottom of her cup. Her eyes were cast down, and her lips trembled from time to time as she spoke.

" Miss Baker. I . . . I am afraid I owe you an apology."

" Oh, you can't help the weather, worse luck," said Miss Baker, determined to know what was up, yet equally determined not to have a scene in Mrs. Brown's comfortable Parlour. " Don't you worry. We'll soon be home." .

" That is just why I *do* worry," said Miss Padsoe in the same low voice. " I . . . I am afraid we may not be."

" May not be what ? "

" Home.  You see . . ."

" What ?  Aren't there no buses, then ? " said Miss
Baker, rather louder than she meant to, but really,
it was the last straw; she could have shaken the
woman.

" Oh, there are plenty of *buses*," said Miss Padsoe
eagerly.  " We can *get* to Bassett in less than an hour.
It is just that . . . you see, I am afraid that when
we get there we may not be able to get into the
house."

" Why not ?  What's wrong ?  Have you forgotten
your keys or something ? "

" I . . . I never carry keys.  I keep them in my
desk," confessed Miss Padsoe, now jabbing furiously
at the bottom of the cup.  " No, I am afraid . . . oh
Miss Baker, do *please* believe how *deeply*, how *terribly*
I regret this most unfortunate situation.  I would not
have had it happen for the *world*.  If only my dear
father——"

She stopped, choked, and sipped with a kind of
fierce absent-mindedness at her cooling coffee, staring
down at the saucer and refusing to meet Miss Baker's
eyes, which were now almost popping out of their sockets
with curiosity and rage.

(" Never   mind   him.   He's   well. out   of   it,"
thought Miss Baker grimly.  " He don't know his
luck—not having you to look after, that's a fact he
doesn't.")

" Well—what is it ? " she demanded aloud.  " What's
up ?  Why can't we get into the house ?  Who's to
stop us ? "

" Winifred.  That is . . . Winifred and her mother.
You see . . ."

" *Who?* That saucy cat of a servant? How can she stop us? You're the mistress, aren't you? You don't have to ask her every time you go in at your own front door, I suppose, do you? I never heard of such a thing."

"No . . . that is, yes," said Miss Padsoe faintly but carefully. "I am, of course, *mistress* of the house because I *own* it, but I am afraid I am not always *altogether* mistress . . . that is, I am afraid I have allowed Winifred and her mother *far too much freedom*. Especially during the last eighteen months. In fact, I have sometimes wondered *where* matters would end . . . so much rudeness. Open defiance. And now this. . . ."

" *What?* " demanded Miss Baker, in the extremely controlled voice of a person whose control is trembling on the edge of collapse. "For Gawd's *sake*, Miss Padsoe, *what's up*? Can't you get it off your chest?"

" They've locked us out."

Miss Baker stared at her. She heard the words, though they were murmured almost unintelligibly into Miss Padsoe's cup, but her mind simply refused to accept them.

"Locked us out? What—out of the house? Them two locked us out?"

"I . . . I am afraid so. Or rather, they have not exactly locked us *out*, but Winifred's mother told me that—that if I came back to-night, she would not let me *in*."

"Why not?" demanded Miss Baker, her mouth pursed up like a rat's.

Miss Padsoe hesitated, an even deeper flush burning up into her thin cheeks, her eyes failing to meet the snapping and furious eyes of Miss Baker.

" Why not ? " repeated Miss Baker.

" Well . . . you see . . . Miss Baker, this is *very* difficult for me and *most* embarrassing . . . but the fact is, Winifred and her mother have been with me for two years, and they have come to look on The Tower as their *home*, rather than as a ' *place*.' And they very bitterly resent . . . I am afraid . . . the idea of a . . . a . . . stranger coming to stay in the house—perhaps to live there. I hesitated for a long time before I wrote to *Town and Country*, enquiring for a partner. I was afraid Winifred and her mother would not like it at all. I was . . . really, Miss Baker, I was *afraid* to tell them. But they found out. There was a *shocking* scene—only that morning, the Sunday you first came. It was dreadful. (That class is so *violent* when roused.) And there have been these scenes ever since . . . and to-day, Winifred's mother said that if I came back with *that woman* . . . "

" Meaning me. Well thank you, I'm sure, for those few nuts. Thank you very much indeed. And you can sit there, and tell me that, and let those saucy, good-for-nothing couple of idle cats lock you out of your own house because you bring a friend to stay a day or two. Why, you ought to be ashamed of yourself, Miss Padsoe—a woman of your age. It isn't as though you were a young girl just married. Shut you out of your own house—! Said they'd do it if I came along to-day, I suppose, did they ? "

A silent nod.

" And you came along to meet me (in all this pouring rain, too, and you just out of bed with a bad cold) knowin' when we got back that most likely we couldn't get into the house ? "

Nod.

"Gawd stone me up a gum-tree," cried Miss Baker loudly, to the obvious interest and amusement of the rest of Mrs. Brown's Parlour, "you must be as balmy as they are. Why *on earth* didn't you stay in the house, so's you could let me in when I came?"

"I . . . I wanted to warn you," said Miss Padsoe faintly, looking up for the first time and showing Miss Baker her large eyes drowned in tears. "I . . . I thought perhaps you wouldn't want to come when you heard there was likely to be unpleasantness. I have had a very terrible time since that day I first saw you. During my illness . . . it was dreadful. I was quite alone. Alone for hours and hours. I thought I should never recover. I even *hoped* I never should. But God's ways are not our ways."

She stopped abruptly. For once Miss Baker had nothing to say. She was embarrassed by Miss Padsoe's last sentence, but her silence was due to more than that. The low hoarse voice and tear-drowned eyes and the story they told awed her. My word, she thought, the poor old girl must have nearly gone west. Looks half-way there already. She's had an awful time. What a rotten shame. Poor old nannygoat.

"Oh, you mustn't talk like that," she said cheerfully, her rage put aside for a moment. "We all feel like that after 'flu. I did meself. All you want is a tonic. Phosferine's very good, they say. We'll get a bottle before we catch the bus. Now, pull your socks up. What are we going to do? Can't stay here all night, can we? We've got no money."

For she was not going to admit to her twenty pounds. She would try any other plan before she paid a night's hotel bill for herself and Miss Padsoe.

"No," murmured Miss Padsoe.

"Well . . . what, then? How about goin' back there, and trying to get in? P'raps they won't dare not let us in. P'raps it's all bluff."

"Oh, I am *sure* they meant it. They were so . . . so *threatening*. Winifred's mother shouted at me from the hall as I came away. 'Remember' she shouted 'you come back with her and we put the chain on the door.'"

"I'd give her 'remember,'" said Miss Baker grimly. "Who does she think she is—Hitler? I'd 'remember' her. Chain on the door! As though we was mad dogs! I never in all my born days—well, come on. No use stickin' about here."

And having extracted threepence from Miss Padsoe as her share of the coffee, Miss Baker paid the bill, picked up the suitcases, told Miss Padsoe to put up the umbrella and off they went.

While they were crossing the streaming Square to where the Bassett bus waited, without having formed any plan except that they must first get to Bassett, Miss Baker said:

"Excuse me askin,' but haven't you got any friends in Bassett? Someone you could go to, for to-night, I mean? Then p'raps we could go round to The Tower to-morrow and show those saucy bitches (beg your pardon it slipped out but they make me so wild) where they get off."

"There is only Mrs. Shelling," began Miss Padsoe doubtfully.

"Shelling? That was the nice-looking young fellow who gave me a lift the first time I came, wasn't it? She his wife?" (For if he was married, what was that plump, shabby, silent girl doing so familiarly in his car? Miss Baker's agitated mind played pleasantly with scandalous possibilities before it returned to the main matter in hand.)

"Oh, *no*. His mother. Mr. Shelling is not married, nor is his sister. I have known them for *many* years."

"Then off you go to them," said Miss Baker decidedly, thinking that when Miss Padsoe did so she would certainly go off with her and share anything that was going or her name was not Hilda Baker. "She can put you up for to-night, can't she? They got a big house?"

"No . . . Baines House is quite small. It was formerly our house, you know. My grandfather's, that is. My dear father built The Tower, you know."

"Well, she can make room for you, then. Won't hurt her, for once."

"The Shellings," said Miss Padsoe delicately as they climbed into the bus, "are not exactly *friends*. They are more *acquaintances*. I would *really* rather not. . . ."

Miss Baker, peering out gloomily through the steamy windows of the bus into the rainy dusk, pointed out that we (and this time she used the plural firmly) couldn't sleep under a hedge in this rain, could we? and Miss Padsoe reluctantly had to agree. So to the Shellings it was decided that they should go, and even as they came to this decision, the bus started, and soon it had left the tawdry streaming streets of Reading behind and was forging through muddy lanes and sweet-smelling darkness filled with rain towards the folded hills hiding Bassett.

Miss Baker sat with her icy wet feet poised on one of her suitcases. She was damp all over, seething with outrage and fury, starving hungry, and sure that she and Miss Padsoe would both get pneumonia as a result of this evening's work.

But in spite of all these things, and of the general awfulness and maddening discomfort of the situation, one fixed determination began to grow in Miss Baker's mind. She was going to give Winifred and her mother something to " remember " *her* by.

# CHAPTER IX

IF the evening had been fine, the arrival of Miss Baker
and Miss Padsoe at Baines House would have been
described as a confounded bore, and discussed for days
afterwards in that tone of polite surprise in which
people do discuss social gaffes. But the rain and wind
had successfully blighted a party for which George and
Bell had issued invitations : since tea-time there had
been a succession of telephone messages from people
who swore it was blowing a gale in town and were
afraid " she'll never do it."

Mrs. Shelling heard each successive ring from the
telephone with a melancholy nod. She had known it
would be like this. Had she not said so to Miss Catton ?
" Yes, Mrs. Shelling," said Miss Catton, who was sitting
on a humpty before the drawing-room fire with *The Origin
of Species* open across her knees.

" No one gives parties in March in the country. I
knew how it would be. I told them so. No, they will
not listen. Now no one will come except that Bertie
Barranger. He will come. Mark what I say. That is
a nice dress, Miss Catton. You look very nice. It was
made at home, yes ? "

" Yes, Mrs. Shelling."

" It is your only evening dress ? "

" Yes, Mrs. Shelling."

" That is quite right. A young girl who does not
go out much and whose parents are not wealthy does

not need more than one evening dress. Isabella spends
too much on her dresses. Always I am telling her so.
Ach, there is the front-door bell. It is that Bertie
Barranger. I knew he would come."

But it was not Bertie Barranger, as George and Bell,
who had been reduced to standing with their noses
pressed miserably against the dining-room window, had
already discovered. Bertie would probably come by
car : these people, whoever they were, came on foot.
As they entered the rays of the light over the porch they
were seen to be female, and rather wet. They seemed
to be arguing.

"It's old Padsoe," said George, flying out of the
dining-room followed by Bell, and brushing past the
maid who was on her way to answer the ring. "Must
have gone balmy at last."

And he flung open the door and effusively welcomed
Miss Padsoe and Miss Baker, who were nearly at the
end of their respective tempers. He and Bell had been
wandering about the house like starving lions since five
o'clock, and now fell upon this crumb of excitement
with avidity.

"I say, you're pretty wet," said Bell, surveying them
curiously. "Have you come over in all this ? I do hope
nothing's wrong ? "

"Anything we can do ? " asked George ; then
suddenly recognizing Miss Baker, he added, "Hullo—
we've met before, haven't we ? "

"You very kindly gave me a lift in your car," said
Miss Baker, who was, for the second time in her life,
subdued by the grandeur of her surroundings : the
white paint, Persian rugs, etchings and gleaming brass
of Baines House seemed palatial to her. "About a
month ago."

"So I did," said George, and just then the drawing-room door opened and out came Mrs. Shelling, buoyed up by a melancholy hope, bred of the most unusual delay at the front door, that Bertie Barranger might have had an accident and be unfit to attend what was left of the evening's festivities.

Mrs. Shelling's hand was outstretched and upon her lips were trembling the words "Good evening, Bertie. How is your poor father?" when she caught sight of the group at the front door, and she changed the sentence to "Ach, Miss Padsoe, what is the matter? Who is this?" pointing to Miss Baker.

"Miss Baker. Miss Baker, this is Mrs. Shelling," said Miss Padsoe faintly, and looking, by this time, so insane that George and Bell quite forgot about the party and stared at her with a satisfying mixture of excitement and compassion. For both were too intelligent not to be easily moved by sympathy for the obviously old and poor and afflicted.

"Pleased to meet you," muttered Miss Baker, sticking out a hand in a damp fabric glove, and then half withdrawing it, and finally re-arranging it upon the handle of Miss Padsoe's umbrella. Mrs. Shelling did not move.

Miss Padsoe suddenly gave a deep, deep sigh and seemed to pull herself together. She began to speak tremulously, but in the voice of a woman who had herself well in hand, and related the facts of their plight.

Mrs. Shelling decorated her narrative with cries of "Ach!" and murmurs of "Himmel!" and once, when Miss Padsoe came to the part where Winifred's mother had shouted "Remember!" Mrs. Shelling said "Jesu-Maria!" Miss Baker, whose spirits, though awed, were reviving from their depression in the quiet

and warmth of Baines House, chimed in at intervals with
" That's right " or " That's a fact."

Mrs. Shelling's face did not change its expression
until the very end of Miss Padsoe's speech. Then, when
she began to see that she was going to be asked to put
up two tiresome women for the night, a shade, the
beginning of a creeping shadow of polite, cautious
excuse, began to appear.

She parted her lips, as Miss Padsoe finished speaking,
but before his mother could get a word out, George
cut in authoritatively.

" Of course you can. We're delighted to be of use.
I never heard of such damned insolence ; they must be
mad or drunk. Typical, of course. I get the same thing
at the factory ; just sheer, stubborn malice. I hate that
class ; it stinks. Look here, you must be starving. Bell,
see about some dinner, will you ? " and he put a friendly
hand on Miss Padsoe's shoulder and began to shepherd
the two women upstairs.

His mother stood still, looking up at them as they
went. She heard Miss Padsoe murmur " Are you *sure*,
Mr. Shelling, we are not giving *too* much trouble ? "
and George's easy reply " Of course not. Don't
you fret," and saw them ushered into the spare
room.

Bell looked at her mother and smiled rather
maliciously.

" The King will see to it," she said. " And he
has, too. Rather a bore. · I suppose I shall have
to have your divan : shall I tell Elsa to make it
up ? "

" Do as you please," said Mrs. Shelling. She swept
back into the drawing-room where Miss Catton was
sitting staring into the fire, swept *The Times* off the sofa,

announced " I am going to bed, Miss Catton.  Tell Elsa
to bring me my milk at half-past nine," and swept out
again.

It was perhaps unfortunate that the luckless Bertie
Barranger should have been chosen by Heaven to ring
the bell at this moment.  Mrs. Shelling stopped as
though shot, opened the door very vigorously and
said :

" There you are again, Bertie," in a tone that made
Bertie blink.

" Rather," said Bertie uneasily.  " Not the first arrival,
I hope ?  George anywhere about ? "

" George is with two old fools in the spare room.
He is a very naughty boy.  Good-night," said George's
mother, and, with her back as straight as a fishing-rod,
climbed the stairs to her bed.

   .   .   .   .   .   .

Miss Catton had switched off the light in the drawing-
room.  The dance of the firelight over the white
walls was so pretty, and the distant music from the
morning-room sounded sweeter if listened to in the
half-dark.

" How Deep Is The Ocean ? " asked the electric
gramophone, very tenderly and softly.

That tune was a favourite of George's, whose taste
in popular music leant towards the Edwardian.  This
was the first time Miss Catton had heard it on George's
gramophone, but she remembered the pretty, haunting
tune from her own dancing days, which were now (she
kept on telling herself) over.

She sat staring sternly into the fire, whose light danced
too much to permit her to read *The Origin of Species*,
thinking that it was half-past ten, that she was twenty-

two and had not yet found her life's work, that George and Bell and Bertie Barranger had been sitting over salted almonds and sherry in the dining-room for a good hour after Miss Padsoe and Miss Baker had gone up to their beds, and that the morning-room floor, so empty and shining, must have tempted Bell and George and Bertie to dance, because a quarter of an hour ago she had heard them laughing and talking as they crossed the hall. She had just decided, with an unconscious sigh, that she must really go to bed, when the music suddenly swelled into loudness, and she heard steps crossing the hall.

George opened the drawing-room door, and stuck his head round it.

" Miss Catton, do you dance ? "

" Well, I do, but I haven't for years," she answered. Her voice was very serious, and fresh as the voice of a child ; she pronounced all her words with a beautiful clearness.

" Well . . . will you come and dance with me ? Do."

She hesitated before replying " Well . . . I was just going to bed."

" Oh, nonsense ; it's only half-past ten. Come on. I'll teach you the rumba." (This was cunning of George, who did not know the rumba but guessed that Miss Catton had a thirst for all kinds of knowledge.)

" Very well, I will, then. Only I must warn you, I'm very out of practice."

" Doesn't matter. So am I."

Bell, whose party dress of lilac and black plaid taffetas looked strangely gorgeous in the large empty shining room, waved in a friendly way at Miss Catton and called " Sherry ? "

But Miss Catton, who was a teetotaller, politely declined. "Really," thought George, looking down at the top of her dark head where the very white parting lay exactly down its centre, "she *is* a little prig. No doing anything with her. Awful little bore, but undoubtedly bedworthy."

And full of surprises, he thought, when he discovered after a few turns that she was as light as a cloud on her small plump feet.

"You dance very well," he observed. "You don't try to lead. I hate a woman who tries to lead."

"Do you?"

He was still trying to decide if there had been an expression of irony in the hazel eyes lifted to his, when the music stopped.

"How high is the sky?" asked the gramophone, on a final softly plaintive note; and ceased. And Bell came drifting down the room to her brother, holding out her arms, thin and graceful as wands in their huge puffed sleeves.

"My turn."

Bertie was attending to the gramophone, and the brother and sister drifted away together.

"They look like one person," suddenly said Miss Catton to Bertie, who was guiding her round the room.

"They are," replied Bertie simply. He was so used to being treated as a fool by the brilliant George that he now said just whatever he thought without dreaming anyone would remember it, comment on it, or believe it.

"You and I aren't, though," thought Miss Catton, who was discovering that Bertie breathed heavily, rammed his tummy against her, had hot hands, bumped, and committed other dancing sins.

And when the music stopped for the second time, she was too busy resenting Bertie to realise that she resented George and Bell dancing as though they were one person.

# CHAPTER X

GEORGE was quite sorry he had to go to town next day, there were so many interesting things going on at home.

There were Miss Baker and Miss Padsoe, refreshed by a night's sleep, and eager for his advice and Bell's upon the Winifred-and-her-mother situation. There was Bertie, who had passed a wretched night upon an inadequate sofa, and who was obviously anxious to impart to George the latest complicated developments in his newest love affair to date, in spite of George's skilful stalling of three previous attempts the night before; and there was Miss Catton, who had met his eyes once at breakfast when she passed him the honey with a severe, almost sorrowful, look which he was most unaccustomed to seeing in the hazel eyes of a young girl. An interesting wench, the Catton.

But it was no use; he had to go. Routine was routine; and besides, Bertie had to be carried back to town in order that he might arrive at his father's office at eleven o'clock. Mrs. Shelling insisted on Bertie sticking closely to this rule every time he came to spend the night; she would never have him in the house an hour longer than was necessary, and George had learnt that if he wanted that atmosphere of idle, rather mocking peacefulness at home which best suited his temperament, he must usually defer to his mother's wishes. They had touched on the subject that morning,

when George went into his mother's room to discuss
with her the business he must do in town during the
day.

"I can't understand what you've got against old
Bertie, Ma. He's human, like the rest of us."

"We are all God's creatures, I hope," said Mrs.
Shelling severely, dismissing her son with a wave of her
hand. But as she turned her attention once more to
her toast and coffee and von Bülow's *Memoirs*, the
thought of Miss Baker and Miss Padsoe flitted through
her mind, and her face expressed a doubt.

Bell was pleasantly divided about her plans for the
day. Should she racket up to town with Bertie and
George, shop, lunch with the boys, do a concert, and
let George drive her home in the evening, or should she
stay at home and watch the Baker-Padsoe-Winifred
battle fought to a bloody conclusion, and pump Miss
Catton about George?

"Well, for god's sake make up your mind," said
George, who was bored by her ditherings, putting on his
muffler in the hall. "What's *her* name?" he added
in a whisper, jerking his head at the closed breakfast-
room door.

"Who . . . Miss Baker? Minnie, I should
think."

"No—Miss Catton."

"Oh—Queenie."

"Nonsense!"

"It's quite true. I saw it on a letter she was reading
at breakfast. 'My darling Queenie' it said. Just figure
to yourself!" .

"Was it from a male, do you think?"

"How should I know? No, I don't think so; it
was on Woolworth notepaper and very carefully written

. . . you know. And why should you care if it's from a male, anyway ? "

Bell always made a feeble splutter of protest before George embarked upon any new affair, but she knew from experience that nothing deterred him.

" Well, I do care," said George teasingly.

" Do you like her ? " Bell was almost on tip-toe, anxiously searching his face with her huge grey eyes.

" M . . . m . . . m . . . yes, I think I do. I don't know. . . . She's a queer little boring prig, but there's something . . . oh, I don't know. Look here, *are* you coming or not ? I must go."

" Coming ! "

She flew upstairs lightly as a fountain-jet and re-appeared incredibly quickly in her outdoor things.

" Do come, for god's sake," bawled Bertie dismally, who was already in the car. " I shall be as late as hell, and Pa will flay me."

Miss Catton, Miss Baker and Miss Padsoe, sitting in constrained silence in the breakfast-room, saw the car go past the window. The occupants waved rather ironically, and shrieked " Good luck ! " Bell was wearing Bertie's hat and he hers ; and Miss Baker observed that they were regular Bright Young People, weren't they ?

" So gay—so young. I like to see them," said Miss Padsoe softly ; she was one of those nice women who accept the fifties without a sigh, and to whom twenty-six seems childhood.

Miss Catton said nothing. She disapproved of exchanging hats and wasting one's time dashing up to town on the spur of the moment when one might have been at home walking in the awakening woods ; or mending one's stockings. Bell had a hole in one grey silk heel.

" Well," said Miss Baker with a loud sigh, having drunk off the last drops of her cold sugary coffee, " now, Miss Padsoe, what about it ? What are we going to do ? "

" Do ? "

" Yes, do. About that Winifred and her mother ? We can't stay here, can we ? Mustn't eat Mrs. Shelling out of house and home," and Miss Baker gave one of her false, toothy smiles at Miss Catton, whom she regarded (quite wrongly) as vice-reine in Mrs. Shelling's absence. But she was not afraid of her—not she. Miss Catton wasn't anybody ; she was only a paid mother's help ; like a sort of servant, really. No better than Miss Baker was—not so good, come to that. What did Miss Catton earn a week ? Fifteen shillings, probably. What Muriel earned, at Haddon's.

But therein Miss Baker erred ; Miss Catton earned twenty.

Miss Catton returned the smile politely but she felt she could not take it upon herself to say that she was sure Mrs. Shelling would not mind how long they stayed or how much they ate, for Mrs. Shelling had made it obvious that she minded very much indeed.

Had Mrs. Shelling been another kind of woman, Miss Padsoe might have asked her, as a prosperous and experienced matron, to cope with Winifred and her mother. But somehow people seldom asked favours of Mrs. Shelling. And they seldom asked them of George, because he was so rich, so fortunate, so obviously the kind of person put into the world by Heaven to do favours to less lucky beings, that he could not help being aware of this : and he was always afraid people were going to ask, and to " use " him (as he furiously put it) instead of liking him just for his beautiful eyes ; and at the least whiff of favour-asking, he became glacial with rage. And presently less fortunate people stopped asking : such are the penalties of wealth. Miss Padsoe never for a second dreamt of begging this kind, gay, friendly young man to act as knight-errant to herself and Miss Baker.

" Shall we go into the morning-room ? " said Miss Catton clearly, who never murmured or muttered. " There's a fire there."

So they trailed uneasily off to the morning-room, with Miss Baker's question unanswered ; but as soon as they got there, Miss Catton marched away upstairs to see Mrs. Shelling about the day's affairs, and Miss Baker and Miss Padsoe were left together.

Though the one was still simmering with indignation and the other was what she would have described as " much upset," both had been refreshed by night's sleep and by the conventional but undeniable comfort of Baines House ; and they were now far better fitted to deal with the situation.

" We can't stay here, that's very plain," said Miss Baker decidedly, the instant the door had closed on Miss Catton. " *She* " (jerking her head at the ceiling) " doesn't like us being here. Plain as the nose on my face. Aren't some people funny ? "

" I was afraid Mrs. Shelling would be rather put out," said Miss Padsoe timidly. " You may remember, I *did* suggest it to you. In the bus. Just before it started."

"Well, we can't help her troubles now," said Miss Baker, ignoring this gentle self-justification. "What we've got to do is to get back to The Tower as soon as we can."

"Oh . . . but now? I mean, suppose they won't let us in? I am afraid I am hardly *equal*, Miss Baker, to a *scene*; my throat is rather bad again this morning."

"They'll let us in all right," said Miss Baker defiantly, who had no plans at all, and was utterly hazy about the respective legal rights of employer and employed. "I'll stand with my thumb on the bell till they do. We'll say we'll fetch the police. That'll frighten them. That's what you ought to have done yesterday, then we should never have had any of this picnic."

"Suppose they won't answer the door?"

"Then," said Miss Baker with great decision and energy, "we'll bust a window and get in that way. Oh, I'll get even with them. You wait. I'll have them both out of that house, bag and baggage, before tea time to-day. Now, are you ready? We'll just ask that Miss Cat or whatever she calls herself if the bags can stay here for a bit, until we know where we are, and then we'll be off."

But Miss Padsoe's long fly-away face did not express the energy and desire to be off which were appropriate to the occasion. She looked extremely woebegone, flustered, and anxious to stay where she was. She coughed, and spread her long thin fingers over her flaccid neck, eyeing Miss Baker timidly.

"Really, Miss Baker, is there no other *possible* way of dealing with this most *distressing* . . . I mean, *must* we both go? I thought perhaps we might telephone to my solicitor. Only of course he might not be in. . . .

But I do really feel *most* unwell to-day. I hardly think I am equal . . . I have caught a fresh cold, I think." (Here she sneezed into a fragile old handkerchief.) " And I really feel that I could not endure a scene of any kind. After all, Winifred and her mother mean no *harm* ; it is just excessive loyalty, perhaps, do you think ? I don't want to break with them, after two years. Places are so hard to get, nowadays. . . . Especially without references."

"References?" Miss Baker had listened to this speech with sundry impatient twitchings and snortings and jerkings. " You don't mean to say, Miss Padsoe, you was thinking of giving them two *references* ? After what they've done ? Shouting at you like that, and locking you out of your own house ? "

" We are told to turn the other cheek," said Miss Padsoe, mildly and solemnly.

" Gawd stone me up a gum-tree ! " exploded Miss Baker, " if you aren't as bad as they are ! Here, I'm off. You needn't come if you don't feel up to it. (You look bad, I will say that for you, and I don't want you on my hands as well as everything else.) You stay here, see, and keep in the warm, and if I am not back in an hour—well, say an hour and a half—you come along and see what's happened to me, see ? "

" Are you *sure*, Miss Baker, you do not *mind* going alone ? It is a *great* deal to ask of a stranger. But really . . . I do feel that I should be more hindrance than help. I have never been able to do very much with Winifred or her mother, if they once made up their minds to anything. But you . . . I feel sure you will arrange everything."

And Miss Padsoe sank restfully into an armchair by

the fire, leaned her head back on its corduroy cushion, and smiled gratefully, with half-closed eyes, across at Miss Baker.

"Looks as though I shall have to," retorted Miss Baker, wishing she could shake her, but also feeling (most annoyingly) sorry for the old fool, with her thin flushed face and air of being nothing but bones inside an old cloth and braid dress and her patched shoes. "Well, it will all be the same a hundred years hence. Now remember. If I'm not back in an hour and a half, you come along after me, see? Get that Miss Cat to come, too, if you can. She'll be company for you. I'll just go up and get my things on."

"Oh, I am *sure* you will be back in *no* time," said Miss Padsoe earnestly, without knowing in the least what she meant, or why she was sure. Deliciously, responsibility had suddenly slipped from her. She leant deeper into the cushion and her eyes closed.

"Sez you," muttered Miss Baker, surveying her with an expression mingling exasperation and bafflement Then she went out of the room.

Fortunately she met Miss Catton on the stairs, and was able to explain the plan to her, such as it was, and to ask if the suitcases and Miss Padsoe might remain there for a little while longer? Miss Catton, secretly stirred by the prospect of the coming battle, thought that she expected Mrs. Shelling would not mind if they did, and went upstairs to ask. Mrs. Shelling waved her away with a piece of toast, and said yes, yes, she supposed so: how tiresome old virgins always were; it was all they had to do, she supposed, to be a nuisance to their more fortunate married sisters.

"Mrs. Shelling says of *course* she doesn't mind," translated Queenie, standing at the door of the spare

.room and surveying Miss Baker with solemn, enthusiastic eyes.

"Let's hope she doesn't split something," muttered Miss Baker. "Well, I'm off. I'll see you in about an hour."

"We'll be there, of *course*," said Queenie, and suddenly put out her hand to Miss Baker, "Good luck."

"I shall need it. Thanks," said Miss Baker, taking the little hand, and then was surprised to find her own warmly shaken.

"I *do* think it's *ripping* of you to go," said Queenie, so thawed, rippling with feeling and stirred by admiration, that her face was transfigured: George would not have known her.

Miss Baker stared at her. The girl looked downright balmy. Oh, into what a world she had strayed!

"I don't know about that," she said tartly. "*Someone's* got to go, haven't they?"

But Queenie was not deceived. She watched Miss Baker stumping down the stairs and across the hall with as much admiration as though Miss Baker had been The Maid herself. Admirable Miss Baker! She was doing it to help Miss Padsoe, because Miss Padsoe was old, frail and incompetent. I am a beast, thought Queenie remorsefully, as she went down to the morning-room to fetch the housekeeping books. I'm always summing people up at sight, and hating them, and then finding they're awfully decent, really. It's awful. I'll never learn. Every six weeks I look back and I'm *amazed* that I could have done such idiotic things only six weeks ago. It's most discouraging.

The exquisite thought drifted across her mind, as she closed Mrs. Shelling's desk, that she might also have been wrong about George; and Bell. Oh! if they were in reality as good as they were charming! A burst of sunlight rushed into the room, all the wet trees suddenly swung glittering in the wind. She ran upstairs two at a time.

# CHAPTER XI

Miss Baker stepped into a drive whose stones shone from a shower, although the sun was out. But everything was very wet, and when Miss Baker thought how she would have to tramp down one soggy hillside and up another to reach The Tower, because she was afraid of losing her way if she went round by the road along which she and Miss Padsoe had come the night before, she felt furious. She stumped away down the drive between the wet rhododendrons, without the ghost of a plan in her head, wishing Miss Padsoe at Jericho, and wondering where on earth she could find a telephone box, supposing it were necessary to call the police, and how she was going to get into the house at all, let alone have Winifred and her mother out of it by tea-time?

It was awful, downright awful. It seemed a year since she had been in the peaceful (at least, outwardly peaceful, though inwardly it seethed like Tammany Hall) cutting-room at Haddon's. She looked at the wristwatch she had uneasily bought for herself on Saturday. Half-past ten. They would just be putting the kettle on for morning coffee, and Muriel would be reaching down the biscuit tin from the shelf where the old account-books were kept.

Yet somehow, in spite of this vision of ordered and ancient peace, Miss Baker did not wish she were back.

She sniffed, as she came to the end of the short drive;

put her head up and back and drew in a really deep sniff such as she had not drawn for years. There was a lovely smell.

Miss Baker's sense of smell, like that of most civilized persons, was used chiefly to repel odours, not to welcome them. Now it welcomed the scent of wet buds and bark, and the soaked earth. Fresh, it smelled; very nice, thought Miss Baker, with her sallow, lined, busy little face thrown back to meet the huge sky, blazing with colourless light. No, somehow, despite Winifred and her mother, she did not wish she were back at Haddon's.

She came out at the end of the drive, and there was the road, and the abrupt deep drop into the valley that held Bassett, and on the opposite hill, a good half-mile away, she could see the turret of The Tower, above its screen of old firs.

There it sat, looking lonely even at that distance, and no doubt inside it those two saucy cats were still sitting over their breakfast, very pleased with themselves and thinking they had won. Well, they hadn't.

And Miss Baker began to stump purposefully across the road.

She went straight through a wood whose path was a succession of pools, and by the time she was half-walking, half-sliding, down the hillside, her shoes were lost in two large lumps of mud, and her feet were soaking in their black lisle stockings. The sky clouded, and a cold wind blew stealthily against the bare trees.

" Good thing I brought me umbrella," muttered Miss Baker, glancing apprehensively at the sky.

Down, down she went, and reached the strip of road at the bottom of the valley, crossed it, and began to go up the other side. All the doors in the village were shut, and not a soul was to be seen.

Going up was far, far worse than going down. The only way she could get up at all was by deserting the path, and climbing up the streaming grass, which washed the mud from her shoes and soaked her ankles.

"Catch me death," she muttered resignedly. "Oh, well, it's all in the day's work." And on she went, breathing heavily, her calf muscles aching furiously, her face flushed with unaccustomed blood pumped up by her surprised heart, a dew of sweat on her wrinkled forehead. She had almost forgotten the task in front of her. Her one aim was to reach the crown of that hill.

And just as she did reach it, and stumped slowly into the little wood which lay between The Tower's gates and the hill, a most amazing piece of luck happened to Miss Baker.

She heard voices.

They were loud, fat, triumphant voices; the voices of women who are drunk with the joy of asserting themselves and ruling the roost and beating other people's faces into the mud, and who have, as a consequence, lost their sense of prudence and proportion. One, a young, hard voice was saying grossly:

"Oh, do shut up. It's all right, I tell you. She won't be back to-day, and if she does, she can't get in, so where's the harm? Come on, for god's sake. We'll miss the blooming bus."

"S'pose she *does* come back, bringing somebody? Nice pair we should look, going out and leaving the 'ouse with no one in it," said a second, older voice.

"*She* won't find anyone. She hasn't got anyone who'd come. Besides, who'd believe an old fool like her? If she does come back this evening with anyone, I'll just open the door as quiet as you please, lookin' surprised, like. 'Oh, Miss Padsoe, where *have* you been

all night? Cook and me was quite worried about
you. . . .' (I don't think.) That'd make her look a
nice fool, wouldn't it? Who'd believe her—an old
scarecrow like that? Come on; I can hear the bus."

And Miss Baker, who had darted behind a large beech
at the first words, peered cautiously out and saw the
two speakers walking rapidly down the road, away from
the house, in the direction where she knew the bus-
stop to be.

She could not see their faces, but she knew the large,
bustling bottom of the younger woman at once. It
was Winifred. And the large, square, grim back
bouncing along beside her could only belong to her
mother.

" Well . . . *What* a bit of luck ! " muttered Miss
Baker joyfully, staring after them as though they had
been angelic visitants. " Of all the——! Well, if that
isn't too good to be true ! Now where are they off to,
I wonder? Fancy going off like that and leaving the
house ! They must be balmy. (Old scarecrow, indeed !
What a way to talk about the one who pays their wages !)
Well, I never. This beats all."

And as the figures retreated still further, Miss Baker
came out cautiously from behind her tree and stood, in
full view had they turned round, gazing first at them and
then at the open white gates of The Tower.

She was quite overpowered by her good fortune.
Why, the coast was clear ! She had only to break a
window and nip into the house, and the field was hers !
Oh, if Miss Padsoe had only been with her ! It was just
like the old nannygoat to collapse exactly when she
ought to have been on the scene of action ; and now it
was ten to one Winifred and her mother would come
back before Miss Padsoe and that Miss Cat arrived from

Baines House, and if that happened, Miss Baker would indeed be in a hole, because she would have two people outside the house whom she wanted to let *in* and two whom she wanted to keep *out*, and heaven help them all if they met on the lawn.

She would have to be quick.

She nipped cautiously across the road, glancing warily from side to side (really, it was like being a gangster on the pictures; she could just imagine how they felt) and slipped through the gate, and had run half-way up the drive before she turned round to see if she were being followed.

No one. Only wet, swaying trees, the watery flash and retreat of March sunlight, the slow sigh of wind in the fir branches, and, fading reassuringly into the distance, the sound of the bus's engine.

Miss Baker resumed her march at a brisk stump. She had forgotten she was tired and furious. All her former feelings were drowned in a sea of excitement. Oh, if she could only find some way of letting Miss Padsoe know what had happened, and telling her to come to The Tower at once!

She reached the end of the drive and faced the house across its wide lawn of sodden winter grass. All the windows, of course, were shut. A thread of smoke wavered from one chimney, spread almost flat over the roof by the wind. Miss Baker had never seen a house looking so locked up. It seemed to have been shut with a snap.

She wasted no time at the front door, but left the path just beyond it and followed a flower-bed round the left side of the house, which was hidden from the drive. She was looking for a low-lying larder window which she could break and scramble through. Or if there was no larder window, a Somewhere Else window would do ; they often looked out on to the garden.

Her luck was in. There were no low windows on that side of the house, nor any facing another broad expanse of lawn and its sighing cedar at the back, but right on the other side, the side furthest from the front door, she pounced upon a window set low in the wall, beside a green-painted door facing a bedraggled kitchen garden.

On the other side of the door was a bigger window, but its curtains were drawn, and it looked too imposing to smash. The little window had only a single pane.

" I bet that's the kitchen," said Miss Baker, surveying the large window. "Where's a stone? Puzzle, find one. Here, this'll do," and she pounced upon a rusty trowel lying on a heap of boughs and last year's roots, and thus armed, went up to the little whitewashed window.

If you are not used to smashing windows, they seem very tough. Miss Baker, hampered by a natural horror at smashing anything, made two attempts before the trowel shattered the pane.

It made a shocking noise, and at last fell tinkling on to a stone floor on the other side.

" Must be a larder, not Somewhere Else. They never have stone floors," thought Miss Baker. She smashed away the rest of the glass until not a fragment was left in the surrounding frame ; then she cautiously advanced, and, pushing her head and shoulders through the opening, peered inside.

It was a large cold pantry, smelling of mice, fresh milk and stone. About three feet below Miss Baker was a broad shelf loaded with food and a large bowl of milk ; this ran all round the four walls of the narrow room and another shelf ran high above it. A door directly

faced the window, at the top of three stone steps.   It
was shut.

" If it's locked, I'm done," thought Miss Baker.
" Now, here goes."

And she thrust herself as far into the window as she
could, and began, with the aid of the trowel, to shift
on one side such jars and bowls as she could reach, for
she did not want to step into them when she climbed
through.

She mnaged to move every dish except the milk
bowl ; that was too heavy.   When she tried to push it
sideways with the trowel, it rocked threateningly, and
when she put both her arms inside as far as she could
reach and tried to lift it, she nearly overbalanced and
fell into it.

" Drat," said Miss Baker, giving it up.   " Oh, well—
just have to chance it, that's all.   Won't half be a waste
of milk, if I kick it over."   She drew cautiously back
into the garden again, took a quick glance all round and
saw nothing to alarm her, looked at her watch and saw
it was ten minutes to eleven, and then set herself to
consider how she should go through the window
frame.

There was plenty of room for her little skimpy body.
It was just a question of which should go through first,
her legs or her head.   If she went head first, she would
have to rely on her hands to balance her on the shelf :
if she went feet first, she would have to risk kicking
over the milk.

" I'm glad Lily isn't here.   She wouldn't half laugh,"
thought Miss Baker, and suddenly decided to go feet
first, without really having weighed the advantages of
either method.   She usually made her decisions like
this.

There was a nasty moment when one of her feet dipped into the milk, but nothing more spectacular happened. Quickly she lifted her foot out again, slewing herself round to the left of the bowl. She dropped both feet (the hem of her skirt fell into the milk) on to the shelf, felt its limit with her toes, curled up her legs until her knees rested safely upon the shelf, then cautiously, very cautiously, drew in her waist, shoulders, head and arms until she crouched on the shelf—inside!

She wriggled round, and pushed tne milk bowl as far away as she could reach. An awful crack came from the shelf, and in a panic, she thrust her legs over the side and landed with a jar on the stone floor.

She felt scratched and bruised all over (though there was really nothing the matter with her) but she was flaming with triumph. Oh! if that door were only open!

It was! She turned the handle, and the next second she was pattering along a dark passage. She flew up a short staircase, opened a door, and found herself peeping round into the hall of The Tower, which she had last seen nearly five weeks ago.

The house was still; still as a church, and its unaired coldness struck right through to her bones. It still looked so sober and respectable that it was queer to think of those two cats shouting threats in it, and leaving the poor old nannygoat upstairs alone when she was ill. Miss Baker, no longer stumping but pattering, flew from door to door, opening them and peering into the large dead handsome rooms, wondering madly what to do.

"I know," she muttered, skimming off downstairs again as the thought flew across her mind. "Lock the larder. Lock all the doors. Lock 'em out so's they can't break a window and get in."

All the doors had keys ; some had bolts. She locked every door she met, after a fiercely inquisitive glare inside, through a four-inch opening. She even locked the coal-cellar door, down at the bottom of a bogeyish flight of wooden stairs.

Finally she darted at the kitchen door and flung it open. A puff of warm air blew out at her, smelling pleasantly of recently cooked bacon. A fire purred in the large gleaming range, a rag rug and a cuckoo clock pleased her at once (" Quite homelike—all wasted on them two.") The red curtains were drawn, and the fire burned out from a warm twilight. Everything was clean, the dresser threw back flame gleams from its china.

" I will say they keep it nice," muttered Miss Baker, and she flew through and locked the scullery window and the scullery door, and then rather reluctantly left the kitchen (" I'll have a good read there this evening, see if I don't ") and locked that, and rushed upstairs again across the hall and into a little morning-room which overlooked the drive. This would make a watch tower, from which she could see Miss Padsoe and Miss Cat approaching, or the enemy when it returned.

As she pushed herself against the large clear window, breathing fast, her nose shining with energy and triumph, and keenly surveyed the windy garden, a thought suddenly struck Miss Baker which was so glorious, so magnificent, such a stupendous brain-wave, that she clapped her hands.

" Their boxes ! " she cried, and flew upstairs to the very top of that huge house and flung open a room which she thought might be the bedroom of Winifred and her mother.

It was not; it was a lumber-room, but the next room had the shut windows and the hair tidies and the smell which belongs to Winifreds and their mothers all over the world. And for the next half-hour Miss Baker was rapturously busy.

Old stays, lace collars, sweaty dresses, family photographs, piles of underclothing the exact colour of washing-up water (from choice, not age or use), trodden shoes and copies of the *Girl's Cinema*—all these were huddled into a sheet from the two beds, and left in the middle of the floor.

And then, rushing insanely into the lumber-room, Miss Baker pounced upon an old wicker trunk cased in worn American cloth, with W. W. home-painted upon it, and she bumped this trunk down the stairs from the top of the house to the bottom, making a frightful row, and encouraging it with shrill cries.

She pulled it across the hall, unlocked the front door, dragged the trunk out well into the middle of the lawn where any rain that was going might fall upon it, tore upstairs again, tied up the sheet, dragged it bulging and flopping from the top of the house to the bottom, pulled it across the hall, out of the front door, and on to the lawn beside the trunk.

With great strainings and heavings she forced it (partly) into the trunk. But she left the lid open, so that, if it rained, the possessions of Winifred and her mother might get wet.

She stood for a second on the grass in the fresh rainy wind, staring down at the trunk with a fierce smile of triumph.

Then she bolted back to the house, slammed the door

behind her, and marched into the morning-room. She collapsed, with a deep, deep sigh, into a chair she had pulled up to the window.

" Phew ! " said Miss Baker, " something attempted, something done, has earned a night's repose. That'll show those two cats. I'll give them ' remember.' They'll remember Hilda Baker all right, or my name isn't what it is."

She leaned back in the chair, and, after a few seconds, shut her eyes. Gradually her breathing grew quieter. The muscles of her little marmoset face relaxed. The final echoes of the footsteps and the bumpings, rattlings and door slammings died away ; they had lingered in the quiet of the house like stains in clear water, but were now absorbed by it. In the silence the hiss of the wind in the firs beat against the windows like the sound of the sea. Most satisfactorily, it began to rain. Miss Baker dozed.

Suddenly the light quick notes of the clock in the tower struck twelve. Miss Baker heard them, and sat up quickly ; she darted across to the window, and was just in time to see the backs of Miss Padsoe and Miss Cat, registering anxiety and excitement, entering the porch.

# CHAPTER XII

"Is it all right?" they demanded eagerly, the instant Miss Baker opened the door in response to their stealthy ring.

"How d'you mean . . . all right?" replied Miss Baker, affronted both by their indecent haste and their lack of faith in her capabilities. "Of course it's all right. They're both out; gone off somewhere by bus. That's their trunk, on the lawn. Mean to say you never noticed it?"

Queenie and Miss Padsoe turned to stare at the trunk.

"I . . . I thought it *looked* like Winifred's trunk, but I could not be *sure*," said Miss Padsoe, not daring to add that she had been afraid to believe the evidence of her own eyes. "Hadn't we better *close* it? It's raining. Their things will get wet."

"'Course they will. What d'you think I left it open for? I'll teach them. Here, come inside. I'm going to keep this door locked."

Miss Padsoe stepped timidly over the threshold of her home, but Queenie did not move.

"I'm sorry; I'm afraid I've got to get back," she said reluctantly. "Mrs. Shelling wants me; she only spared me for half an hour, just to see Miss Padsoe over the valley. Good-bye, Good-luck. I'll walk over this evening, if I may, and if I can be spared, to see how you're getting along."

"Oh, we shall get along like a house on fire, don't

you worry," said Miss Baker, who disliked Queenie.
" I don't expect the old girl will be able to spare you.
Keeps you on the hop, don't she ?  So-long."

And Miss Baker firmly closed the door in Queenie's
face.  Miss Padsoe murmured that Queenie seemed a
dear girl, but Miss Baker only retorted that all that fat
couldn't be healthy.  " Now you come on downstairs,
and get a warm-up," she said, shepherding Miss Padsoe
along the icy hall.  " Don't you worry about them two.
If they do come back they can't get in.  Where would
they have gone off to like that, now ?  They must be
barmy—leaving the house alone, when they know we're
outside, wanting to get in."

" To see old Mrs. Pim, I expect," said Miss Padsoe,
trying to repress a qualm at undoubted indications that
Miss Baker was about to give her a warm-up in front of
the kitchen fire.  It was a year since Miss Padsoe had
been in the kitchen ; it was a place of dread to her
because of the two who reigned in it, and this, added to
an Edwardian gentlewoman's natural state of genteel
inexperience about kitchens, made her most anxious
not to go down into it.

" Who's she, when she's at home ? "

" Winifred's mother's mother.  She lives in Fan's
Green.  Winifred and her mother tell Mrs. Pim . . .
I'm afraid . . . everything.  It is most annoying . . .
all one's affairs. . . ."

" They'll have something better still to tell her
next time they see her.  There ! isn't that a lovely
fire ?  Now  you  just  sit  down  here,  and  get
warmed up, and I'll pop up and keep an eye on the
front door."

Miss Baker had been dragging up a chair to the fire
as she spoke, snapping on the light (for she would not

part the curtains in case those two should come round and peer in at poor Miss Padsoe) and snatching up a soiled copy of *Answers* which she slapped firmly on Miss Padsoe's dazed lap.

" There you are ! snug as a bug in a rug. Now don't you move. Just you stay quiet and warm and have a bit of a read. I'll see to them. If they're not here by half-past one, I'll come down and get us some lunch. Lucky there's that lovely fire."

And with a smile, no longer false and toothy, Miss Baker pattered away, leaving Miss Padsoe uncomfortably close to the roaring fire, embarrassed at her most unaccustomed surroundings, and much repelled by the egg and mustard stains on the copy of *Answers*.

But before the sound of Miss Baker's patterings had dimmed away upstairs, another sound made Miss Padsoe sit bolt upright, her face working, her heart banging against her side.

It was a long, imperious, thrilling peal at the front door bell.

Miss Baker, mounting the stairs on her way to Miss Padsoe's bedroom window whence she could survey the field, also heard the sound, and increased her pace to a run.

" That'll be them ! " she thought, and in her mind's eye made a lightning survey of all the windows in the lower part of the house. All were locked, and with the exception of the kitchen and the morning-room, all the doors were safely locked as well, with their keys on the outside.

The Tower was in a state of siege.

She unlocked Miss Padsoe's door and went across to the window. This was slightly to the left of the porch and overlooked it ; one could not see down into the

E

porch, but one could hear what people were saying as they stood inside.

Cautiously, very cautiously, Miss Baker slid up the well-fitting frame, and leaned out into the wind.

The first word she heard was " disgustin'."

" Disgustin' " repeated the voice more loudly. " I'd be ashamed. That's a lady, is it ? That's what we slave for. Well, if that's a lady, I'm glad I'm not, that's all. Don't you stand it, Gert. The law " and here the voice mounted another semitone, " the law's on your side, girl. Compensation. All your things dragged down and left in the wet . . . spiteful, I call it. Down-right spiteful. Nobody minds havin' a fair up-and-a-downer ; we all feels better for one. But goin' behind your back when you was out, like that, and couldn't stand up for yourself . . . oh, I *do* call it narsty."

" Shut up, will you ? " said Winifred's voice savagely. " Jaw-jaw-jaw. Fair give me the sick, you do. Ring the bell again, Mother, can't you ? "

Miss Baker did not hear the second peal (though Miss Padsoe, trembling in the kitchen, did.) She was over at the washstand, picking up a soapdish.

She threw it out of the window.

It smashed, in a satisfying way, out of sight but not out of sound, on the path immediately before the porch.

There was a second's stunned silence ; and then the first voice broke out again, shrill and undoubtedly rather frightened.

" 'Ere, shut up. Throwin' things. Oo d'yer think you are ? Might 'ave 'it somebody. Might 'ave cut somebody's 'ead open."

" Come on out," shouted Miss Baker, leaning out of the window with wisps of hair blowing Valkyrieshly in the rain. " I've got a message from Miss Padsoe."

In another stunned pause, voices were heard observing that it wasn't 'er so it must be The Other One, and asserting that they didn't take orders from The Other One not if they was killed for it, and what business was it of hers anyway? But finally, after Miss Baker had shouted again, she observed a dark point detaching itself from the end of the dark surface of the porch's roof; and this point elongated until it was a small old lady, crowned by a skimmed-off sort of bonnet, and draped in a bugley mantle and the matronly folds of a huge old green skirt. A tiny face, given humanity by two large pale protruding eyes and one of those sucked-in and drawn-down old mouths which seem made to grizzle at street-corners, was lifted to Miss Baker.

" Brought your poor old grannie along, have you? " shouted Miss Baker to the unseen Winifred. " I'd be ashamed if I was you—a great cow like you——"

" 'Oo are you calling a cow? " screamed Winifred, rushing suddenly out of the porch and lifting a furious face to Miss Baker. " You dirty bitch from god-knows-where, 'oo are you calling a cow? Where's Miss Padsoe, that's what I want to know? 'Oo brought my box downstairs? Where's all my things? You don't know what you've done, Miss Smarty; you wait. You won't look so funny when I come back with a policeman."

" Compensation," said old Mrs. Pim, nodding vigorously and sucking her mouth in until it almost disappeared. " All them things. Spoilt."

" Never mind about a policeman," said Miss Baker, leaning her elbows insultingly upon the window sill, and maddeningly surveying the three (for the group had now been joined by Winifred's mother) with her head on one side. " We'll soon see who'll get a policeman. Wait till Miss Padsoe's lawyer begins asking where all the money's gone.    All the money she had to pay for meat she never got, poor old dear, while you was stuffing away like a couple of prize pelicans.    Wait till he comes to see the housekeeping books (oh yes, *Miss Winifred*, I've got them all here, see ?) and hears how you left her alone upstairs when she was ill for hours on end, you pair of dirty idle lazy good-for-nothing saucy useless robbing thieving sluts you, and how you kept on about me coming to stay here more as though you was a couple of duchesses than two dirty servants."

" Bastard ! " shouted Winifred's mother suddenly, lifting her broad, rage-reddened face to the window. " Dirty bitch ! "

" Same to you *with* knobs on," retorted Miss Baker imperturbably.    " When gentlefolks meet, compliments fly, as they say.    Now if you've quite finished giving yourself away, I'll just get a word in edgeways, *if* you please.    Miss Padsoe's given you the sack.    She don't want ever to see you again, neither of you.    Here's" (and Miss Baker flung a screw of newspaper straight at Winifred's mother) " a week's wages between you, and that's a fat lot more than you deserve.    Still, if we all got what we deserved, none of us would escape a good whipping, as they say.    Now you be off.    I've got to get our lunch."

And Miss Baker began, with dignity and without haste, to withdraw from the window.

" I'm going straight off to Reading by the next bus," shouted Winifred, " and by three o'clock I'll be back 'ere with a policeman.    See if I'm not ! "

" We'll have some tea ready for you," promised Miss Baker, elaborately readjusting her hair.    " Pleased to see you both, I'm sure."

" Compensation," said Mrs. Pim.    " That's it, Gert.

That's what you got to get. Compensation. Like Aggie."

" Ow'm I to get my box 'ome ? " asked Winifred, sullenly and suddenly, looking round at the sodden garden, and then down at her own coat, through which the rain was beginning to seep. " It's 'eavy."

" P'raps the policeman'll help you," said Miss Baker, once more re-arranging herself upon the window sill and surveying the group almost benevolently. " Give him a kiss, then he'll do anything for you, I'm sure."

" You go to 'ell," piped old Mrs. Pim suddenly, roused by the low turn the conversation had taken. " You got a dirty mind, that's what you got. Putting ideas into a girl's 'ead. You're no better than you should be, I'm sure."

" And how long since *you* retired from Piccadilly ? " enquired Miss Baker, which so enraged and shocked Mrs. Pim that she could only stand and stare up at Miss Baker, mumbling her mouth in and out like one of those india-rubber faces sold by hawkers at Christmas.

During this exchange of opinions, Winifred and her mother had been holding a conference in undertones ; and something—a subtle change in the smell of the battle, a sudden increase in the strength of the rain, which now quickened to a downpour—conveyed to Miss Baker the fact that the fight was over and the field hers.

" Been thinking it over ? " she enquired. " Going home, like good girls ? "

" I don't want none of your bloody lip," shouted Winifred's mother, coming across the lawn until she stood immediately under the window. " We're goin' 'ome now because it's rainin' and we can't stay 'ere. But we'll be back again—don't you make no mistake. We'll have our rights off Miss Padsoe. She'll be sorry,

later on, she didn't stand by us and keep in with them
that meant well by her. Gawd 'elp the poor old fool,
with you after her money."

"Goodness knows I don't want her money. I've
plenty of my own," said Miss Baker, with a kind of
heavenly sorrowfulness and an oh-if-you-only-knew-
what-an-ass-you're-making-of-yourself note in her voice.
"It's a good thing I *am* here; she'd have been dead,
in another six months, if she'd been left alone with you
two."

Whether this was true; whether some sudden vision
of how their battening might have ended swept over the
gross women and frightened them, Miss Baker could
never know. But, suddenly, they collapsed. Their
flamboyant plans and bullying pride blew out like fuses.

"Oh shut up," said Winifred's mother, in a kind of
yawning snarl. "Come on, Win. Give us a hand
with this."

Miss Baker observed all this with the greatest delight,
but her face did not betray her feelings. A thought
suddenly struck her and she shouted :

"And before you go I want that latch-key, too.
None of your sneaking off with it and coming back some
fine night and helping yourselves to anything you fancy.
You leave it on the grass, if you please, where I can
see it. Come on—quick ! I want to see about our
lunch."

There was a moment's hesitation and Miss Baker did
just wonder what she should do if they refused to hand
over the key. But the battle was over; there was no
fight left in them. Winifred half-turned, with a hand
in her bag, and sent something spinning towards the
window. Miss Baker saw that it was a key, before it
fell on the path and was hidden from view.

Winifred took one handle of the trunk, and together they staggered off slowly across the streaming lawn, followed by old Mrs. Pim, who kept on making ineffectual dabs at the two handles in an attempt to help which brought cries of " Stop it, messin' about, will you ? " from Winifred.

Rebuffed, Mrs. Pim turned back for a final spar with Miss Baker.

" Compensation," shrieked Mrs. Pim, going so far as to shake her fist at Miss Baker. " You wait. Compensation. We'll 'ave the law on you."

" And I hope it keeps fine for you," shouted Miss Baker, simply : and shut the window.

For a little while she watched the procession receding, through panes which quickly became dimmed by rain-drops and her breath. Once she wiped the pane clear, and when she had to do so a second time, the three with the trunk had disappeared under the shade of the trees in the drive.

Miss Baker gave a sigh of satisfaction. She knew that they would never come back. She had dealt with rude women for too many years not to know the look of defeated insolence when she saw it ; it had been in every feature of Winifred's coarse young face, and in every gross limb of the older women.

The Tower belonged to Miss Padsoe again.

An imaginative woman might almost have fancied that she felt the oily yet troubled waters of the servants' reign retreating from this Ararat. The house (she might have fancied) seemed less cold, smelled sweeter, boards dared to creak and doors to swing in the spring winds. Presently someone might come in, hatless and humming a tune, carrying a bunch of buds and kingcups : the house felt like that.

But Miss Baker, uncursed by fancy or imagination, went pattering downstairs to tell Miss Padsoe the gorgeous news.

" Miss Padsoe ! " she called, at the top of the kitchen stairs.  · " Miss Padsoe !   It's all right.   They've gone ! They've gone ! "

But there was no reply.

" It would be just like her to have kicked the bucket," thought Miss Baker, with a little uneasy feeling, " just when everything's all right."

" Miss Padsoe ! "

This time there came a sort of stifled sound in reply.

" Crying.  Do her good," thought Miss Baker, pushing open the kitchen door.

The room was in twilight.  In the red fireglow Miss Padsoe sat bent forward over *Answers*, her face buried in her two hands, and painful sounds coming out of them.

Miss Baker stood quiet for a moment, not knowing exactly what to do.  " Must be awful for her," she thought, but the word has lost its strength, and could not convey to Miss Baker the misery, the shame, the frightful and icy loneliness which were ravaging Miss Padsoe.

" There, there, dear," said Miss Baker, at last, putting a too-heavy but very kind hand on Miss Padsoe's shoulder.  " Don't cry.  They've gone now, for good, and they won't be back again.  Everything's all right. I'll just make us a nice cup of tea, and then we'll see about some lunch, shall we ?  Let's have a little light on the subject," and she crossed to the window and drew back the curtains.

The glare of light seemed to restore Miss Padsoe a little.  She sat up, and drew from a pocket in her petticoat another of those frail old handkerchiefs which were so like herself.

". . . So sorry," she muttered, ". . . losing control of myself . . . so foolish . . . in the k-k-kitchen, too " (a slight shudder). " Have they gone . . . really gone ? "

" Half-way to Reading by this time, I shouldn't wonder," said Miss Baker cheerfully, putting coal on the fire. " Now, don't you fret. Everything's all right."

Of course, everything was not all right. Miss Padsoe was sixty, her friends were scattered, poor, dead, the world of her deliciously gay and gentle youth had vanished more horribly than any dream. She had not a thing to do in the world but move uselessly about inside her body, waiting for death.

Yet, when Miss Baker called her from the scullery whence she had gone to fill the kettle " to see something pretty," she rose, mopping her eyes, and went.

It was a cluster of narcissus, nodding in a bed of dark earth outside the scullery window on a level with the two women's eyes.

" *Narciss*. Lovely smell," said Miss Baker, sniffing. They stood side by side, in a strange little fit of quietude, looking at the flowers which danced in the wind, with the rain-globes rolling springily down their petals. They seemed to repel sorrow by the delicate abundance of their life.

# CHAPTER XIII

IT was not Queenie's fault that she was a prig; she had been born into a family of them, and example had proved too strong for her.

In 1900 an earnest young man just entering for his final examinations in dentistry had married an almost equally earnest young woman who taught English in a National school. Each was a Socialist, each a blushing but resolute advocate of sexual equality; each desired with ardour to be a good citizen and to put the world to rights.

Six children were decided upon: and six were duly born. If Mr. Catton was inclined to doubt his right to bring six children into a world already beginning to suffer from over-production and over-crowding, his wife had no doubts at all. One could not have too many embryo good citizens; and that was what she was there for, wasn't it?

But Mrs. Catton, fortunately for Queenie, was just three shades less earnest than Mr. Catton. Despite Marx, she had a lingering and secret interest in, and affection for, the Royal Family; and she retained (a legacy from a mother who had been the daughter of a prosperous builder, and who had married a nurseryman) an ideal of what gentlemen and ladies should be.

Queenie's own delicate and stately name, never used, was Alexandra; she was called after the Sea King's daughter from over the sea, in face of the solemn and often stated disapproval of Mr. Catton, who objected to her nickname nearly as much, and compromised by calling her " my girl."

" Alexandra. Such a mouthful, but very pretty—if I had time for it, which I haven't," said Mrs. Catton, who never had time for doing anything thoroughly. She galloped conscientiously through reports of meetings of the Anti-White Slavery Society, the Anti-Black Slavery Society, the Society for Extending the Age of School Leaving, the Association for Promoting the Increased Production of Beet Sugar in Great Britain and Ireland, the Anti-Betting Association and the Round London Column in her morning paper, all with equal concentration, zest, and failure to remember what she had read.

The household should, logically, have been vegetarian, but was not. Everyone had plenty of good plain food which gave them strength to join societies, sit on committees, organize clubs, carve their careers, and argue. The eldest girl, Gertrude, was a mistress in a National school as her mother had been ; she organized and ran a club for the local wild girls, and was herself a Girl Guide. Mr. Catton disapproved of this, as well as of his second daughter's name, because Guiding had uniforms, ranks and badges, and all the trappings of militarism. So Gertrude and Mr. Catton used to argue rather a lot about Guiding.

Stan, at eighteen, attended a Polytechnic. He was to be a wireless engineer, and in his spare time he played with an incredibly complicated set of his own making, in his bedroom. But he did not really have much spare time, because on the evenings when he was not rehearsing for the plays got up by the Islington Barnstormers he was drilling with the Territorials.

Mr. Catton disapproved terrifically of the Territorials. He and Stan used to argue a good deal about it.

Fred was sixteen, and captain of the local grammar school. He was to be a dentist, like his father, but was devoured by ambition and wanted to be a 'doctor. He cut up a good many minor animals in his bedroom, which added smells to the noises which pervaded the house ; and he, too, argued a good deal with Mr. Catton about his future, and also about the existence or non-existence of God.

Ted, at fourteen, was affectionately called Our Handyman. To the disappointment of Mr. Catton, who had wanted him to go in for commercial flying, Ted hated commercial flying, and simply wanted to be a carpenter. The noises made by his fretsaw and numerous files and other implements, could be heard, in the pauses of the arguing, on most evenings, proceeding from a shed at the bottom of the long walled garden. Pending his fate, he designed and made far too many plain, rather beautiful tables, small bookcases and cupboards, for which there was no room in the house.

As for Don, aged nine, he was still too small to argue much with Mr. Catton, who rather thought he would like him to go in for journalism, but he argued about everything he was told to do in the course of his day's routine ; clear, logical, sensible arguments, which frequently led to the sudden and surprising smacking of his head at school.

Fortunately, the house was large enough even for this tribe. It was a huge grey barrack of a Victorian house, incredibly shabby, used as relentlessly as the scabbard of a sword. It was never quiet. It was always full of footsteps, voices arguing, bathwater running, saws working, voices enquiring where they had put the report of the Society for Promoting or Suppressing something, the thunder of patched boots rushing up or down carpetless stairs, and the distant noise of wireless.

Did Queenie argue?

Never. She was " our quiet one "—not a difficult title to earn, if you lived in the midst of a family which did not often pause to reflect before it spoke, and if you yourself were given to reflection.

Queenie was a Disappointment. Nobody said so, because they were all very kind people, but there was a growing feeling among the older Cattons that Queenie *was* a Disappointment.

So far she had effortlessly resisted all attempts to make her be anything. Mrs. Catton had wanted her to take a two-year course in Social Science at the School of Economics, and try for a post as a Care Committee worker with the London County Council, but Queenie had, somehow, managed to avoid doing either of these things; and she made herself so useful at home that, after her eighteenth birthday, her mother had confessed with a sigh that really she had got so used to having Queenie about that she did not know what she would do without her.

Queenie was deft. When she washed up, dishes came from her hands shining and unsmeared. She never broke things. She sewed plainly and beautifully, cooked admirably, was never late for appointments, could do gay, clever little tricks with cards and string and matches, amuse children and control them without effort, do up parcels strongly and neatly, and she never forgot anything.

All minor accomplishments, and liable to be over-looked (except for a vague feeling of comfort when she was near) by a family which set so high a value on arguing.

But Queenie had not been altogether a drag on the family's finances. Twice she had taken a post as companion, once to a rich old woman in Highgate and once to the busy wife of a South Kensington vicar: both posts had been recommended to her by fellow committee-women of her mother's (Mrs. Catton sat on two local committees) and both ladies had professed themselves charmed, delighted, thoroughly satisfied with Miss Catton. In each case she had left at her own wish and under dismayed protests.

She took these posts because, when she reached the age of nineteen, she felt that she would die (only of course, that was a hysterical and foolish way of expressing herself, due to over-strained nerves) if she did not get away from endless cheerful noises, smells, and arguing. No one else seemed to mind; but she minded.

She did not want beauty and luxury, for she was not very susceptible to the former, and the latter repelled her rather austere young spirit, but she wanted peace, orderly routine, and *quiet*. Stories of convent-life where the measured stroke of the bells broke upon a sweet-smelling silence seemed to her like stories of heaven.

" Mummy," she said once to her mother, " don't you ever get sick of the *noise*? "

" I'm used to it, pet," said Mrs. Catton, and she put her work-spoiled hands (about which she did not mind at all) absently on Queenie's firm young arm for a moment and there drifted across her active mind a vague memory of herself at nineteen. She had been earnest, it is true, but not always arguing. She had admired the lovely Princess Alexandra and had been secretly very anxious that her children should grow up into ladies and gentlemen. Now, of course, she knew that putting the world to rights was more important than rearing ladies and gentlemen; and her former admiration for the Princess was something of which to be a little ashamed; though even now she simply *could not* help liking all the bits in the paper about the Prince of Wales, in spite of the things Mr. Catton said about him.

" It's me, not them, that's wrong," thought her daughter penitently.

Mrs. Catton dared more than once to say that no doubt Queenie would marry. " Dared," I say, because marriage was not regarded in the Catton household as it is regarded in most households. No one wanted anyone else to get married, but this was something more than the dislike which might be felt by an affectionate family at the thought of its circle being broken.

Like most happily married Progressives, it was Mr. Catton's joy to make savage darts at the monster Marriage from within the cosy circle of the wedding ring. He and Mother had got married because it was the most convenient and obvious thing to do, as they were placed at the time. No one would have wanted to have their teeth pulled out by a dentist who was living in sin; and if no one had wanted to have their teeth pulled out, there would have been no money with which to afford a family. And they had wanted a family, badly.

But because he and Mother were married, that was not to serve as an example to the children. *They* need not marry at all, and if they did, they must first carefully walk all round the monster Marriage, and examine it coolly. Marriage was tottering, obsolete, degrading and doomed. He had sooner (almost) that the children entered into a lifelong partership *without* marriage, than embark blindly upon it (here there was a low murmur, unnoticed by the family, from Mrs. Catton).

And all the young Cattons except Queenie promised that they *would* walk all round the doomed, degrading and tottering monster before getting married ; but Stan, who was at times visited by strange gleams of some emotion which in a less earnest being would have been irony, felt suddenly sure that his father's indignation against marriage in the abstract would only be equalled by his pain and shame should any of his children decide to do without it in the concrete.

Except as a subject for intelligent argument, marriage did not interest the young Cattons much, because all their instincts were adequately sublimated into arguing ; and it did not interest Queenie because she was so physically fastidious that the coarse, kind hand of a boy placed on her waist at a dance made her shudder, and shrink rudely away.

But love interested her. She thought often of love, seriously and rather painfully. Her secret heart sometimes seemed to her full of love, which she must give away, or die. " I want to help," was the form this longing took. " I *must* help the whole world."

Yet she did nothing ; would not be trained for any useful work, would not decide whether she believed in God, nor what she wanted to do. Gravely, after reading all the conflicting literature about Russia which she could obtain, she decided to become a Communist, and did so. Communists seemed to want to help everybody, too. And with the extreme, grinding seriousness she had unconsciously acquired from associating with her family, she settled into a steady disapproval of the rich.

All the time she was revelling in the silence, the routine, the smell-lessness of Highgate and Islington, she was steadily disapproving of her employers' comfortable way of life. She finally left both posts from a sense of duty because she felt that she must return to the arguing, noise and smells in which her family lived. If she, a Communist, were weak enough to mind such details, she must be disciplined by living among them, until she did not mind them, perhaps even liked them. So back she went, and did not emerge again from her prison until unbearably tempted by the prospect of a post in the country.

During her self-martyrdom, she consoled herself by sternly thinking that no doubt Communism, when it ultimately conquered England, *would* be all arguing, noise, and smells, so the sooner she learnt to like it, the better.

Yet all the while the love burned softly, like a painful flame, in her breast. It turned inward, and burned her, and she wanted it to turn outward and warm the world.

· · · · · ·

A walk which she took that same evening with George was the beginning of a closer acquaintance. Mrs. Shelling said that she had best go over to The Tower and see what those two silly women were up to, and whether they were likely to make any more embarrassing demands upon the hospitality of Baines House. So after tea she set off.

She met George coming round from the garage through the rhododendron bushes. He had been putting the car away. He had been quarrelling with Bell all the way down from London. One of the black fits of boredom and depression which occasionally ravaged him had descended; and he had turned and rent Bell.

George was walking moodily, with his head down, kicking at the gravel, but he looked up as Queenie crossed his vision-line. His face did not change. She said " Good evening " clearly.

" Hullo. Where are you off to ? "

" The Tower. Mrs. Shelling thinks I had better see if they are likely to bother us again to-night."

" Doesn't matter if they do," said George truculently. " It's my house, isn't it ? Pity I've put the car away ; I might have driven you over."

" I like walking, thanks."

She had turned, and was making her way to the road when he came striding after her.

" I'll come with you."

" You've no hat . . . suppose it rains ? "

" Good job if it does," said George gloomily, implying that if he caught pneumonia and died, people might be sorry.

They walked in silence. The clouds had broken and wild gold light flooded the wet trees and the road. Queenie did not once glance at him, but knew exactly how moodily beautiful his face looked, with lowered eyelids and lip thrust a little outwards ; his hands were jammed into his pockets. He said suddenly :

" I suppose you don't ever feel that nothing's worth while, and you can't enjoy anything, and wonder what we are here for, do you ? "

She hesitated before replying, a habit with her. She liked to say exactly what she meant. It was strange ; this was the first time they had been alone and talked together, yet the silence between them was easy, comfortable, natural. She did not feel she was with a friend, but with a stranger whom . . . as yet . . . she need not fear. I do not know him, but I shall, she thought.

" No . . ." she replied at last. " I don't think I do. I never feel nothing's worth while, though I often can't enjoy things and I *very* often wonder what we are here for."

"So do I," said George.

"I've noticed you do," she replied dryly. She was longing to add sharply, "you need some real work to do," but did not quite dare to; and suddenly the unspoken phrase seemed silly. George robbed her of her thunder by his next sentence.

"I work hard enough, god knows. I've got everything I want, and I'm enjoying life, and quite suddenly, down comes this, and everything's hell. Just plain hell. Now go on, say I've got too much. I know I have. But that doesn't make it any better. I shouldn't feel better if I gave it all to the unemployed, should I?"

"You might. But the unemployed" (proudly) "might not want it. You—rich people always seem to think the poor would be grateful for that sort of charity."

"So they would. You try them and see."

"I don't believe they would. The poor aren't like that at all."

"What do *you* know about the poor?" asked George, intrigued, despite his depression, by her stern profile and averted eyes: he drew a little closer, and peeped under her hat brim.

"A lot. I've lived among them. . . . Well, not exactly *among* them, but in a poor neighbourhood."

"Well, so do I live among them. At least, I manage a factory full of them. So I know a bit about them, too."

"Not properly. You can't; you're a boss—an employer, I mean. They can't be themselves when you're anywhere about, because they're afraid of you."

"Tripe," said George, looking as though he would have liked to say something even less refined. "That's just sentimental rubbish. I suppose you're a Communist ? "

" Yes." This time she did not hesitate.

" Well, I respect you for it," said George gloomily. A second later he added " No I don't, though. I think you're a sentimentalist, like the rest of them. Communism is easy, nowadays. It's being a good capitalist, and hanging on to your theories, and making work in an unsympathetic world, that's the difficult job to-day. Like being a militarist. Pacificism's easy ; it's sensible capitalism, imperialism and militarism that are difficult jobs. The other things—the crank things—have got world sympathy with them."

She was silent. His words glided off her mind. With a deplorable lack of Catton earnestness, she ignored words which should have been red rags to her, and her mind wandered below their surface, pondering on his discontent. She despised him for it. He reminded her of the young man in the Bible who had great possessions ; and she could not feel sorry for him.

They found Miss Baker triumphant and cheerful and only too ready to send a message to Mrs. Shelling that they were comfortably settled, and would not disturb her again. Miss Padsoe had gone to bed with a hot bottle and a cup of hot milk.

Having declined Miss Baker's invitation to warm themselves at the kitchen fire, they walked home together, in silence.

" This is wonderful," thought Queenie, keeping step with him through the twilit woods, " I've found a young man who doesn't want to talk. Oh, how lovely and quiet the evening is ! Don't let him speak . . . don't let's say a word. I'm so deadly tired of listening to people talking."

He was not thinking of her at all. So easy, so natural, was their pacing side by side that he had fallen into a reverie, blessed by silence. Gradually his sullenness lifted, leaving only a settled melancholy. Unfortunately the former was brought back in full force by Bell, who met them on their return at the front door with a brilliant smile, and the remark as she ran her glance over the two of them—" Nice walk ? "

George looked at her in a very ugly way, and pushed past her on his way up to his room.

" Can't have been much fun for you," said Bell, standing in the last sun-rays and looking at Queenie through lids narrowed against the glare. " My little brother's pretty grim when his moods are on him. What did you talk about ? Come to my room and have a cigarette before dinner ? "

" I'd like to come," said Queenie, following her across the hall, " but I'm afraid I don't smoke."

The coolness between the brother and sister lasted for a week, during which each turned to Queenie for companionship and society.

One of her few discontents with the post at Baines House was the fact that it gave her no regular leisure time to walk, a pastime of which she was very fond ; Mrs. Shelling's commissions, though reasonable and not uninteresting in themselves, were many, and so arranged that she had no regular leisure time. But sometimes at lunch Mrs. Shelling would announce " This afternoon I go to see Mrs. Ryder—or Mrs. Croft—or Lady Benson. I shall not need you, Miss Catton " and then Queenie knew that she could gladly escape into the woods.

But now even these occasions were monopolized by Bell, who would come up just as Queenie was ready to start, saying half arrogantly, half timidly, rather as a

wild gazelle might have offered itself as a stable mate—
" I say, are you going to walk. May I come ? " and of
course Queenie could not say, no ; and indeed, did not
often want to. She was very nervous of Bell, in her
own silent and seemingly composed way, and yet
fascinated by her.

Recollected in tranquillity, it seemed to her that on
these walks they had talked of nothing but trivialities,
Bell drifting along, and frequently tripping over a
root, as Shelley used to do, or staring vacantly up
at a tree while Queenie painstakingly expressed her views
on some point, and then suddenly turning her huge grey
eyes on her companion, looking not at all vacant but
dazzlingly bright with intelligence and mockery.

They did not often mention George. " My little
brother " Bell always called him, in a disagreeable voice.
" I'll lend you that—my little brother's got it for the
moment," she would say of a book or a poem. " As
my little brother says "—when she quoted one of his
maxims.

Queenie learned nothing, by direct statements, of her
tastes, preferences or prejudices. Bell had that manner,
so maddening in a *tête-à-tête* and supposed to alienate a
woman from men, of never appearing to listen to what
was said to her. Her mind seemed busy (but only as a
kitten plays with string) with some other subject than
that under discussion. Yet Queenie was surprised, on
more than one occasion, to hear her own views accurately
repeated by Bell some days later.

In Bell's case it was painfully plain that men had not
been alienated by the kitten-and-string manner. Desperate little letters in small masculine handwritings appeared,
too frequently to please the tender-hearted Queenie,
beside Bell's plate at breakfast.

"Him again!" Bell would murmur, to no one at all,
flicking the note aside and bending right down over her
plate to pinch up breadcrumbs, with an abstracted
expression. This was a trick of hers. She would stare
at her own pinching, moulding fingers as if hypnotized,
and then come out with a trivial remark. A maddening,
unbelievably charming creature, Queenie found her,
with more than a little malice in her make-up. Queenie
was rather afraid of her.

In the evenings it was George's turn. Bell went up
to the nursery and sat alone in the lengthening April
twilights, playing Bach very beautifully. George would
get behind Queenie as she was following his mother out
of the dining-room, and mutter "Like to help me clean
the car?" and, fifteen minutes later, she would slip out
to the garage.

She did not like cars nor understand them, though
she would have been quite willing to clean anything that
was really dirty, so she was relieved when she found
that helping him clean the car meant sitting wrapped in
the rug inside the car, watching him fuss with it and
replying when he spoke to her. She sometimes saw
nothing of him for an hour but his fair head bent over
the radiator.

If she learned nothing of Bell's views, she learned of
George's at length. They discussed (George was too
undecided in his views to argue) Communism, capitalism,
romanticism, classicism, free-will, predestination, everything except sex, in which George was not interested.
But once, during a discussion on the ideal State, they
got on to free love and trial marriages, and Queenie
(no longer nervous of him) told him she was glad, as a
Communist, that he did not seem to fuss about whether
people lived together without being married. "So

many people do fuss," she said. "I think it's so boring."

"Oh, I got over *that* when I was twenty," said George, breathing lustily on the back mirror. "Doesn't worry me a bit."

"But you *are* queer, you know," she said, watching him. "You say one set of things, and you do quite another. I mean, you don't live by your principles."

"I," said George rather sadly, "live by the intellect."

He put down his polishing rag, and coming over to the window of the big Daimler, leaned his elbows on the ledge, and looked in at her, where she sat cosily inside.

"And what do *you* live by?" he asked her, smiling.

"I don't know," she replied after her usual little pause for right reflection. "I'm still trying to find out. I think—like Keats, you know—'I am certain of nothing but of the holiness of the heart's affections.'"

"Oh . . . affections," said George, going back to his polishing, "I change mine every week."

No one, overhearing his light pleasant voice saying that in the growing dusk, could say that Queenie had not been warned. The may tree in the yard outside, in full leaf and waiting for its flowers, stood like a cold dark-green fountain, and down over it wandered the notes of music from the open nursery window.

At the end of the week the two were suddenly reconciled. Queenie, returning from a dull drive on Saturday afternoon into Reading with Mrs. Shelling to choose bridge cakes, found that George and Bell had taken his car and dashed up to London to hear a concert.

"Now," she thought simply, with a little irony but without bitterness, "I shall have some time to myself again."

She was surprised to find, during the week-end,

that it was not so. The pair were back to dinner; she came down and found them in their places, looking a little sheepish but their ill temper gone; and they greeted her pleasantly. Evidently they had both grown so intimate with her (even Bell, in her curious way) during the estrangement that their good manners would not permit them to ignore her now that they were reconciled.

"We're all right, you see," said George.

"Delightful for you both," said Queenie with intentional sarcasm.

They laughed delightedly. She had discovered that they both took great pleasure in a semi-mocking style of conversation, and they hated anyone to cringe to their charm; they enjoyed being bullied.

"But I can never keep it up," she thought despondently, helping herself to an almond.

PART II

# CHAPTER XIV

BASSETT was not the isolated village which Miss Baker
had at first supposed it to be. It was served indirectly
by no less than five bus services, and directly by one.
None of these services saw fit to run direct to Bassett
on Sunday, but all had their terminus at Fan's Green,
outside *The Chairmenders' Arms*. Those who took their
glass at *The Chairmenders' Arms* derived an idle pleasure,
and occasionally a little profit, by speculating upon
which bus would be selected by some traveller,
embarrassed by the rich bus-life offered him in Fan's
Green.

"It's too much . . . five buses in a place this size.
Upsets people" was the general verdict.

Miss Baker soon chose her bus, and was not to be
tempted from it and its conductor and driver, however
rich in interesting idiosyncrasies the personnel of other
buses might be. She first made sure on which bus were
the conductor and driver who had laughed at Miss
Padsoe's appearance on the evening of her first visit
to Bassett; and then she chose the bus which stood
furthest from this bus on the stand, and each time she
mounted the steps of her own bus she bestowed a long,
steady, meaning stare on the puzzled driver and conductor
of the offending bus. "Showing them," Miss Baker
called this ritual, and it gave her much satisfaction.

She used her bus, on an average, every other day,
when she went into Reading to buy the baked beans and

147

sardines, sausages and chops upon which she and Miss
Padsoe chiefly lived.

For Miss Baker could not cook, nor could Miss
Padsoe. They could, it is true, each boil an egg and
fry chops (although Miss Padsoe's usually got burnt)
but they did not know how to turn out a dish of creamy,
well-seasoned mashed potatoes or a fruit tart, or even a
nourishing stew. Miss Baker had lived for nearly thirty
years on meals in restaurants or meals cooked at home
on two gas rings, and Miss Padsoe, being an Edwardian
achievement, rather than a late Victorian one, did not
think it necessary for a lady to know how to cook.

So for the first four days of their setting up house
together, Miss Padsoe did not fare much better than she
had fared under the régime of Winifred and her mother,
although she did get plenty of what there was to eat ;
and she indulged, at first shamefacedly and afterwards
with a fierce recklessness, her passion for cups of China
tea at all hours of the day.

Miss Baker shared this passion, though she hated
China tea (" water bewitched and tea begrudged " she
called it) ; during one of her many exploring expeditions
in the basement cupboards of The Tower she found
a teapot small enough to make tea for one without
waste, and this was filled with strong Indian tea, as
many times a day as Miss Padsoe's own little Dresden
one was filled with China. Side by side on the cool part
of the range stood the teapots, and three or four times a
day Miss Baker and Miss Padsoe paused in their labours
to refresh themselves from their pots.

They worked hard. On the first strange, rather
uncomfortable evening after the rout of Winifred and her
mother, Miss Padsoe had sat opposite Miss Baker at the
kitchen table, doubtfully eating her supper and wondering

whether she had not exchanged one form of tyranny for another? But it soon became plain to her that Miss Baker was no tyrant, no parasite with a nest to feather, no borrower or sponger.

Miss Baker, having announced on the following morning that they both felt better for their night's rest (a statement with which Miss Padsoe scarcely agreed) proposed to talk business.

They must first arrange about money. They had to live while they were getting the house to rights for the boarders. (Miss Padsoe started nervously. She had quite forgotten the boarders). Miss Baker had three hundred and sixty pounds in the Post Office and twenty pounds upstairs in her suitcase. She didn't want to upset Miss Padsoe, nor to seem nosey, but how much had Miss Padsoe got?

Miss Padsoe, blushing extremely and trying not to sound haughty, faltered that she believed her income varied between two hundred and two hundred and seventy pounds a year. It used to be over five hundred, but the dreadful Crisis had upset everything, and then the bills had been so heavy lately, with Winifred and her mother you know, that she had not been able to keep her balance in the bank at Reading as high as she would have wished. She believed she had about fifteen pounds there, and a dividend was due in a few days (something to do with railways, she believed) which should bring her in about thirty-three pounds. She had a pound note and some silver in her purse upstairs.

Miss Baker was much relieved to hear these facts. Miss Padsoe's income seemed to her an extremely comfortable one: she, Hilda Baker, would neither have to lend Miss Padsoe money nor to support her.

Now that those thieving sluts had gone, there would be
no more huge bills to pay and no wages, and they would
be able to live in comfort.   Winifred and her mother,
Miss Baker was stunned to hear, had received respectively
fifteen shillings and a pound a week, *and* their laundry !

Miss Baker suggested that they should both put
twenty-five shillings a week into a pool.   She and
Miss Worrall had had a pool that time they went to
Clacton, and if Miss Worrall had remembered to put
back into the pool the petty cash which she drew out
from it for her private use, the plan would have worked
very well.   This time, Miss Baker would carry the pool
round with her, like Miss Worrall had done at Clacton,
and all would be well.

Miss Padsoe asked timidly if twenty-five shillings
would be enough.

Well—say thirty-five, if they had a woman in to clean
up a bit every day.   They could do a good bit themselves, but not heavy work like scrubbing.   Besides,
the house needed a bit of a spring-clean.   You couldn't
ask people to come and live in a house unless it looked
nice, could you ?

Miss Padsoe agreed eagerly to this proposal.   Mrs.
Partner would come, she was sure.   Mrs. Partner was
the sister-in-law of Mr. Partner who kept the general shop
and post office in Bassett, and she used to come in twice a
week in my dear father's time.   Mrs. Partner would be
delighted to come for fifteen shillings a week.   Mrs.
Partner could also cook.

Miss Padsoe said this with seeming artlessness but
with actual guile, for she disliked extremely this living
in the kitchen to which Miss Baker took so naturally
and joyously, and wished very much to return to her
former existence in the airy, icy drawing-room and bed-

room. She was also bored by, and terrified of, the cooking, at which Miss Baker was beginning to make experimental dabs ; and she thought that if Mrs. Partner came, the mistress of the house and her guest would naturally retreat upstairs to their proper realm.

She very much hoped that this reinstatement would occur before the actual arrival of Mrs. Partner, or else it would be all over Bassett that " they was living in the kitchen up at The Tower. What would the old gentleman have had to say to *that !* "

Yet life in the kitchen was not slovenly. Miss Baker abhorred a sloven. She was a creature of twenty years' office routine, and lived by the clock.

At eight-thirty precisely the two ladies, washed, dressed and trim (at least Miss Padsoe was as trim as she could ever make her lacey, bitty Edwardian self) sat down to their eggs or sardines. After a morning which seemed to Miss Padsoe to be spent entirely in washing up, making two beds and climbing up and downstairs, it was time to cook sausages for lunch at one. The afternoon was passed in more washing up and in cutting bread and butter for tea at half-past four, and then at half-past six it was time to begin preparing for supper at half-past seven. By ten Miss Padsoe was ashamed to find herself hungry again, but curiously relieved to find that Miss Baker was hungry too, so they ate cocoa and cake like schoolgirls, and fell into bed at eleven, drunk with unaccustomed work, and slept all night.

A feeling of surprise once flitted through Miss Padsoe's mind that servants so frequently " got into trouble." How did they ever find time ?

Both women would have been much surprised if anyone had told them that for years they had been tyrannised over (the one by family and domestic ties,

F

the other by the economic machine) and half-starved.
Yet they had; and their curious peacefulness, their
disinclination to take sensible and definite steps about
the future, was due to the relaxation of their bonds.
Death and Money, the great liberators, had now freed
them; and unconsciously they enjoyed their first days of
freedom.

Miss Baker enjoyed the housework. She did it
shockingly badly, and loved it. This was probably
inherited from her house-proud mother. She enjoyed
the spaciousness, too. She had lived for fifteen years
in one room, but now roamed from bedroom to hall,
from garden to kitchen, as naturally and happily as a
lady; except that a lady does not spend whole mornings
nosing into someone else's cupboards, and Miss Baker
did.

It cannot be said that a cloud lifted from Miss Padsoe's
eyes during their first week together and that she suddenly
saw Miss Baker as her deliverer and sister. Miss Baker
continued to get on her nerves, and a dozen times a day
she thought, with a dreadful sense of grief and loneliness,
what a state she had fallen into, to be sharing life in the
kitchen with such a vulgar, if good-natured, little
woman. Her past seemed more than ever like a lovely
dream.

But Miss Baker was certainly better than Winifred
and her mother, and she was businesslike, and she fussed
over Miss Padsoe's chest, wet feet and rheumatism in a
manner that was strangely warming. And she was
*very* anxious to make the boarding-house scheme a
success. The question of her stay being a temporary
one was now altogether dropped; she was a fixture,
and it even became difficult for Miss Padsoe to remember
what The Tower had been like before she came.

" Company. That's what you needed. We all do.
I do meself. Lily Worrall, my friend, does. It's
natural," said Miss Baker, complimenting Miss Padsoe
upon her improved spirits.

On the fifth day Mrs. Partner arrived, all eyes, and
took up her duties, and Miss Baker and Miss Padsoe
retreated to the drawing-room and took up their position
as ladies.

Mrs. Partner installed for three hours daily, and a
gardener from Reading re-engaged with doubtful and
tremulous joy by Miss Padsoe, it became necessary to
think about advertising for the first paying guest.

Miss Baker decided that it must be a quiet gentleman,
who should pay them two and a half guineas a week.
He could have the best bedroom which used to belong
to Miss Padsoe's father, and his laundry would be
extra. And as soon as he was nibbling, Miss Padsoe
must dash into Reading and engage a girl, but not until
he *was* nibbling, or they might find themselves landed
with a girl with no work to do, if the quiet gentleman
decided not to come after all.

" Must it be a gentleman ? " asked Miss Padsoe
timidly, " I would really *rather* . . ."

" Ladies give trouble," said Miss Baker decidedly,
with dim memories of ladies who had done this in her
mother's boarding-house. " Finnicky, ladies are. Can't
eat this and can't bear the other. Besides, they always
make a fuss about their bills."

Miss Padsoe subsided. She felt she could not bear
the idea of anyone making a fuss about anything.

Accordingly, the young Shellings and Queenie were
startled one morning at breakfast a fortnight later to
hear Mrs. Shelling snort and exclaim :

" That old woman ! She is mad, I tell you. They

are both mad. Now what would that poor old Mr. Padsoe have said, could he have seen his child trying to keep a lodging house? She is quite mad. I shall speak to the Vicar. She should be put away; it is not safe for us all."

George, mildly interested, reached over and picked up the local paper which his mother had thrown down. Miss Baker, in drafting the advertisement, had had no false shame about concealing their address ("a good address makes such a difference") and there it was, for all the world to see.

George read it with a gloomy lift of his fair eyebrows. For the last week he had been extremely silent, and had taken to staring tragically at Queenie when she was not looking at him, and then quickly turning his eyes away when she did look. A far less conceited young woman than Queenie would have wondered what on earth ailed him. Bell watched these tactics in cynical silence, and Queenie was extremely embarrassed by them.

"Hope she gets somebody," he said at last, passing the paper to the craning Bell. "Probably they will be too ruddy, but if they should be at all bearable, it will be useful to have a fourth for tennis. You play tennis, Miss Catton?"

"Yes."

"Well?"

"Fairly well. Quite well, I think."

"Good," said George, letting his fine grey eyes rest steadily, this time, upon her face. "We must have some games when the weather gets decent."

He went out into the hall to get ready for his drive into Reading, leaving Mrs. Shelling indignantly re-reading the advertisement, which she regarded as an insidious invasion of the privacy and dignity of Bassett: and when Queenie came out, five minutes later, he was still there, loitering at the door opening on the drive, with his hat on the back of his head.

As she passed him on her way to the morning-room, he deftly slipped his arm round her waist and pulled her towards him, whispering " Who's my girl ? "

He was quite unprepared for the violent spring she made away from him. She struck his arm down so violently that it stung.

" Don't do that ! "

" I say—I'm frightfully sorry ! I didn't know you'd mind."

" I do mind. I hate it. I *loathe* being touched by anyone I don't know, and even when I do know people I don't like it very much."

She was nearly crying, and turned her head away so that he might not see. He was very penitent and honestly surprised, and came a little closer to tell her as much, quite innocently. She sprang away again.

" *Don't !* "

" All right—I wasn't going to touch you. I won't ever again—if you don't want me to. You are a funny girl. Don't you like being kissed ? "

" I hate it. No one ever has. I wouldn't want anyone to, unless I really loved someone."

An expression of boredom mingled with suspicion came over George's face. He said, rather impudently :

" Most of the girls I've kissed usually get to love me."

" That must be too marvellous for them," snapped Queenie. " Well, I'm not like most of the girls you've kissed. It makes me feel sick."

And she ran upstairs and left him.

She certainly was not like most of the girls he had kissed : and he was not a young man who thought each new girl unlike all the others. He usually knew, too drearily, at exactly which moment he would begin to tire of kissing. Girls fell into his lax hands like plums, and their bloom was brushed off as quickly.

"Bell always said," thought George gloomily, putting in the clutch, "that one day someone would smack my face and then I'd fall in love with her. Am I in love with Queenie (god, what a name !) ? "

He toyed with the idea all day ; and it grew. It warmed him with a pleasant melancholy ; he hummed Schubert to himself as he inspected semi-finished rib-shears, and on his way back through Reading he stopped at a florist's and bought a small bunch of yellow roses.

" I say, I'm awfully sorry about this morning," he said, encountering Queenie that evening by design outside her bedroom door. " Look—these are for you."

She took them and stood looking seriously down at them in the dusk of the corridor. Her face was charming in its frame of short curling dark hair, and a strange pain moved George.

" I believe I am in love with you," he muttered.

" Rubbish ! " said Queenie, and she laughed and gave him back his pretty roses, which annoyed him but not very much.

She went back into her bedroom and began methodically to freshen her appearance for dinner, and her usual deft movements did not betray that she was disturbed. Yet a curious agitation filled her thoughts. She had been sincere when she said " Rubbish ! " at George's serious face ; she did not believe for one instant that the rich, elegant, selfish and decidedly flirtatious George was in love with her, even a little bit. It interested him to imagine he was, that was all.

But she was flattered by his attempt to kiss her, his apology and his roses. The two incidents made her feel curiously gay and malicious ; she wanted to tease him and lead him a dance ; and because this healthy reaction to a little male attention was new to her, she found her own feelings strange and disturbing. A delicious lightness flowed into her solemn little mind, and even invaded her body ; her stomach felt disturbed, and her heart sent a faint flush up into her clear pale cheeks. Her hands were chilly and the tips of her fingers moist, and more than once she picked up a hairbrush or a face towel and put it down again without quite knowing why she had picked it up.

" Silly ass," she muttered to her own neat reflection in the dark pool of the mirror (for her vocabulary was sternly school-girlish). " Pull yourself together, can't you ? "

But it was so delicate, so enchanting a feeling, and so new ! When she entered the dining-room and saw the light glinting across George's fair head as he stooped over the table to inspect a wine label, a freezing thrill rushed all down her diaphragm. He looked up, and she gave him a demure yet mocking smile. George retaliated with a look of pain ; genuine, naked pain.

" Heavens . . . this is frightful," she thought, slipping into her seat in a sudden panic.

" Had a tiring day ? " Bell asked her brother. " You look somewhat yellow." She was leaning forward over her plate, her fingers already busy at their pinching and kneading of her bread, and staring lazily at him through half-shut lids.

" You'd look yellow, if you'd got to do what I have."

"Well, what have you got to do except fuss over the hock like a head waiter or something?"

"I've got to teach Uncle Fritz's little boy to manage a factory, that's what I've got to do."

Mrs. Shelling and Bell both cried out and Bell stopped her kneading.

"Albert? Is he coming here? Who said so? When did you hear?"

"This evening. He wrote to the works. Uncle Fritz, I mean. Damned nuisance. Uncle Fritz wants him to be here six months and see something of our methods, he says. As though a foreigner (all right, Ma, but he *is* a foreigner—born in a hotel or something, wasn't he?) or anyone, for that matter, could learn to run a factory in six months."

"Is he musical?" asked Bell, going round to her mother's side to read the letter written in a stiff Continental hand which George had handed over.

"Oh, I expect so. Sure to be, with a mother like that. You'll have someone to play Bach with, now. Such fun for you."

"What a filthy rage you *are* in," said his sister, looking across at him rather curiously. He avoided her glance, and bent over his sole.

"Why did he not write to me?" demanded Mrs. Shelling, much offended. "It is I who should have been asked whether Albert could come. It is always the same. That Fritz—he has no sense of what is right and proper and due to his brother's wife. Because I am a woman, I cannot know about business—I cannot do this, I cannot do that. You are a young boy, inexperienced and wild, and yet he writes always to you."

"Well, if you feel like that about it, why don't you write and tell him Albert can't come? God knows

I don't want Albert round my neck day and night, just
as all the best concerts of the season are coming on.
He'll probably be a most frightful little tick—all over
scent, I shouldn't wonder. Probably be a nancy,
too. Most of them are, I'm told, nowadays."

Bell giggled, and Mrs. Shelling looked consciously
blank.

" I am sure I do not know what you mean, George.
Poor Albert . . . poor boy. No mother to look after
him, no father to guide him in right ways. It is very
sad, I think."

" You're quite right," said George, helping himself
to an olive.

" All the same, Fritz should have written to me.
It would have been only polite. But there . . . I do not
mind. Perhaps I shall not be here for long."

George, Bell and Queenie all stared at her, the first
two in blank surprise and Queenie in concern.

" Silly children," and Mrs. Shelling laughed her
rare laugh. " I do not mean to die (though no doubt
you would be pleased if I did, for then George could
manage the factory as he pleased, and Bell play the
gramophone all night). No. I shall perhaps go away
on a little visit. To Innsbruck, perhaps, to see Auntie
Katt."

" Dammit, Ma," exploded George, flinging his
napkin on the table. " You can't do that, leaving us
with Albert and everything. Suppose he's a frightful
nuisance and gets into messes ? I haven't the time to
haul him out, and Bell hasn't the sense."

" All the same, I think I shall soon go," said Mrs.
Shelling tranquilly.

(" And then I shall have to go home," thought
Queenie in a sudden dismay that was overwhelming.

" Oh I *can't*—I can't go back to everything, just as I'm beginning to be so happy here. Oh, *please* don't let her go.")

" Where will he sleep ? " asked Bell, again busy with her bread pinching.

" With you, I expect, if he gets half a chance———"

" George ! I *will* not have you speak so ! Albert will sleep in the spare room. It is a great nuisance. I like to have the spare room empty in the summer ; it makes the house feel so cool. I shall tell Albert it is a nuisance. He must learn to have right feelings."

" He *is* going to have fun," murmured Bell. " Must he sleep here ? Can't he go and board with the old fish-faces at The Tower ? "

" We will see. I do not like Miss Padsoe to think that I approve of old Mr. Padsoe's child keeping a lodging house. It is all very tiresome. When does Albert come ? Oh, he comes in a fortnight, Fritz says. It is a silly letter, I think, but then Fritz's letters are always so silly."

" How old is Albert ? " asked Bell.

" About twenty-five. I expect he'll fall insanely in love with you, so watch out. Dirty little dark men always like tall fair girls ; they attract them like a lot of beastly little beetles."

" How do you know he's dirty and little and dark ? "

" Bound to be—born in a hotel, with a Russian mother and a dancer at that, and as mad as a hatter. She led old Fritz a dance, didn't she, Ma ? Isn't it true he lost stones in weight and thousands in cash during the time he had her ? No wonder old Fritz could never settle down after she died."

" Well, I'm glad we're going to see him at last," said Bell comfortingly. " I've always wondered what he was like. Poor Albert—dragged round the world from hotel to hotel! I expect he *will* be *most* peculiar."

"Your Uncle Fritz," said Mrs. Shelling sombrely, "is a much injured man. That Natalie spoiled his life. Never did I see a man so dazed as your Uncle Fritz on his wedding-day. We all said (your Auntie Katt and Auntie Isabella and I) that if he had been another man and not Fritz, we should have thought he had had too much to drink. He was like one in a dream. And there was she . . . that Natalie . . . laughing and talking, and so gay, and even dancing a little in her wedding gown. She had no right feelings. We all said so . . . your Auntie Katt and Auntie Isabella and I. And then, to lead him such a life—making him go round with her while she danced, and look after her son by another man, who had deserted her. No rest, no good home life, no little children. And the business was neglected, too. Ach, it was dreadful. We all said so."

"I'm sure you did," drawled Bell. "But the business got all right again, didn't it? I mean, Uncle Fritz isn't poor, is he?"

"Oh no. Of course not. Your Uncle Fritz is very comfortable, because he has found a good manager. Mr. Fuller. Mr. Fuller does everything and keeps everything in order, and it will all be ready for Albert to go into when your poor Uncle Fritz dies."

"Nice for him. Does he want to go into it?" asked George.

"Your Uncle Fritz does not say so. It does not matter, even if he does not, because it is all he can do, he is not educated for any other work. For twenty-five years, that boy has done nothing but enjoy himself."

"Have you ever seen him?"

" Once I saw him, when he was about four years old, before your Uncle Fritz went to Brazil. He was a very plain child, poor boy. Very fat ; a large plain little boy, always talking——"

George groaned.

" —and telling lies. I used to speak to him very severely. It was dreadful to hear a little boy always telling lies ; and when I told him he would go to Hell if he went on telling lies, he said—that child !—he said that he would not mind going, because he would like to see what Hell was like. Only think ! "

This story cheered George and Bell somewhat, as showing Albert in a more interesting light, and Bell, who would not have the responsibility of looking after him, began to think that perhaps Albert might prove an amusing addition to their party.

George was chiefly concerned with the problem of keeping enough evenings free from Albert to attend some of the excellent concerts which were to be held in London during May, and told Bell that to-morrow, which was Tuesday, she must go up to town with him and buy tickets for every concert worth hearing at the Queen's, Aeolian and Wigmore halls during the next fortnight. After the arrival of Albert, they could make other plans. The main point was to get in as many concerts as possible during the next thirteen days. If there were any to be had, she might also get some for " Fledermaus " at Covent Garden, and for " Turandot."

" How many shall I get for each concert ? " asked Bell, looking meaningly across at him. They were sitting in the drawing-room, where the curtains were still undrawn and the lights unlit, and the lingering daylight filled the room with softest shadows ; it was like still, clear water. George had the *Telegraph* on his knees, and was searching it for coming concerts.

" What do you mean—how many ? "

" Well . . . two . . . or three ? " she asked, lowering her voice.

" Oh, twos, as usual," he said casually, not glancing at the corner under the old gilt mirror, where Queenie sat nursing *The Origin of Species* and staring out of the window at the shadowy distant woods.

Mrs. Shelling looked up from *The Times*.

" I should like to go to a concert," she announced.

" Oh, Ma, you *can't*," cried George and Bell together. " You know you only want to go to concerts when we start talking about going. You never want to go any other time. Besides," added George, " what's to stop you going by yourself ? You've got the car, and Bennett can always run you up."

" I should *prefer* to go sometimes with my children," said Mrs. Shelling, going back to *The Times*. But she did not sound hurt, and Bell and George took no more notice of her.

Bell had thought that George would certainly wish to include Queenie in one or two of the concert parties (he always improved the minds of his young women) and was resigned and rather amused, but when she heard him say " Twos, as usual," she was lulled out of her suspicions. It never occurred to her that he would want to take Queenie alone. She was used to being a frequent third when George took his girls out; the wretched girls secretly raged and wished she would have a long illness, but she never did. There she sat, thin as a flower stem, dressed with her own careless elegance in her pet shades of violet or lilac or blackest purple, listening to every word that was said and letting not the tiniest shade of meaning in incident or phrase escape her large lazy eyes and keen intelligence. It was plain hell; and after they had been dropped by George, it was of this aspect of their affair with him that the ex-young women spoke most bitterly. "If it hadn't been for that beastly sister of his, things would have gone on" was the most frequent remark made by the dropped ones.

So when, a week later, George told Bell that he was taking Queenie to hear Schnabel at the Queen's Hall, alone, Bell could hardly believe her ears, and at once became very jealous. She was too wise to stare, but just glanced at his moody face, now a little lightened by malice, as he sat opposite her on the old nursery sofa. She had noticed that he had been miserable for the last two days, but put it down to one of his periodical fits of discontent; and sat waiting, like a snake-charmer, for the music of her silent sympathy to make the reptile of his grief unfold. But no confidences had been forthcoming.

"Well this *is* serious," she said at last. "Are you going to propose?"

"Don't be a fool."

"Well . . . what *are* you going to do? What's the matter? You've been like a sick monkey, my dear, since Sunday."

"I don't know what's the matter," muttered George, standing up, and staring at his shoes. "At least, I suppose I do, but I'm not sure. All I know is, I'm taking her alone on Thursday, and I don't want any of your exquisite wit, thank you."

"Ma won't spare her. And if you ask, she'll smell a rat."

"Ma won't have to spare her, and she won't smell

a rat, either," said George, with a kind of spiteful triumph. "It's her day for going up to see her family, and I shall bring her back in any case (I suggested it to Ma, and Ma approved) and she won't know we've been to hear Schnabel."

"Oh . . . the ghastly family," said Bell musingly. "They sound too frightful—the bits I've heard. It's curious that anything so quiet and charming could come out of all that earnestness."

"You *do* think she's charming?" asked George eagerly, wheeling round and sitting down again beside her. "She is, isn't she?"

"She's so *worthy*, George."

"I don't care. Ding-Dong" (and here he put his head on her thin shoulder for a moment, as he used to do when he was a delicate little boy; he spoke in German, and used the old nickname which he never used unless he was much moved) "*do* like her. You will, won't you? She's so . . . she's like a dear little home-made cake!"

"Never so light as the shop ones," said Bell, running cool thin fingers over his forehead.

"But you will, won't you?"

"I'll see. Anyway," with energy, "I don't at all like being done out of Schnabel."

"Poor sweet. I'll take you to hear Schumann when she comes in June. Oh hell, there's the gong and I've never put the car away," and he flew up and tore out of the room.

Bell sat still for a little while after he had gone, her long arm lying along the cushioned top of the old chesterfield, where it had supported her brother's shoulders a second ago. She looked like a spirit, in her full-skirted pale dress, but her face wore an angry, troubled look which was not spiritual. She was considerably alarmed.

She was that rare creature, a happy human being. Untroubled by passions, satisfied to her cool, shallow depths by music, malicious and intelligent, she was content. She tried to imagine as she sat there, a life which would please her more than this one in Bassett with her brother, but failed.

It was true that her imagination was unexercised, because she so rarely thought about her own character and tastes, but she was intelligent enough to be able to paint other possible worlds for herself : and none pleased her so well as this one.

Now there seemed a possibility that this one might be changed and spoiled.

Quickly she got up, and crossed to the window, and stood looking down at the great hood of the may tree, smothered in tiny snowy buds. A fainting fragrance wavered up to her. She thought " Best to let it have plenty of rope. Then it'll burn itself out. God, what a metaphor ! "

# CHAPTER XV

GEORGE asked Queenie to go to the concert with him on Tuesday morning, and she was so amazed and embarrassed that she said " yes " before she knew she had (if I had stopped to think, she afterwards decided, it would certainly have been " no ") and George muttered " That will be lovely " and gave her his beautiful smile, as embarrassed, this time, as her own.

" I'll call for you at home, shall I, about half-past six ? "

" Oh . . . no . . . I think perhaps it would be better if we met in town."

" Outside Oxford Circus tube ?  That's near the shop, and I won't keep you waiting.  I promise."

So it was arranged, and he went off, *not* beaming triumphantly, as he would have done a month ago.

Oh, it was all most alarming !  How she wished she had declined !  A thousand difficulties presented themselves to her mind during the morning, which she spent gardening with Mrs. Shelling.

It would mean lying to her parents, a course which offended her desire " to let all things be done decently and in order " and telling them that she had had instructions to return early.  It would undoubtedly mean deceiving Mrs. Shelling, which offended her sense of what was proper in the relationship between employer and employed (except that Mrs. Shelling would probably guess ;  Queenie always had a curious conviction that

Mrs. Shelling knew everything that went on in the house, from larder to garage). Then he would almost certainly try to kiss her again . . . but at this point such a feeling of solemn, trembling agitation overcame her that she made a great effort, and turned her thoughts away from the problem, and concentrated them on the greenfly.

But by Thursday her agitation had almost gone, and the mood of teasing gaiety had returned. It was heightened by the pretty place to which George took her for dinner; one of the more expensive Italian restaurants of Soho, gay with rosy lamps, and mirrors, faded gilt and claret-coloured plush. All the windows were open, letting in the air of a London summer evening; the traffic roar dying down, the smell of dust and warm stone, and the feeling that all London was driving off in taxis to a party, past the baskets of fading flowers at the street corners.

George would not let her eat much.

" You can't appreciate Beethoven if you're full of dinner."

" Nor can I if I'm hungry. I want a sweet."

" I'm taking you out, and I say you shan't have one."

She demurely drew out a little purse, pleasantly fat.

" I've got some, too."

" I wouldn't care if you did pay . . . much. That sort of thing doesn't bother me—women paying for themselves, I mean : I don't seem to have many of the normal he-man reactions. I don't get jealous, either."

" Possibly," she said maliciously, " you've never had cause to be."

" Not often, it's true, but even when there was reason to be, I wasn't. That's why " . . . he hesitated a second

. . . " that's why I should be a bad person to fall in love with."

" Because you don't get jealous ? I should have thought most girls would have liked that. Jealousy," said Queenie very sternly, " is loathsome. It's barbarous."

" I agree. No—I meant that I don't have very violent feelings about things—nor about people. That's why I'd be a bad person to fall in love with."

" I'll remember," she said impertinently, but her heart was beating very hard. He gave her a quick, almost plead-ing look, strangely at variance with his confession, and changed the subject.

The hall was crammed, and the concert excellent. Queenie listened solemnly and intensely, and found herself very tired at the end of the first item, a concerto. She greatly liked parts of it, and in parts her mind wandered shamefully, and she was not sorry, though surprised, when George said abruptly at the end of the next item—two short pieces—

" Do you mind if we go ? I'm not in the mood for Beethoven to-night, I'm afraid. And we ought to start soon, if we're to get back at a respectable hour."

They drove away from Oxford Circus just after ten o'clock ; and almost immediately there fell between them one of those silences which Queenie found so curiously peaceful and intimate ; it remained unbroken while they passed through the old suburbs and then the new ones immediately outside London, and at last entered open country.

She did not look at George, but knew that his expres-sion was aloof and rather grim. The sky had clouded during their time in the concert hall, and now the watery moon sent a diffused light through a drifting coverlid of pearly clouds, which darkened and softened the whole heavens. Infinitely high, slow-moving and soft, those clouds looked; the dark trees had no details, only their silhouettes and their sweet leafy smell. The car dipped into hollows still full of the day's warm air, mounting into coolness again on the heights, and the headlights struck the still trees, for a second, into livid emerald. Oh, I do wish we could drive home like this, in silence, she thought, and stop outside the big white rhododendron bush, without anything being "discussed." Yet another part of her nature was eager for the car to stop.

When at last George did stop it, still without speaking, they halted on a hill some eight miles from Bassett.

The noise of the engine died into the silence; and, as once before on that first time when she had ridden with him, the tiny noises of the woods flowed into the quiet. Now they were the sighings and scents of a May night, as then they had been the frosty alertnesses and crackings of a winter's noon, but now, as then, George sat still without saying a word, his profile turned from her.

She looked timidly at him. She was afraid he was unhappy.

At last he said, slowly and almost unwillingly, and still without looking at her—

"I'm afraid I'm falling in love with you."

Her heart gave a heavy throb. She tried to speak lightly but her voice sounded to her anxious and pleading.

"Why 'afraid'? I mean, I'm sorry if it makes you unhappy, but . . ."

"I don't want to fall in love. I don't need love."

"I don't want to, either," she said, very seriously.

" And you're the kind of person," he went on, " who'll fall in love so deeply, when you do. That's why I'm afraid."

" But surely " (she was still timid and overcome with embarrassment, but very bent on getting matters straight) " if two people love one another—I mean, if one loves first; and then the other loves, too, that's all right, isn't it ? Not that I want to be in love. . . . I'm sure it upsets things frightfully."

" Haven't you ever been ? "

" No. Have . . . have you ever ? "

" Not properly. Not like I'm afraid I'm going to be with you. I get sick of people."

" And are you afraid you might get sick of me ? "

" I don't know."

There was another long pause. She was frightened to find how much the thought of his getting sick of her could hurt. She pushed the thought to the back of her mind, and tried to speak gaily, this time with more success.

" And what are you afraid I'll do to you, if you *do* fall in love with me ? "

He turned to her, responding eagerly and at once to her change of tone.

" You'll try to change me ; women always do. You'll want to boss me about and always be with me, and dominate me."

She was laughing at him. Her small teeth gleamed tantalizingly in the darkness of the car, and, suddenly moved by desire, he bent over to kiss her.

She was so soft to touch, and so tender and silent as she gently returned his kisses that he forgot his doubts and everything they had just been making him say. He caressed her gently, peering through the dusk at the

small pale moon of her face, in which her eyes were
soft shadows.

"Oh, Queenie, you *are* a darling! I *am* falling in
love with you—I can't help it. Do you love me?"

"How on earth could I love anyone so quickly?"

"Well, I do."

"No you don't—you've just been grizzling about
how afraid you are. You don't love me at all."

"I do—I do!"

"Say it, then."

George tried, but the words would not come, and
he laughed foolishly. She laughed too; a gay, rather
prim little sound which he had seldom heard. Their
spirits were rising rapidly. George said confidently:

"You know, I'm sure we've been taking this much
too seriously. I expect everything will be all right.
Don't let's get all earnest about it; shall we? I do so
detest intensity."

"So do I. No," she corrected herself at once, "I
don't detest it. But I don't like talking about it."

He missed this, because he was kissing her neck, and
immediately afterwards exclaimed that they must go, or
there would be a scandal.

"Do you mind scandals?" he asked, as they coasted
smoothly down the moonlit hill.

"I've never been in one. What kind of a scandal?"

"Well . . . suppose I asked you to sleep with me,
without our being married?"

"If I were in love with you, I would," she said,
lightly but steadily. "Otherwise . . . not."

"Then I do ask you to."

"But I'm *not* in love with you, so the answer doesn't
apply."

"I shall ask you again, when you are."

"Ah, but I shan't be."

"Ah, but you will!"

Their seriousness had vanished like morning mist. The car spun home cheerfully, and stopped outside the big white rhododendron bush exactly at twelve o'clock. George would not let her linger an instant for a last kiss (not that she was trying to linger) as he whispered that Ma and Bell had ears like spiders, and would be sure to note that seven minutes had elapsed between the stopping of the engine and George's key in the lock.

Bell, lying awake reading, heard the car enter the drive, and stop. Slowly she put out a long arm, extinguished her lamp, and lay back on her pillow, arms behind her head, staring at the waning moon.

Queenie lay in that same position, with arms behind her head, for a little while when she awoke the next morning. She was still so young and the deep, calm resources of her body so untried, that awakening from sleep was a slow unfolding, a delicious return from one sweet world into another, as it is to a healthy child.

She thought of last night, and of George's tenderness, no longer feeling tantalizing and malicious. She was beginning to be lost in the maze of love, and did not wish to tease him and lead him a dance. She wanted everything to be quite clear and happy between them, without fits of foreboding or sudden alarmed withdrawals. "It's too good to last . . . if it *does* come to anything . . ." she thought. I could never hope to hold such an attractive person. He only wants me now because I didn't take him seriously at first. As soon as I do, he'll get sick of me, as he has of all the others.

And she knew that, if she wanted everything to be light and happy between them, she must not wander further into the maze of love, but stand just outside, on

guard. I'll do that, she thought, with a sudden gush of
gaiety and mischief which made her curl up her toes.
It'll be hard, but worth it . . . if he really gets to
love me.

Her thoughts just touched the possibility of his asking
her to marry him, then flitted away from it again like
butterflies. From the beginning, she never for one
instant, in her innermost heart, believed that he would
ask her; such an event would have been slightly
out of perspective, just a little too wonderful, too
beautiful, to fit into her rather sober picture of life.

" Miracles don't happen," she was fond of saying,
.and that little phrase arose from the central rock of her
character. They do, of course; radiant and ridiculous,
they happen a dozen times a day all round us, but
Queenie was still too young to know this : and perhaps,
for her and others like her, quick miracles never do
happen. Such people's miracles are of the slow kind
covering years. " I'm healed," someone thinks in
surprise after ten years ; and recognizes a miracle.

She was not shocked by his casual suggestion that they
should become lovers.

The Catton family discussed such unions without
horror ; they kept their horror for marriages without
love. It was true that none of their immediate friends
lived as husband and wife without being married, but
the younger Cattons knew one or two wildish, studentish
people who knew other people who did ; and Gertrude's
teacher friends often made robust allusions to, and
threats of, living in sin, week-ending, going the whole
hog and going off the rails. Protected by their looks and
virtue, they jested comfortably within the pale, and
were not nearly so distressed about their own celibacy
as some people liked to imagine.

So Queenie was used to such talk; and compared with the boisterous, ugly phrases used by the teachers, "sleeping together" was poetry.

She chiefly thought of marriage as a means to an end: that of gently persuading a wild, moody, selfish but beloved creature to remain quietly grazing at one's side. Besides, marriage was safer for the children, and made social life easier; and in short, she knew nothing about it and was just the kind of woman for whom marriage, as a holy order, was ordained.

There she lay, solemnly dismissing marriage as a mere expedient, a formula, a mumbo-jumbo, of next to no account beside its towering brother Love; while her whole body and nature were especially made for no other end than to adorn and edify the sacrament which she dismissed! It was enough to make angels laugh.

As for George, it was the custom in that intellectual, slightly raffish circle on whose outer circumference he and Bell revolved, to ask any personable young woman to sleep with you, after you had once expressed admiration for her. If boredom or fastidiousness had, in every former case, stepped in and prevented George's carrying out his casual intention, that was due to George's rather unusual mental and nervous make-up, not to scruples or the pressure of convention.

Unlike Queenie, George took marriage very seriously indeed; too seriously ever to wish himself married.

It was unfortunate that her plan for keeping the affair on a light, gay level should have been broken by no less a person than George, but it happened.

"Damn you, don't laugh at me," said George, very pale and with eyes full of pain, the first time he tried to kiss her in the garage and she told him not to get intense.

"But you said . . ." stammered poor Queenie, too

willing to become intense and going into his arms with
a fatal readiness.

" That was last night.  Don't always be quoting me :
I hate it."

" I can't *understand* you.  It's awful.  First· you don't
want me to·be serious, and then you do, and whichever
I do, you don't like it.  What *do* you want ? "

" How should I know ? " said George.

And after this there was no more effort to keep matters
light ;  hand in hand, and with only an occasional nervous
twitching from George's fingers, they wandered deeper
and deeper into the maze ;  and of course, as soon as
George stopped trying to engineer a false security and
gaiety spread over a volcano of love, gaiety came as
naturally as scent to a flower ;  and the days before
Albert's arrival flew in a delicate pageant of absurd
jokes, arguments, long glances, longer kisses and
exquisite reveries.

Mrs. Shelling was wrapped up in her frightful annual
battle with the greenfly, and Bell seemed inclined to be
amused and sympathetic.  So there was nothing to
spoil the month of May in Bassett.  Blind and drugged
and light-headed with happiness, Queenie wandered
deeper, ever deeper into the groves of the maze.  The
thread of common sense by which she had once hoped
to find her way back had long since been dropped
and lost to sight.

She was soon too much in love to be troubled by the
deception which was the inevitable companion of their
love-making.  At first it distressed her very much.  She
did not like Mrs. Shelling but she respected her and
was curiously sorry for her (though goodness knows
Mrs. Shelling seemed to have everything a woman could
want, including a husband who was dead) and even if

respect had been lacking she would have scrupled to deceive an employer.  And she had disliked deceiving her family, though it was true that she was so apart from them in spirit and interests that she felt almost entitled to cultivate a little hidden garden of her own and eat her secret bread in peace.

But she felt, very strongly, the contrast between the comfortless, earnest atmosphere of her own home which was kept going by gruelling hard work, and the easy cultured pleasantness of that home in which her love was flowering.  It seemed to her like an insult flung at her home ; as though she had rejected her family, whom she honestly loved ; and deception added to this was just insult added to injury.

But at the end of that fortnight before Albert's arrival her scruples had almost vanished.  In that strange ironical mood which sometimes came to her, and which later was to help her, she would smile maliciously to herself because she was in love with a rich young man, and have spiteful thoughts about spoiling the capitalists as a good Communist should.

Her malice was only matched by her fiery determination to accept neither presents nor treats from George. He might give her roses off the garden bushes, and she fell for a copy of Whitehead's *Adventures In Ideas* (which her father had fretfully told her she should be reading instead of wasting her precious time with dead Darwinism), but then she stood firm.  Presently George, rather hurt, stopped buying her scent and other small gaieties ; and told her that she was an obstinate, boring girl.  He added that all the same, he had never loved anyone so much before ; never, in all his experiences, which had begun when he was fifteen and at school in Geneva, had he found a girl he so loved to kiss.

He never discussed his love in detail. Sometimes she asked timidly and casually why he loved her . . . (if he was sure, that was, that he really did?)

"You're so sweet," was all he would say. "You're a darling, and so funny. So *serious*—enormous eyes, simply popping with seriousness! And I do love you . . . to-day, at any rate. I can't answer for next week, so we'd better make the most of things while we can."

These warnings began to hurt her, as time went on. But if she adopted his own light tone; if she resisted his kisses, withdrew her spirit from his (for they were becoming close friends, as well as romantic lovers) he suffered. He would look at her steadily, his eyes darkening with pain from clear grey to a troubled blue, and say "You're far away to-day, aren't you?" and she could never stay away for long. Back she would go, and forget prudence in the tenderness and silence of his kisses.

# CHAPTER XVI

On the day of Albert's arrival, the society of Bassett was further enriched by the arrival of another gentleman.

At twelve o'clock in the still, fragrant morning Miss Baker was carefully coming down the stairs into the hall of The Tower, carrying a stuffed crocodile. It was only a head, but it was so large that it was nearly as long as a small crocodile's whole body, and it was smothered in dust and Miss Baker was going to give it to Mrs. Partner if Mrs. Partner wanted it, which Miss Baker never for an instant doubted she would.

There had been a few words with Miss Padsoe about the crocodile. Miss Padsoe had not wanted it to be taken down from its place above Mr. Padsoe's bedroom door, where it had hung for thirty years. She explained that it had been hung there by her dear father himself, on his return from a visit to Egypt in 1900.

" All the same, it'll upset people," said Miss Baker, looking up at the crocodile with a condemning eye. " It fair gives *me* the creeps, sticking out up there. It's a dark bit of landing, too, and if anyone was coming up to bed a bit late, after reading one of those thrillers, it's enough to give them a heart attack. Besides, it must be filthy dirty."

Miss Baker added that boarders were easily—too easily—put off, and the crocodile might do The Tower's reputation harm—give it a bad name. She really thought it had better come down and be thrown away or given to

179

Mrs. Partner. Miss Padsoe, with a little colour in her
thin cheeks, said that she supposed perhaps it had, and
went off rather quickly to bed out geraniums under the
sitting-room window. Miss Baker, after a slow ascent
and even slower descent of the step-ladder, bore the
crocodile's head in triumph downstairs.

She was half-way down when she saw somebody
sneaking into the hall.

"Sneaking" was the regrettable word afterwards
used by Miss Baker to describe to Miss Padsoe the
shy, charmingly undecided progress down the hall of
Mr. Christopher Mildmay. A very fat retriever bitch
had preceded him, and lay at ease, looking up intolerantly
at Miss Baker, on the narrow mat at the foot of the stairs.
The front door had been left open to air the hall, and this
was what happened. Men and dogs sneaked in.

"Here, what do you want?" cried Miss Baker loudly,
stopping in the middle of the stairs. "Get up—go
away—shoo—shoo," she added to the dog, waving the
crocodile's head. The dog put its head down on its
paws with a deep sigh and looked up insolently at
Miss Baker.

The gentleman also looked up, and a whimsical smile
lifted one corner of his mouth.

"Enter lady, carrying a crocodile," he said, surveying
her with his head on one side. "No . . . don't move.
It's perfect—quite perfect. It's too good to be true. I
get out of a bus full of Bensusan characters, I climb a hill
that looks like the gateway to Faery . . . I find an open
door and now . . . you, carrying a crocodile. Tell me,
lady with the crocodile, you *are* real, aren't you?"

The tilted head, the eyes wrinkled up in the whimsical
smile which was tinged with a vague melancholy, the
loose tweed jacket and grey undergraduateish bags, all

these had automatically smoothed a path for Mr. Mildmay
through the British Isles ever since he was twenty-one.
He was now nearly fifty, exactly the right age for someone
like him to be. He had been born fifty, too, though his
friends were not of the kind who say such things. They
called him Kit, baptizing him in good ale, of which
they were all connoisseurs, and he described them as
his pals, preferring the gipsy word to the Teutonic
" friend."

Unfortunately, Miss Baker did not belong to the class
that breeds and admires Mr. Mildmays. She just thought
he was not quite right in the head.

" Do you want to see someone ? " she asked, con-
tinuing her careful descent with the crocodile. " Or "
(another thought struck her, and she looked at him as
sharply but less belligerently) " is it about the advertisement ? "

" *Was* there ever an advertisement ? " he asked,
tilting his head even more on one side. " Are you
sure . . . quite sure ? Isn't it difficult . . . a little . . .
to fit the word ' advertisement ' into . . . all this ? "
He half-turned, and indicated the shimmering, motionless green of the garden which shone through the open
door. " No, lady with the crocodile, let us forget the
sour ' uses of advertisement.' The gods sent me here—
Pan, perhaps, or he of the winged heels. I followed the
track of a gipsy's wheels or the flight of a stonechat. It
doesn't matter much, does it ? "

Miss Baker stepped distastefully over the bitch's back,
which was quite flat, as the back of a too-fat dog often
is ; and the bitch growled at her.

" Lady, shut up," said Mr. Mildmay, " and get off
that mat. Have you *no* manners ? "

Lady took no notice.

"I mean the advertisement in *Dalton's Weekly*" explained Miss Baker carefully, as one explains to somebody deaf and rather silly. "Miss Padsoe, my friend whose house this is, wants to get some paying guests, and we put an advertisement in the *Bucks Recorder*, and I thought more people would see it if we put one in Dalton's, so we had one there, too. Did you think of staying?"

"I did 'think.' I certainly did," said Mr. Mildmay softly, looking round the cool, pleasant hall. "It's all too good . . . oh, but you've put down your crocodile! I say, you mustn't do that! It's all part of everything, your nursing the crocodile. Do, please, pick it up again, won't you?"

"Don't touch it, it's filthy dirty," said Miss Baker, observing his movement towards it. She was wondering if he was ever violent? Even the soft kind often were. If not, she did not mind his staying. He could always be locked into his bedroom if he began behaving very queerly.

"Would you like to see Miss Padsoe?"

"'Padsoe'? But that's perfect, again. I say, this is all *too* marvellous. May I see a room, if you have one? And I suppose we had better talk about 'terms,' hadn't we—I believe that's the word, in the queer jargon the agents use."

"I'll fetch Miss Padsoe."

And Miss Baker, not caring to leave Mr. Mildmay alone in the hall with the old copper bowl on the carved linen chest and sundry other small portables, bustled to the front door, put her head out into the porch and cried:

"Miss Padsoe! A gentleman."

Miss Padsoe was not so immediately charmed by

Mr. Mildmay as one might have predicted. If she was silly, it was in the older, Saxon sense of the word rather than in the slighting contemporary sense, and her likes and dislikes were surprisingly strong and well-founded in such a fragile, wandery-minded creature.

She may also have been a little prejudiced against poor Mr. Mildmay by the warning faces which Miss Baker, who remained standing at the door with her back to Mr. Mildmay, was making. It is not possible to jerk the head over the shoulder without moving a muscle, but Miss Baker almost achieved the feat. The effect was both disturbing and stimulating to the curiosity.

Mr. Mildmay's manner to Miss Padsoe was different from his manner to Miss Baker. He verbally wrapped her in lavender. His subtly modulated voice suggested that he was physically bending over Miss Padsoe's extended hand. Her fragility, her timidity, called forth all his chivalry, and he had lots. And it was with relief that he found his prospective bedroom airy, spotless and charming and decided to stay for two months, as he could never have brought himself to back out after he had sympathetically pigeonholed Miss Padsoe among his gallery of types, and poured all that charm and chivalry over her.

" I cannot say I care for that fanciful way of talking," said Miss Padsoe to Miss Baker, as they opened a glass of tongue and prepared a lettuce in the scullery. " To me, there always seems something *insincere* about it. But perhaps I am being a little uncharitable."

" Well, I think he's—you know," and Miss Baker significantly tapped the frizzy wave of hair which decorated her forehead. " But he don't seem to mind paying what we ask, does he ? and he's certain for two months, anyway. Now, how about a girl ? Could you

G

go down into Reading this afternoon and see about it, or shall I ? Or what say we do without one for a bit longer, and see how we get on ? He's only one extra to cook for."

" But he is a Man," said Miss Padsoe solemnly, " and that makes all the difference. They cannot eat what we eat . . . eggs, and so on. I think perhaps we had better try for a maid. I will go down this afternoon, then, shall I ? "

So by the two-thirty bus Miss Padsoe rattled away into Reading, looking (only she did not know it) rosier, plumper, less strange than she had looked two months ago. It was really curious (she thought, as the bus bounced between swishing hazel hedges) how most of the things which had been worrying her so dreadfully only two months ago had just faded away, like forgotten attacks of toothache. It was like looking back on a nightmare : she felt quite ashamed to think that she could have let herself get so run-down, so depressed and despairing and frightened.

There had been nothing to be frightened of, really. Winifred and her mother had simply vanished : there had never been another word from them. And the house was peaceful and well-kept once more, as it had been in her dear father's day. Only yesterday she had climbed into the clock tower, as she had not done for a year, and sat there pleasantly for half an hour in the quiet and the sunlight, looking across the valley at the massed, slumbering blue woods on the far hills, quivering in the heat haze.

And the garden was really beginning to look nice again, and she had had a letter from an acquaintance only that morning saying that they had missed her from the last four W.I. Committee meetings, and that they did trust and hope she was not thinking of giving up the work altogether.

" *Indeed*, no," thought Miss Padsoe warmly, watching the passing hedges with bright interested eyes which did not see them, " I will write this evening, and apologise for my idleness."

She had several errands to do in Reading beside the important one of trying to interview a prospective maid, and she did them with pleasurable absorption. She bought a little lace collar with cuffs to match, and a chocolate cake and a copy of *The Lady*, and saw several amusing little incidents which she stored up to tell Miss Baker when she got home.

They had fallen into the habit of doing this. After either one had been into Reading, she arrived home pleasantly conscious (without realising it) that the stay-at-home was agog for news and ready to comment fully, satisfyingly and good-naturedly on the afternoon's events, as related by the traveller. Only someone who has lived with a superior beast who will not gossip can realise what a comfort such an interested stay-at-home can be.

Miss Padsoe would soon have been depressed, and her vitality lowered, if Miss Baker's comments had been spiteful. But they were not. They were just sufficiently full of smug wonder at the odd ways of the rest of the world to be spicy, but spiteful they were not.

Miss Baker was coming off the defensive.

So Miss Padsoe, having spent a pleasant afternoon and interviewed a likely girl or two, only paused on her journey to the bus to buy a bunch of cornflowers for Miss Baker.

She had noticed Miss Baker often wore a scarf, and sometimes a dress, of that same regal bright blue which inevitably kills a sallow complexion, such as Miss Baker's was, stone dead. Evidently Miss Baker liked blue, so Miss Padsoe took her home some blue flowers.

Miss Baker was surprised to receive them but quite pleased. She put them carefully on the dresser while thanking Miss Padsoe for them and enquiring what luck Miss Padsoe had had about a girl, and after she had been reassured by the news that two girls were coming over from Reading to-morrow morning to be interviewed, she picked up her flowers and went upstairs to tidy herself in preparation for tea.

She climbed the stairs to her bedroom, which was on the third floor, at a comfortably slow pace, mounting through shafts of brilliant sunlight pouring through the landing windows ; and opened her bedroom door with the feeling of pleasure which never failed to come to her at that moment. She closed the door behind her and just glanced round her room as she crossed to the mirror. She had not had a room to herself, used solely for sleeping in, since she was nineteen ; and she took a pride now in keeping her bedroom spotlessly clean and tidy.

All was peacefully in order. The clean faded chintz curtains, patterned with tiny bunches of dark-red carnations, moved a little in the wind. A sweet smell came from a pot of pinks and French marigolds on her dressing-table. Her little pile of papers—*Christian Novels*, *Smart Novels* and the *Red Letter*—lay neatly on the bedside table with her clean candlestick and matches beside it (there were no bedside lamps at The Tower ; at Baines House they shone wherever the lazy George and Bell could persuade their mother to have a point inserted). All was cool, airy, fresh and silent.

"Nice," Miss Baker called it to herself; everything in the room was "kept very nice."

She began quickly to smooth her hair in front of the mirror without really seeing her own face. She never noticed it much at any time. It was a subject for facetious comment between herself and Miss Worrall rather than a cause for 'anxiety or for experiment. Its alert, pugnacious expression had scarcely changed since she was a shrimpy, sallow, boy-hating creature of seventeen.

Yet there was a change. It had come in the two months she had lived at Bassett.

She was just about four pounds fatter, to begin with; the lines on either side of her mouth were less noticeable. Her sallow complexion was one and a half shades clearer that it had been in February. Her voice and movements were not so emphatic; she no longer looked quite so suspiciously and belligerently at people, though her eyes still darted all over things and persons like busy exploring beetles.

In short—very slowly, so slowly that only a person engaged in the unlikely occupation of a life-long study of Miss Baker's character and appearance would have noticed the change at all—Miss Baker was losing that air of nervous tension which had stamped her as a woman who had earned her living by hard, honest work in a city for twenty years.

If she felt different, she never thought about the change. She was too busy exploring the house, arranging, working, managing, tidying. The days flew. For the first week they had seemed long, if not empty: she had been on the alert, as a town-dweller usually is in the country, waiting for something to happen which never did. Now she was too absorbed and busy to wait for anything.

She hummed a hymn as she brushed her ill-cut bob of hair. This Mr. Mildmay . . . now he was queer, if you like! And that nasty fat dog (Miss Baker was very afraid of dogs) where would it sleep? Could Mr. Mildmay eat sausages for supper, with an apple charlotte to follow?

What would the girls be like who were coming to-morrow? She must have breakfast well over by half-past nine, so as to be quite ready for them by ten.

She glanced out through the open window as she crossed the room on her way downstairs. The far woods shimmered in the heat; all the wide valley behind the beech screen lay dreaming in the delight of early summer. Peas: we ought to grow peas, thought Miss Baker. Nothing nicer than your own-grown vegetables; give the place quite a name. I must speak to her about it.

Miss Padsoe had long since become "her" in Miss Baker's mind.

She stumped busily and happily downstairs to help prepare tea.

If Mr. Mildmay was disappointed that neither Miss Baker nor Miss Padsoe had recognized his name, he did not show it. He probably consoled himself by thinking that if he had simply said "I am Mohican" they would have known it at once. In this he was wrong, for neither lady was what is cosily called "a great reader": Miss Baker read nothing but weeklies dealing with the cinema and twopenny and threepenny novels, and Miss Padsoe read books on gardening and, occasionally, the New Testament and the Beatrix Potter books.

Yet nearly everyone in England who liked reading had heard of "Mohican."

Mohican was the only essayist alive in Great Britain

who made nearly enough to live on by writing essays. He whimsically called himself Mohican because he was, he said, the last of the English : the last man left alive who knew the lost downland paths, the ancient sites of gipsy camps, the fairs and highways, the lore of tramp and thatcher, about which everybody in England, of course, used to know by instinct.

And oh! what a fat piece he made out of being the last man to know these things . . . if he really did know them, which one or two sour and reticent scholars who made a hobby of their knowledge but did not exploit it, seemed inclined to doubt.

There was his bi-weekly essay for *The Comet*. There was his weekly essay for *Men and Affairs*. There were his frequent contributions to *Woman's Sphere* (usually on Some Old English Recipes for Cordials or Elizabethan Designs for Embroidery). There was his yearly novel about fairs or circuses. There were his lecture tours, dealing with the Musical Instruments of The Open Road. There were his prefaces, contributed oh! so gracefully and just the least bit condescendingly and perhaps a shade too frequently, to other people's novels about fairs, circuses, otters and polecats.

And finally—and this looked as though it was going to rake in the fattest piece yet—there were his contributions to the Wild Life of the Home Counties Series. He had done one on Sussex last year which had sold ten thousand copies, and was still selling steadily, and this year he was going to do one all about the few luckless badgers left alive in Buckinghamshire, and that was what he had come to stay at The Tower for. He was going to watch badgers.

*Brother Brock*, he was going to call it. All his essays and novels were full of brotherliness for animals, expressed in that polished, whimsical, tender style which made so many people lyrically enthusiastic, and a few soured persons feel sick. He was a great one for polishing. He went for long walks, and polished. He shaped, he carved, he inset and inlaid. He talked about The Craft of The Word. Words, he said, were his mosaic. But in fact they were much more like nails, which Mr. Mildmay kept on tapping, but never quite knocked them slam on the middle of the head, so that they went home into the wood of a sentence and expressed precisely the meaning which common, unliterary people attached to them.

It was very lucky for Mohican that, as the English people moved into towns, they wanted to hear about the country. The more they pulled up primrose and bee-orchis roots, the more they liked essays about bee-orchises and primroses in flower. The fewer circuses there were to go to, the more people wanted to read about them.

To read Mohican's essays, you wouldn't think there was an idle colliery, a cinema, or an unmarried mother in the length and breadth of England. England, apparently, was peopled by mole-trappers (usually the last one in that particular county), gipsies, thatchers, hedgers, ditchers, and reapers. These circulated between little old pubs, cathedral closes, circuses and village greens on which cricket was always being played. Praise of good ale ran like a theme-song through the essays, lectures and novels.

He wrote easily, but messed his sentences about so much that a book took him twice as long to write as it need have done. He did not intend to write much during the months he was in Bassett : there would be no time. He meant to go for long walks, and sit outside pubs with his eyes twinkling, collecting copy and polishing.

And one or two fine, still evenings, of course, must be devoted to watching badgers. In a few days he was most comfortably settled at The Tower, with the Lady of the Crocodile and the Lady with the Trowel (for so he christened Miss Padsoe) and had almost decided to put them both into an essay.

# CHAPTER XVII

WHEN Queenie returned from a walk with Punch the Alsatian, about four o'clock that afternoon, she found the family at tea under the big chestnut tree on the lawn. With them was a dark, unfamiliar figure who could only be Albert.

His general blackness was the chief thing she noticed about him, for she was momentarily distressed by the idea that Mrs. Shelling might have wanted her to stay at home that afternoon in honour of Albert, and she accordingly felt a little guilty and confused and not inclined to observe anyone closely. But her embarrassment soon passed, banished by Mrs. Shelling's calm and even approving air. No doubt if Mrs. Shelling had wanted her to stay at home, she would have said so ; and Queenie accepted a cup and some cake, sat back in her chair and looked across at Albert.

Albert was staring at her, brassily, steadily, rudely as a child. On being presented to her he had carefully put down his cup, risen, and made a stiff bow, and apparently had not taken his eyes off her since.

He was a smallish, square young man, very sturdily built, with a large pallid face and a bold yet calm expression. His dark eyes were disagreeably prominent, his chin was bluish and his mouth too small for a man's mouth.

She stole a glance at the wide, sweet curves of George's mouth ; he was very elegant in his pale grey flannels, balancing cake on Punch's nose and looking secretive and amused. He seemed so cool and detached that she felt wretched for a second; she was beginning to love him so painfully that she could bear less and less easily those frequent retreats which he made into the fastnesses of his own mind. There were whole days when, despite his avowed love, he did not seem to need her. Her heart felt full of pain as she looked at him; she might never have seen him agitated and heard him muttering pleas for her kisses, so little comfort did those memories now give her. She lowered her eyelids, just as George suddenly gave her his beautiful friendly smile.

Bell seemed amused, too, and a little excited and stimulated. She said very little, but lay back looking graceful and fascinating in a deck chair. Albert's eyes moved solemnly from her face to Queenie's and back again, and Mrs. Shelling kept up a placid flow of enquiries and comments, to which Albert politely replied.

Queenie thought that she had never seen a young man who seemed so sure of himself, so solemn, so humourless and impudent-looking. She thought him perfectly horrid, and hated the way he stared. Most grown-up people decently wear a mask of reserve and good manners and self-consciousness. Albert had no mask. His face was a child's face, topping a man's thick body in a dead black, ugly foreign suit.

He ate half a cherry cake and drank five cups of tea, and when Mrs. Shelling was not talking, he was describing his recent travels and the state of his father's health in a loud, precise voice which had little accent and few unfamiliar turns of phrase, yet was withal indescribably foreign. He hissed his s's, and had a curious habit of

giving a long-drawn little expulsion of his breath,
almost like a sliding groan, when he complained of
anything, and adding " It was offal." ' The first time
he said this was almost too much for Queenie, whose
nerves were not so steady as they had been a month ago,
and who was beginning to laugh uncontrollably and
sometimes to cry, with rather frightening ease.

Fortunately neither Bell nor George looked at her.
George went rather red ; Bell sank her lip hard
between two tiny upper teeth. The moment trembled
on the brink of disaster, but it passed, and they were
saved.

By the end of tea, Albert's gaze had shifted from
Queenie to Bell once and for all, and remained there.
The evening sun-rays glittered in her coronets of hair
and her eyes shone too, like grey water. Her ankles
were tucked under the frills on her lilac print dress, her
arms were crossed comfortably across her small breast
and her light lazy voice, which always sounded to Queenie
as though it came from behind a fencer's mask, rose and
fell easily. Did Albert care for music ? Was he fond of
walking—of tennis—of parties ?

" Of Wagner, yes. I heard much Wagner when I
was in Vienna last month. I went almost every night
with some student friends. Oh, it was very fine.
Very fine indeed. I do not like to hear anyone much
except Wagner. I like to walk, but not very much.
There are some pretty walks here, I should think ?
When I was in Belgium last year, some friends took
me every day for our dinner in the woods. I think it
is called a picnic in England. O-oooh, it was offal.
I hope you will not do that much while I am here,
Isabella ? "

" Oh, we take our supper into the woods sometimes,"

said Bell, glancing across at her brother. Queenie
thought she knew why; those summer evening picnics
in the woods were one of their earliest shared memories.
So far, they had not yet been on a single such expedition
this year.

"... but you needn't come if you don't like picnics,'
finished Bell.

"Yes. You asked me if I played tennis. Yes,
I do. I like it very much. I played a lot in Vienna.
I see you have a court here, so I hope we shall play a
great deal; every day, I hope. You also ask me if
I like parties. Oh yes, I like parties very much. Whenever I stay with friends, there are always parties. I
am very friendly, you know. I like to be gay, and to
dance, and to meet many new people. I have always
been so. I have looked forward so much to coming
to stay here, Isabella, because Father has always told
me how gay you and George are."

"Well, that's lovely," said Bell comfortably, "but
won't you call me Bell, instead of Isabella? Everyone
does. It's so much easier."

"Thank you — thank you. I will do so with
pleasure," he returned eagerly, and smiled for the first
time.

Everybody felt how the smile transformed him.
Queenie immediately, without any reason, felt sorry
for him. George, who had been a little depressed
because his cousin seemed so poised, mature and well-
read in comparison with himself, was cheered to find
that Albert, when he smiled, looked six years younger
and even ingenuous. Mrs. Shelling thought a smile
improved his looks—which needed improving, goodness
knows, and her eyes wandered complacently in her son's
direction—while Bell, who had thought that his egotism

was going to make him an impossible scalp to bag, decided that he would probably be easy in the long run . . . after an amusing tussle. And she felt like a tussle. She was eager for any excitement that would take her mind off the spectacle of Queenie's growing absorption in George and George's gradual surrender to Queenie.

"Does your father never speak of settling down and making a real home for himself?" asked Mrs. Shelling rather severely. "It is time that he did. He is an old man now. He will be seventy on his next birthday, in October."

"He speaks of it sometimes, but he never does anything about it. We have a house, you know," said Albert simply. "In the Stubaitaal, above Innsbruck. Very pretty. But we only stayed there for a month when I was twenty. Papa prefers to live in hotels. Well, in some ways I prefer it, too. It is very gay, and we have no domestic troubles, and one meets very interesting people, only they do not always stay long enough to get truly *gemütlich*. I was born in a hotel, you know, and I expect I shall die in one."

"Nonsense," said Mrs. Shelling roundly. "You should not say such things. A man should have a home, a wife, and some nice little children. There is nothing so sweet as a good home life, and I think all this talk of being gay and meeting such interesting people does not show right feelings. It is not your place, Albert, to tell your father so, but I shall tell him when I write to him on his birthday. Now while you are here, *this* is your home, and I hope you will be very comfortable and happy in it. These naughty children will amuse you, and you must work hard and show an improvement to your father when you return in November. Now I shall go to write some letters."

And much to everybody's surprise Mrs. Shelling went over to Albert, placed two firm hands upon the shoulders of the ugly black suit and bending her head, kissed him thoroughly on his unappetizing forehead.

" There ! " she said, drawing back and surveying him, " I feel as though you were my own nephew."

Albert rose gallantly, and, in his turn, kissed her hand ; and she went back to the house looking rather pleased. The others sat in amused silence, but after she had gone George said, " What's biting Ma ? She never kisses anyone."

" Oh, I kiss people very often," said Albert eagerly, turning to him. " I have no inhibitions sexually, I am pleased to say. I was told in Vienna I was not a fitting subject for analysis because I have so few complexes."

" Nice for you," said Bell, catching George's eye and beginning to laugh. " Would you like to play tennis before dinner ? How about you, Queenie ? "

" Very much," breathed Queenie. This was the first time Bell had used her absurd nickname, and she could not help being pleased. Oh, how painfully she wanted Bell—Mrs. Shelling—even Punch !—to like her, because they were part of the pattern of George's life and if they liked her, she might hope to creep into that pattern, almost unobserved, and become necessary to it !

George glanced from one to the other. He carefully guarded his expression, but put Queenie on his left arm and his right round Bell's waist, and steered both girls up to the house. Albert, staring solemnly first at the garden's beauties and then at Bell's braids, followed slightly in the rear.

Queenie and Bell were surprised to find that Albert played an excellent game, but George was not. He was a good judge of character and of potentialities, and he had seen, from his first glance at Albert, that here was a young man who would do well everything which he attempted or would not do it at all. He was extremely vain, and could not endure to play tennis or Bach badly, waltz clumsily, or fail to talk interestingly.

At the end of a week the brother and sister had decided that he was a pleasant addition to the very limited society of Bassett. Queenie wavered between a foolish feeling of repulsion before Albert's general blackness, prominent eyes, habit of staring, and extremely complacent manner, and a most irrational pity for him, for which there seemed no cause.

Complacent he certainly was. When taxed with it by Bell, who never minded what she said to people, he rather floored her by asking her, why should he not be complacent? He said that he knew his own mind, had mastered four languages and some difficult games and music, and always earnestly tried to cultivate his mind. Why should he be deferential, doubt his powers and be vague and sentimental?

" It's so middle-aged to be complacent."

" So you think, because neither you nor George nor Miss Queenie have the courage to be sure of your own desires and opinions. Miss Queenie is the most sure of the three, but I think her desires are so strong, and also her opinions, that she is afraid to admit they are so. When she is a little older, she will admit them. But George—he has no opinions, only an interest in everything. He has no desires ; he has only a taste or a distaste."

" And how about me ? " She seldom asked people's opinion of herself; she considered such questions vulgar, but Albert amused her and she was mildly curious to see how far he had fallen in love with her.

" You are not a human being at all, and therefore you would be very dull to sleep with," he said calmly looking at her with a mingling of desire and contempt in his expression which she found very diverting.

" Yes," he continued meditatively. " I like to talk with you, to look at you, and often I think what it would be like to sleep with you. But I always think: no, she is too unkind. I cannot enjoy myself with an unkind girl. You are too intelligent to be openly cruel to the humble and the stupid and the tender-hearted. Only stupid people are cruel. You have good manners, so you will not be unkind openly. But oh! your heart is very unkind." ·

" It isn't," protested Bell, who was enjoying all this hugely and saving it up to tell George, amid shouts, later on. " It just hates fuss, that's all."

" It is the same thing. All real life, all warm human life such as the great poets—the *dichter*—love to tell of—is filled with fuss. What is birth? Fuss. What is death? Fuss. And love . . . more fuss. If you hate fuss, you hate life."

" You *do* know a lot, for one so young," said his cousin, suddenly bored with him. Despite his words, his round eyes were fixed steadily on the owner of the " very unkind " heart with an unwilling devotion.

" I am only twenty-five but I am mature. You— George—Miss Queenie—none of you are mature, so I seem old to you, that is all."

Fortunately he could never perceive irony, and this

afforded his cousins-by-courtesy much quiet joy and
made them put up with long and rather boring speeches
which they might otherwise have quenched : they could
cap them with ironical comment, appreciated by an
amused but rather disapproving Queenie.

He quickly adopted the Shellings' ribald yet cold
manner of discussing sex. His natural habit was to
say exactly what he thought or felt, and as they did
not reprove him, he spoke as he pleased. Good manners
sometimes checked George and Bell : save that he never
swore nor used ugly expressions before the girls, nothing
checked Albert.

Their freedom of speech arose from coldness and
indifference, his from warmth and a preoccupation
with his natural desires, but the effect in conversation
was identical.

This used at first to distress and embarrass Queenie.
She was not interested in lust ; these ugly bald phrases
and the cold acceptance of lust as a joke made her writhe.
And the brother and sister seemed a little ashamed of true
love. It was not to be discussed ; only hinted at with
tender, indulgent, mocking laughter such as might be
heard behind the back of a well-beloved " natural,"
so she imitated their lightness, laughing when they
laughed at love.

Her natural instincts were social and sound. She did
not like laughing at serious, tender and intimate feelings.
She liked sex kept to heel, like a well-trained dog.
She wanted her life to have a shape and a purpose.

But these instincts shrank before George's influence.
They smelled of washing-up water and cooking. She
had never met people who wore culture as mockingly and
casually as a flower, and the example was too much for
her. Her family had the painful reverence for culture

of the half-educated : George and Bell used it to feed their instinct for pleasure.

She became quite pleased with herself as May wore into June : an ironic, flippant second self was satisfactorily masking " the little stodge " of six months ago. She grew quite familiar with Bell, growing closer and closer to that sprite's side as Bell graciously permitted her to come. Bell was too wise to be stiff and keep her at bay : she had never seen George so much in love, so fierce to defend a girl, so tender and reticent. Queenie shared their jokes, their concerts and idle evenings, and was deliciously, exquisitely happy.

During the two most beautiful months of summer, Bassett looked like a village in a fairy story.

The elms, heavy in full leaf, stood round and hid the church, inn and single row of cottages from any gazer on the hilltops, and up the sides of two hills marched forty or more little may trees no higher than a girl's waist and for a fortnight these dwarfs were buried in snowy, hauntingly-perfumed flowers. To walk among them at evening after the sun had set was like walking in the middle of a poem. All the wide, shallow valley was full of long rays and peace and divine silence ; and sentry beech woods, still now, but in the day brilliant and restless and green as the sea, stood four-square on the circling hills. No one ever seemed to come there except the faithful daily 'bus, and the valley looked and smelt and felt like an earthly paradise.

# CHAPTER XVIII

At the end of June, Mrs. Shelling decided to leave the paradise and pay a visit to Auntie Katt in Innsbruck, hoping to see her once more alive before those Nazis got hold of her, as they seemed to do, in the long run, of anyone who could read, write, and think for themselves.

George and Bell were terribly pleased because they felt the need of giving some parties : and parties could be more *gemütlich* when Ma was away. Like old Mr. Woodhouse, Mrs. Shelling thought that " the sooner every party breaks up the better," and such an attitude is scarcely conducive to the success of an evening. Albert was sorry she was going, and told her so. He liked his Aunt Minna and she liked him. Despite his odd upbringing, he was not a naughty boy. He was a good boy. It was a pity George was not more like him. And so on.

Queenie heard Mrs. Shelling's calm announcement at breakfast, and a thrill of alarm rushed through her body. Would she be sent home ?

A month ago she would have gone about her morning duties silent and apprehensive, waiting for Mrs. Shelling to speak, but now that she had persuaded herself that irony, courage and a little impudence could conquer charmers and manage life, she behaved differently. She broached the subject. She said to Mrs. Shelling, while they were looking out clothes to be packed:

" Shall you want me to stay here while you are away,
Mrs. Shelling ? "

Mrs. Shelling, kneeling in a strangely girlish position
in front of a chest of drawers, did not look round nor
did she immediately answer : and when she did the
pause, though tiny, had both shown Queenie her mistake
and given an additional coldness in her ears to Mrs.
Shelling's reply.

" That is as you please, Miss Catton.   If you wish to
stay, do so.   There will be letters to forward, and bills
to pay as usual or, if you prefer to go home, you can go.
It is just as you please."

" I would like to stay here, please," said Queenie
rather boldly, though her face reddened and for a
second she felt to the full the misery, and discomfort,
and even the vulgarity, of deceiving her employer and
abusing her trust.

" That is well, then," said Mrs. Shelling, going on
sorting out combinations : but her voice was dry, and
somehow Queenie did not feel that it was at all well.

I'm sure she knows all about it, she thought, watching
Mrs. Shelling get into George's car to be driven to the
station three days later.

Yet there was not much to know.

Only a record of kisses which had increased in
violence, and of silences which became longer as words
became less necessary.   No harm had been done.
None.   None ?   Her depressing thoughts, which took
place at the open morning-room window whence she
was looking out at the drive, were interrupted by
Bell.

Bell was at the telephone.   She had flown to it
almost before the car was out of sight, and was now
impatiently giving Bertie Barranger's number for the

second time, on tip-toe with impatience, swaying a little to and fro, and frowning into space.

"Oh Bertie, there you are! What frightful ages these people take . . . look here, Ma's gone off to Innsbruck to-day for a month, and we're giving a party on Friday night. Can you come down?"

"Oh curse your pa. He always does.

"Oh about eight, I suppose.

"Yes.

"Yes.

"All right; that'll be lovely. Good-bye."

This conversation was repeated with variations during the morning; the house echoed to Bell joyously telling people for whom she did not care a hoot that Ma had gone away and wasn't it marvellous and yes they were going to have some parties, and could you come to one on Friday about eight. Yes, dress, please.

It was true that a weight seemed lifted from the house; the servants went about smiling and eagerly agreed when Queenie remarked that it was a beautiful day, and Punch gambolled on the lawn and upset the deck chairs, and Albert trotted round after Bell listening to everything she said and remarking frequently, "How gay we shall be!" until Bell told him that if anything could damp her pleasure at her mother's departure, that remark could, and shut him up.

The three had a noisy and cheerful lunch, Queenie talking as loudly and commenting as freely on Mrs. Shelling's absence as did the other two. She was a little fey with arrogance and love: she had climbed right into the hearts of two capitalist charmers and sat there enthroned and welcomed, free to preach Communism to amused and tolerant ears if she liked, loved by the brother and liked by the sister. Her first timid jealousy

of Bell had vanished : there was nothing to be jealous
of. They made a harmonious three, and when George
wanted to be alone with her, Bell never sulked, so what
more could she want ?

Bell took her arm after lunch and drew her out into the
garden through the french windows. They began
slowly to pace up and down beside the delphinium
bed, Bell suiting her long stride to Queenie's shorter
pace.

Queenie, who did not know that Bell never discussed
dress except with her dressmaker or the maid who did
her mending, had begun talking about clothes ; she,
since she had fallen in love, was beginning to take a
serious interest in dress and to experiment a little with
her own appearance.

" What shall you wear on Friday ? " she asked happily
and eagerly, her vowels broadening just a shade as they
always did when she grew excited. She was so happy
that she did not observe a tiny pause before Bell's
reply : " My lilac tulle. What shall you ? "

" Well . . . I only have my old black ; I really
need a new one. I wish my day off came before Friday,
I would go up to town and get one."

" My dear child, you aren't a black slave," laughed
Bell. " Your time is your own now Ma's away. Come
up with me to-morrow : we'll go to May Mason
and have our faces done."

" Oh . . . but isn't she terribly expensive ? Besides,
what would she do to us ? "

" I'll treat you. Oh, tidy our eyebrows (yours
don't really need it but mine do) and show us what
make-up to wear on Friday."

" I should *love* that. You *are* a saint to treat me.
One day I'll treat you." She laughed a high, excited

little laugh and threw a joyous, almost defiant look round the garden which trembled with delicate colour and heat-shimmer. ¬

"I am going for a walk. Would anyone like to come with me?" said Albert politely but without much hope in his voice, appearing at the window in his too-correct plus-fours. George had screamed at them and told him that only Ikes wore them nowadays, but he could not bear to abandon them.

No one wanted to so he went off briskly with Punch, who was not in a position to refuse.

"Then we'll go up to-morrow, shall we, by the ten-thirty? George will run us in—what a bore it's not his day for going up."

"Will he be home earlier to-night?" asked Queenie, thinking with a thrill of happiness that this evening she could sit quite openly on the lawn and sew, waiting for him, instead of lurking behind her bedroom curtain and sadly watching Bell go up to him and pull his ear or thump him in the chest.

"I shouldn't think so. Why should he?" asked Bell rather sharply. She had her own game to play but sometimes her unconscious opponent's manner grated so sharply upon her nerves that she almost gave her plans away by an outburst.

"I only thought . . . as your mother is away . . ."

"Oh mercy, George isn't like that at all. He's much more likely to kill himself with overwork than do that sort of thing. You don't know him very well, do you?"

She could not resist trying to discover how far the affair had gone, though she awaited the reply with pain and distaste.

Queenie was flung, for a second, back into her old

mood of silent, humble love.   She said a little timidly,
looking up at George's sister :

" He's not easy to know, is he ? "

" No.   He's a very complex person."   And that
was all she would say, although she thought with
satisfaction, " but I know him, if you don't."

After dinner that evening when the four were sitting
on the little stone terrace outside the drawing-room
windows, George said in a low tone to Queenie, " Shall
we go for a walk ? "

She nodded with shining eyes and slipped away to
get a coat, under cover of Albert's loud monologue
about his experiences in a Berlin night club.   It was
all excessively boring, and Bell was not listening to a
word of it ; she was lying back staring into the high,
deepening blue of the night sky in which the stars
were beginning to show.   All round the back of her
chair glimmered the massed horns of a white rhododendron, a heraldic device on a shield of dark green bush,
and Albert (on being asked to do so) had put her
feet on to a little white-beaded Victorian stool to keep
them from the dewy flag-stones.

" So then," went on Albert, " she put her arm round
my neck.   Excuse me, I said to her very politely,
excuse me, I do not care . . ."

With smiles at Bell which she faintly returned, George
and Queenie slipped down the little path behind the
flowering bush.

He took her arm and drew it into his, covering her
fingers with his kind warm ones.

" Happy ? "

" *Perfectly*.   Oh George I've had such a lovely day ;
Bell's been so kind.   She's going to take me up to town
to-morrow.   I'm going to buy a new frock for your party."

" Are you ? "

But he did not seem to have fully taken in the meaning of her words ; he spoke in a quiet, dreamy tone that matched the look on his face as he bent over her. The light was the clear, lingering one of a June evening which is a marriage of coming darkness and reflected day, and it gave his face, always beautiful and a little remote, a strange, tranced look. She put up her face to be kissed, and he stopped for a moment, and putting his arms round her, kissed her with so much passion and in a silence so trembling with feeling, that she lost, for a moment, all sense of where she was. She felt nothing but the pressure of his body and warm lips, and closed her eyes and went into darkness. It was strange to see the tiny, high stars sparkling over George's dark shoulder in the huge dome of the sky when she opened her eyes again ; for a second they made her feel frightened and sad.

He put her arm in his again and they went out through the drive gates, across the dusty white road now dim in the owl-light, and into the beech coppice which looked over the valley and Bassett. It led down on to the hill where the little may trees grew.

Oh, the blue and dimming green in the beechwood ! High, high ran the slender stems and ended in motionless traceries against the sky. The highest leaves were bathed in a lingering transparent light, and looked as though they were under warm grey water. The boles were in shadow, a sweet cooling smell crept out of the few briars and wandered along the paths, warm air blew in puffs from the open hill beyond, and all was still and shadowy. The dark path sloped downwards ; they could see the little may trees glimmering between the branches lower down.

It was too lovely in the copse to talk, but when they
came out into the great expanse of lingering light
and darkening woods and hills, where coolness rose
from the long grass, George said, " Let's go and walk
among the little trees, shall we ? " and they went down
towards them.

But the tiny flowering trees grew closely together in
groups ; one could only walk between them, not round
the single trees. It was strange to look down on to their
snowy foamy hoods, to put one's face into them and feel
their feathery red stamens brushing lips and nose and
smell their sweetly haunting smell.

George sat down on a turf, and Queenie walked
silently from tree to tree, brushing their hoods with her
palms.

" George, they *are* so soft, and quite cool. Do
come and feel."

" I like to look at you. Darling, come here a minute."

She came slowly over to him between the trees,
dark against the pale sky, her own face now transfigured
by the owl-light, and stood looking down at him.

" Well ? "

" We can't go on like this, you know."

" Can't we ? " she murmured : and her very voice
was softened by love, and changed from its cool non-
murmurous note of two months ago.

" Of course not. It's bad for both of us. Will you
come away with me ? "

He said it almost lightly, but his face, lifted to her,
was terribly pale and full of feeling. She knelt down
beside him, drew his head down against her shoulder
and said, without a thought of refusal :

" Of course. I want to, too."

" We'll go on Saturday, shall we ? We'll take the

car and just go off and have the whole week-end together.
Oh love . . . my sweet love . . ."

They stayed quietly for a little while, she stroking
his bent head and staring solemnly down at Bassett
in the valley. Two lights, clear and gold, suddenly
shone out in the inn and the last cottage opposite the
church.

She was not thinking of anything at all, except how
much she loved having his head against her shoulder,
and comforting him. She thought, too, how lovely
it would be to have him for a whole two days to
herself. But she never thought of what she had promised, nor of rules and rites and consequences. It
was the natural reply to give, and so she gave it.

When they got back to the house it was dark. The
terrace was deserted, the bead footstool abandoned,
and through the windows of the lit drawing-room Albert
could be seen sternly playing César Franck to Bell,
who did not seem to be listening as absorbedly as she
usually listened to music.

# CHAPTER XIX

THE delightful plans for the party were so well advanced by Thursday morning that everybody felt in a state of slightly maudlin benevolence towards the world, and it was decided to ask to the party those two old fish faces from The Tower and that extraordinary looking male who was apparently living with them. The poor old things would probably love being invited; and, after all, it was not as though a few older people were not going to be there: Mrs. Minister must be getting on for sixty and old Mr. Barranger was coming which was a simply crashing bore, but he was so fond of us both because he knew us when we were kids and when he heard Bertie was coming, he said he would so love to come too that we simply had not the heart to refuse: he and Mrs. Minister would be company for the fish faces.

So on his way to work that morning George left an invitation at The Tower which threw Miss Baker and Miss Padsoe into a pleasant fit of agitation, and made Mr. Mildmay even more acutely conscious than usual that he was a public character. Now he was pleased that he had packed his tails: his house-keeper had warned him that a popular and famous gentleman like himself was almost sure to want them, and the excellent woman had been right.

" Chains, Cartwright . . . chains," he had murmured to her, wagging a finger and twinkling, as she packed the tails under his direction.

"*Sir?*" breathed Cartwright interrogatively; she knew exactly what he meant but held her job down by pretending to be a bit housekeepery and fuzzy on the uptake, thereby providing Mr. Mildmay with many delightfully whimsical anecdotes about her obtuseness.

The personnel of this party was more agreeable than that of most parties held at Baines House. George was feeling softened by the exquisite weather, by his feelings for Queenie, and by the approach of the week-end, and he suggested to Bell that it might be a good idea to ask all the really nice people whom they knew. Bell in her turn, watching his serious happiness with a mixture of jealousy and unselfish joy, suggested that they should return some of the hospitality given them by older friends of their mother. She could not help being influenced by his gentle mood. She hated its cause, yet its manifestations charmed her; and the charm worked itself out in her suggestion.

So one or two young professional women with very few frocks were surprised and pleased to get invitations from this elegant pair whom they hardly knew: and one or two talkative bounding persons who practically lived at parties because they were so miserable at home in their ill-kept bachelor and spinster dens were puzzled but pleased to be asked. Shy, learned people crept out of their holes, feeling flattered. A number of feckless souls who could make a party " go " on water-cress and dillwater were invited, and finally, a sprinkling of people whom Bell and George had known for many years but never thought about: these gave a comfortable, do-you-remember feeling to the party.

A more dreadful collection of guests a sophisticated mind could barely conceive . . . and yet, from the very beginning, from the first note of the violins played

by the string band which George had hired from town,
from the first bite at the first cold duck sandwich—that
party was a shimmering, a radiant success.

The weather helped. All day, sighing through the
middle of a heat-wave, a long steady breeze blew flowers
and scent off the lime trees, and pollen off the flowering
ash, scattering seed-keys on the shaved lawns and
cooling the house. Evening came like a new part of
the day, not like an exhausted end to it; rays and wind
fell together through the ever moving trees, that tossed
and turned their silver undersides to the blue sky.

George skimmed about examining wine, drawing
Queenie behind doors to kiss her neck and look long
into her bright eyes. Albert tied and retied his bow before
his glass, solemn and correct. Bell drifted from drawing-
room to supper-room, saw that the band had stout and
cold beef in the servants' parlour, arranged great sprays
of moist lime-tree leaves and flowers in the vases,
floating her frilled skirts of misty lilac tulle after her as
she went, putting an absurd bunch of heliotrope sweet
peas into what she told Albert was her corsage.

At The Tower, there was a frightful scurry going
on, though not a sound betrayed it. It had been
agreed that it would be pleasant if the two ladies walked
round by the road to Baines House with Mr. Mildmay;
it was the longer way, to be sure, but the descent into
the valley would be disagreeable, as it meant crossing a
field of large sun-baked clods. They were to leave at
eight-fifteen; and at five minutes past eight Mr. Mildmay,
elegant in tails and white scarf, descended into the
drawing-room and sat down with his soft black hat
and yesterday's *Comet* for company, to wait for the
ladies.

Upstairs, panic reigned. Miss Baker, wearing a

Locknit petticoat, her hair in even more disorder than usual, kneeled before Miss Padsoe, madly sewing the ultimate frill on to the skirt of a grey floral chiffon dress, which was extremely becoming and fitted Miss Padsoe admirably. Miss Baker had made it in a day; yesterday had been devoted to making one for herself, which also fitted but was not, alas, becoming. Royal blue, printed with very large orange flowers, was Miss Baker's choice; with a cape, a bow on the cape, frills on the hips, frills at the hem and frills on the sleeves.

Frills take time, as any dressmaker knows. Miss Baker had not finished her own frock until nearly one o'clock that morning, and had been up at seven to begin machining Miss Padsoe's.

They had had to have them. Both had decided, ten minutes after reading the invitation, that they had nothing to wear to the party; and they had gone into Reading by the second 'bus to choose materials.

Miss Baker, of course, could cut like a tailor; and with a pattern over which she sniffed contemptuously but which she used successfully as a basis, evolved a graceful dress for Miss Padsoe which gave the latter the purest childlike pleasure.

" It really *does* look nice, doesn't it ? "

" Do hold still; I'm only half-way round. It looks really smart : I'm quite pleased with meself. It's years since I *made*, though it's only four months since I was cutting, of course. That puff on the sleeve looks really lovely."

Miss Padsoe, cautiously twisting her head, looked solemnly into her long glass on the opposite wall.

She saw a tall, very slender lady in a grey dress patterned with shadowy pink flowers. A head silver as honesty topped the grey dress, and blue earrings

picked up the bright blue in her eyes. Miss Padsoe
stared and stared. That's me, she thought. I used to
look at myself like this when I was twenty.

"I'm going to throw all my old clothes away
to-morrow," she suddenly announced, "and buy some
stuff to make new ones. Could . . . could you find
time to help me, do you think?"

"Make 'em for you. I'd like to. It's high time
you had some new ones," said Miss Baker, madly
snapping off her last end of cotton, scrambling to her
feet, diving into her own dress, and smoothing her
hair all in one complicated movement.

Three minutes later they came serenely into the
drawing-room, both smelling strongly of lavender
water, and ready for the evening's gaieties. Mr.
Mildmay gallantly placed himself between them, and
off they went.

They did not get to Baines House until just after
nine o'clock, and found the party already well away.
George had asked people to leave their cars at the
side of the house near the garage, so that they were
partly hidden by the rhododendron bushes and did not
spoil the flowery, romantic prospect of the garden
and the lit windows of the house, and as the three
approached, Miss Baker exclaimed "Well! It's ever so
pretty, isn't it?"

The front door stood open, and the french windows
of the drawing-room; the sweet gay noise of The
Merry Widow waltz floated from the latter room where
the younger people were dancing. Sedater figures,
snuffing the fragrant air and gossiping, strolled under
the tree-shadows. Over all arched the blue darkening
dome of the sky.

"Hullo, my dear souls—how nice of you to come,"

said George, darting out at them on his way across the hall; Miss Baker's prudent beetles noticed that he had already had one or two. "Bell—here's Miss Padsoe."

Bell's huge bright eyes, shining with excitement and mischief, fastened their gaze immediately on Mr. Mildmay. Mr. Mildmay did not like young women as a race, but he flattered them on principle and made himself very agreeable to Bell, who tried to flirt with him and threw Albert into sombre agonies of jealousy which were none the less painful because he knew how trifling and physical was the feeling from which they sprang.

But almost everyone else seemed transformed on that evening, fey and witched out of their everyday selves into a mood of gaiety and heedlessness. The mingling of old people and young ones proved a success : the party became a world in miniature and gaiety gained from contrast with sobriety.

It was Queenie's evening. Transmuted with happiness and joy, she danced as though her small feet had wings, and her face was so solemnly radiant, its clear paleness set off by her dark blue dress scattered with silver stars, that several of the older women looked at her curiously and a little wistfully. Her look of serene health, which was what had unconsciously first attracted to her the delicate and nervous George, was peculiarly noticeable that evening; her firm yet delicate body seemed charged with vitality.

"You look like a bride," said that usually silent young man, Bertie Barranger, suddenly to her, as they walked among the rhododendron alleys after a dance to get cool.

"I'm so happy . . ." she said suddenly, staring straight in front of her and speaking in a low voice

that trembled a little. "So marvellously, incredibly
happy . . ." and suddenly she turned aside, and plunged
her head and shoulders into a mass of snowy and purple
flowers on a level with her eyes. "Oh!" she cried,
laughing and coming out again with dew all over her
face and petals scattered on her shoulders and hair,
"That was lovely! Shall I do it again? I had to—
I must get closer to things, or I shall explode!"

He laughed, standing looking down at her with his
legs a little apart and his hands in his pockets. He was
a little taller than she : a freckled nondescript boy with
a good chin.

"Do it again if you want to, and if it does you good.
I don't mind."

He never minded what people did as a rule, but
he had the quality of sticking to his disapproval if once
he gave it.

"No . . . I must go back. It's George's dance,"
she said more soberly, and began picking petals from
her hair as they turned back to the house.

So that's it thought Bertie, walking silently by her side
and watching her intent little face. It's George. . . .
He had seen more than one girl exalted by George's
favour, but never like this. He felt, to his amazement
and for the first time in their long friendship, something
like anger with George blowing coldly into his mind ;
and obediently and at once, his mind rejected the feeling
and turned its attention to other things.

"Ding-Dong," said George to his sister as they moved
slowly round the room in the paces of a tango,
"I'm going away for the week-end."

He felt her give a little quiver in his arms, and then she
looked up and found his eyes looking down, very
steadily and a little coldly, into her own. For a second

she said nothing ; she did not know what to do or say, because she had never suspected, in her wildest anticipations, that things could go so far as this ; and she knew from his expression that he had made up his mind and nothing, nothing, could move him. He based his will, when he asserted it, not on reason but on caprice. He never had reasons for what he did nor could he analyse his motives ; he just lodged all the cold obstinacy of his nature on a caprice, and refused to argue.

At last she said slowly :

" I think you're very unwise."

" I dare say you do. But you're wrong. I'm being wise for perhaps the first time in my life. I want . . ." he paused a second or two, while they parted and came together in the movements of the dance, and then went on " I want this experience. It's something utterly new, Bell. I can't tell you what it's like, this feeling we have. . . . It enriches everything ; it's marvellous. I wouldn't have missed it for anything in the world."

" Are you going to marry her ? " asked Bell, furiously jealous, feeling shut out and lonely, cut off from the person she loved best in the world.

" I don't know. Perhaps. Not yet, anyway ; nor for a year or two, if we ever do. We don't talk about marriage much : she doesn't seem to want it."

" Well . . . for god's sake be careful . . ." she began coarsely, but at that moment the dance ended and they drew apart and stood clapping, but in silence, neither looking at the other. Suddenly he said, still clapping and not looking at her :

" I wish you didn't mind so much. It would have been perfect if only we could have gone off together knowing that you were happy about it."

"I'm sorry, but I can't be. How can I? When I know you so much better than you know yourself, and I can see this will end in a ghastly mess? It's all wrong, George. She isn't our sort at all, really. I quite like her : she's intelligent and original, up to a point, but all that earnestness and brooding business . . . really, I can't cope with it."

He did not reply ; and she felt that her words had simply glanced off his mind. He had shut her out. He was in a maze with his new experience and his little lover, and she was left outside with wit and reason and music, which he and she had once shared, to console her.

The evening was completely spoiled for her, and she spent the time until the end of the party being an excellent hostess and seeing that everyone had plenty of cup and ices ; and in thrusting her own painful jealousy to the back of her mind. Nothing could be done. She could not avert what would happen to-morrow nor win him back in a few hours to that pessimistic flippancy which used to be natural to him and which had up till now been his armour. She could only hope, bitterly, that he had arranged for their departure to be discreet, so that the servants might not *see* what was taking place, however much they might *guess*.

Another person for whom the evening did not end so pleasantly as it had begun was Mr. Mildmay. He was unwise enough to reveal, during a conversation with George, Bell, Miss Padsoe and old Mr. Barranger, that he was Mohican. This revelation was greeted with loyal if lonely cries of delight by old Mr. Barranger. Miss Padsoe had not read Mohican, and George and Bell loathed his work.

"Then I suppose," said Bell, "you're down here collecting information for a new book?"

"Alas . . . I plead guilty."

"What kind of a book? All about birds?" asked George, who was a little drunker than he had been at the beginning of the evening because his conversation with Bell made him unhappy, and he wanted to forget it.

"Not birds," smiled Mr. Mildmay. "I can scarcely expect you to believe it but at the moment my profession is that of a badger-watcher."

"A *what?*" asked George loudly, and he winked at Miss Padsoe who was rather distressed.

"A badger-watcher," repeated Mr. Mildmay, in his clear voice. (It is odd how foolish quite sensible words can sound, if said loudly and clearly to an uncomprehending audience.) "I shall watch them, and take notes of their habits, and embody them in the essays in my new book."

"Oh I say, what a good idea," cried George, again winking at Miss Padsoe. "We'll all come one evening and watch with you. We'll have a badger-washing party. Now, that's settled, Mr. Mildmay. We'll all have dinner here first, and then go off and wash for badgers. Watch, I mean. Would one evening next week suit you? I suppose it must be a fine, clear night and all the rest of it? Do you know where to look for them?"

"I have made notes of two likely places," said Mr. Mildmay rather coldly, "but I am afraid we cannot make a party of it. There are *some* occasions," said Mr. Mildmay with acid relish and glancing from George's tipsy, amused face to Bell's carefully innocent one, "which by *no* amount of taking thought can be transformed into a party. And I am afraid that badger-watching is one of them. It is a solo job. A man alone with his two eyes and his five senses . . . that is badger-watching in a nutshell."

"Oh, we can't believe that, you know," said George easily. "Surely we can all copy you, and learn how to watch? How would to-day week suit you?"

Mr. Mildmay was much embarrassed and annoyed. He glanced first at Miss Padsoe and then at Bell, but he got no help from either, and was at last reluctantly obliged to tell his young host that to-day week would suit him.

"Well, that's splendid," said George heartily. "How many people can you do with? I'd like to get as many along as possible, you know."

"Three. At the *very* most, three," said Mr. Mildmay, endeavouring without much success to conceal irritation. "And even then the badgers are most unlikely, I fear, to manifest themselves. They are wildly shy; the shyest of our woodland inheritances."

"Oh, they'll be all right," said George, with vague magnificence, and went off to get Miss Padsoe some fruit jelly, leaving Mr. Mildmay to console himself with the slender hope that, by the time morning came and the fumes of claret had evaporated, George might have forgotten all about the invitation. Unfortunately, he misread George's character.

The party ended, as even parties which seem blessed by the very patron saint of parties must do at last; and about two o'clock people began going across the dark dewy lawn in search of their cars, laughing and talking under the soft, starred, summer sky, and pointing out to one another how beautiful was the setting moon whose light was beginning to retreat from the sighing darkness of the elms.

All the elderly rich were taking the youthful poor back in their cars, and the youthful poor, full of patties, gaiety, ice-cream and gratitude, warmly thanked George and Bell and swore it was the most delicious party they had ever been to ; a quite eerily and fairily lovely party. Over the lawn and down the drive died the gay voices and the laughter, and the sound of engines, and the house and garden were left to the sleepy host and hostess and their two lovers, and the dark trees still rippling and rustling in the unearthly wind.

" An excellent ' do,' " said old Mr. Barranger, riding home beside Bertie, with three girls in the back of the Morris. Old Mr. Barranger liked to keep abreast of contemporary slang, but spoiled his spontaneous effects by putting the alien words in inverted commas. " That's a pretty little girl, that Miss Catton. Nice wholesome little girl. George thinking of marrying her, d'you think ? "

" Pa," cried Bertie, " how I wish you would learn that nowadays because a man dances all the evening with one girl, it doesn't mean he's going to marry her."

" It did in my day."

" Oh, *your* day ! Hansom cabs and Lottie Collins ! " said Bertie rudely.

" Bertie's jealous," thought old Mr. Barranger mildly, going straight to the true cause of Bertie's rudeness in a crude, old-fashioned manner. There was not the slightest reason for Bertie to be jealous ; he had only met Queenie three or four times before ; George was Bertie's closest friend and Bertie had been his adoring slave for years, ever since they were at school together in Geneva. Nothing was less likely, on the face of it, than that Bertie should be jealous of George ; and yet old

Mr. Barranger, in his old-fashioned, foolishly sentimental way, was quite right.

.        .        .        .        .        .

At twelve o'clock the next morning Queenie was sitting under a holly tree on a hedgerow bank, some five miles from Bassett.

The morning was quiet; the holly with its dark leaves and unfamiliar flowerets stood stiffly against the pale blue sky, and a sweet smell of elder blossom and dust·floated in the air; all kinds of tiny dronings and sudden dwarf whirrs came from passing insects; the summer day seemed as though it had stopped moving and hung still in time.

Queenie sat staring down into the grass and chewing a stem and wishing her heart would not bang uncomfortably; it was banging, not so much because she was going away with George as because she was afraid he might be delayed or not come at all. He had told her to be under the holly (both had noticed it on a recent walk) at twelve, and here she was, waiting to be fetched by him.

Bell need not have been afraid that George would flaunt their departure. Everything had been arranged with the greatest discretion—a discretion which Queenie found disagreeable. She had told Bell on Thursday, at his request, that she would like to go up to town to see her family for the coming week-end, and Bell had lightly said that of course she must go: Queenie had seen to it that the housemaid knew, too, and George had said something in front of the gardener-chauffeur about going to spend the week-end in town with Bertie, as he occasionally did.

All this was detestable to Queenie. She resented it

H*

with a disgusted feeling of shame, but she thrust the feeling into the back of her mind and tried to pretend that she did not mind there being a need for deception, or what people thought; she told herself that she and George had love, unspoiled by laws or convention or the interference of the social system; and she must be prepared to look on lies and gossip and leering speculation as the mud spattering Love's heels as he walked aloof through the mob, and she succeeded in seeing it so. She was not afraid, for an instant, of " people talking," but she loathed the necessity for deception.

She had even had to walk for five minutes down a broad lane on getting out of the bus a few hundred yards away on the main road, in order that anyone who was casually staring at her might not wonder why she was going over the fields to nowhere. The field-path was a short cut to the road where her holly tree was, but, thanks to the social system, she might not walk along it unremarked.

(It was thanks also to the social system that she sat on the grass a free woman, in small danger of assault or of having her purse stolen, but this fact escaped her notice.)

She was transformed by love. As she sat there, staring seriously down into the grass and busily chewing her stem, she was defenceless as a flower. The armour of irony, common sense, and honour which had protected her two months ago was cast aside, and she wore instead, nothing but love's blinding bandages over her eyes.

She did not think of George as she used to think of him before she loved him : now, his nervous tiredness, his fits of sudden disgust at the aimlessness of life as he saw it, his discontent, all seemed to her to be

matters for pity and anxiety. His physical delicacy at
once charmed and alarmed her : she loved to have his
head lie quietly on her breast while she smoothed his
forehead with careful, solemn little fingers. She would
have delighted in taking quiet conferences with Bell
and his mother about his health, and seriously putting
their mutual plans into action for his good : she wanted
to make a tight circle of love and comfort round him
and her and pull the circle ever closer, ever tighter,
shutting out the huge frightening world.

But she never achieved her conferences. Bell did
not encourage such small cosinesses, and Mrs. Shelling's
suspicions must never be aroused. Unfettered love has
countless minor disadvantages : it may sit in the desert
and admire the illimitable prospect but it is quite rightly
told to go back there if it sneaks into the town about
four in the afternoon for a cup of tea.

I wish he didn't get so moody, she was thinking : he
needs more rest; he's always tired. He works too hard,
and I'm not sure that he really likes the factory. He
ought to have some bigger purpose in life than just earn-
ing money to keep Bell and Mrs. Shelling : I'm sure he
would like it, if he had. Those moods would disappear.

Queenie always thought that people would like it if
they had a bigger purpose in life.

With a shock she realised the time : it was a quarter-
past twelve. The one note drifted across the fields to
her from the church clock in a hidden village near, and
she sat upright and looked rather wildly down the long
white road. Oh, suppose he did not come ?

But it was all right; suddenly, there was the car
rounding a curve and coming quickly down towards
her, and she could see him at the wheel. She put her
hand behind her, not looking round, fumbled for her

suitcase and slowly drew it towards her over the silvery notched grass-heads. The car drew level with her, and stopped.

For a few seconds neither of them moved. George sat quietly at the wheel, looking across at her and smiling a little ironically, and she sat looking at him, drinking in his good looks, his fine grey eyes and fair skin now becomingly burned by long summer hours. I love you, she thought. A voice seemed to say it inside her mind, like a little flower suddenly opening. I love you. Seldom she said it to him, but never, never grew tired of whispering it to her pillow and hearing the little flower-voice say it deep in her secret mind. *Darling*, she thought, looking solemnly at him.

" Well ? " said George.

" Well ? "

" I'm very, very sorry I'm late. Were you afraid I wasn't coming ? "

She nodded. George laughed delightedly, and got out of the car and came over to her. He did not kiss her, but sat down by her side.

" I knew you would. She'll be in such a state, I thought, and I nearly killed about eight people, getting away. I had some letters to sign."

" Well, I'm glad you *are* here," she said very seriously, looking away from him because his intent, delighted gaze embarrassed her. " Have you thought where we're going ? "

" Oh, we'll go on until we find somewhere nice. There are lovely places in the hills above Oxford . . . or we might follow the river into Gloucestershire. We'll find somewhere. But first you must have this. . . ."

And he lifted her hand and began slipping on to her

finger a little wedding ring, which he had taken from his pocket. She stared at it for a second, her face expressing delighted pleasure and another emotion—a troubled resentment.

"Oh, George . . . it's so pretty! But must I wear it? I would rather like to—but I don't like *having* to. Would people notice, if I didn't?"

"Bound to. We look so young, you see. Everyone will probably suspect the worst, in any case, and if you have no ring, we shan't get let in anywhere decent . . . and we don't want to go to a beastly rowdy place that doesn't mind what sort of people we are, do we?"

"No . . . oh, no. But I do wish . . . I rather hate having to pretend, that's all. I wish we could just do as we liked. How *beastly* people are! It's just the same as if we *were*, I mean. It seems to spoil everything, having to pretend."

"I hate it too, but it can't be helped. The world *is* like that, and that's all there is to it."

She held her hand out in front of her, moving it this way and that and admiring the ring. The plain, quiet, dignified look which it gave to her hand pleased her very much; it was a look almost of sorrow, so grave was it, but she did not mind that. Her hand looked responsible, matured, and some briar scratches on it seemed schoolgirlish and out of place.

George was watching her, taking pleasure in her pleasure.

"Do you like it, Mrs. Shelling?"

"Oh . . . oh, how funny it sounds!"

"Do you like the sound of it?"

She was so radiantly happy, sitting beside him in the sunlight and knowing that when the night came she

was to belong to him, that his question did not cause
the smallest pang : it seemed to have nothing to do, in
its implications, with those numberless times she had
painfully thrust the thought of marriage with him to the
back of her mind, as an impossibility.

" I do . . . rather."

" Well, we'll see. In about three years, I probably
shall want to marry you. Certainly I've never wanted
to marry anyone before, and there are times when I
can see myself married to you and enjoying it immensely.
But we're so damned young . . . I don't want to marry
until I'm getting on for thirty."

" By then *I* may not want to marry *you*."

" Would you now . . . if I asked you to ? Do you
like the idea of being married to me ? "

Tranquilly, confidently, she looked at him and
answered, again playing with the idea, too happy to
be serious about it—" I do . . . rather."

" That means a lot, from you ! Oh, my love . . .
my sweet . . . my darling, darling sweetheart . . ."
and he drew her down beside him in the grass, " are
we going to be happy together ? We are, aren't we ? "

" I'm very glad," was all she could whisper in reply.
She was never eloquent about her feelings, but she
thought that he understood how much she felt.

Presently the car drove away. She sat beside him,
tranquil with dreams and love, content to be going
forward, with no destination, into the green woods of
summer.

If I live to be an old, old woman, she thought, watching
the bannered trees stream past—the far gleam of sunlight
in the shady woods—the white road unfolding before
the wheels of the car—I will never forget this. I shall
remember it until I die : until the day I die. It will

always be in my heart, and I can always look at it like a beautiful picture. No one can ever take this away from me, for ever and ever, until the day I die.

The arches of the green boughs closed over the road, the sound of the car's engine died into the silence, and the secret wood received them into its heart.

PART·III

# CHAPTER XX

A WET spell followed the last fine week of June ; and was received with gratitude by at least one member of Bassett society.

Mr. Mildmay, who had viewed with considerable dismay the prospect of watching badgers accompanied by a lively party of young and irresponsible persons, felt that his guardian angel had interceded on his behalf ; and that the result was wet, chilly weather. No one watches badgers in the rain (badgers hate rain and on wet evenings will not come out to be watched) and Mr. Mildmay did not feel that he was called upon by heaven to set a precedent.

As the week progressed and it became clear that the weather was not going to mend, Mr. Mildmay's spirits rose ; and he felt sufficiently cheerful to begin his new novel *Hagaar's Portion*, which was about a gipsy woman who ruled a large tribe and had a lovely time exercising her power-complex. Mr. Mildmay would have detested her and have been much repelled had he encountered Hagaar at a dinner party or at close quarters on the Downs, but he loved writing about her, in exquisitely polished sentences. As the gipsies were gipsies, of course they all had violent passions and kept on doing violent things, and as all the things they did (such as killing each other, stabbing themselves, beating their crippled step-brothers and what-not) were described in long, slow-moving, delicately phrased paragraphs, the general effect was rather like slow-motion wrestling as demonstrated by Messrs. Nervo and Knox. But no one minded that, least of all Mr. Mildmay, to whom the comparison did not occur.

He had just got to the part where Hagaar's lovely bastard granddaughter Judith announces that she intends to join a circus as assistant to a lion-tamer with whom she has fallen madly in love, and he was busy describing the shocking rumpus kicked up by Hagaar on hearing the bad news, when a friendly little note from Bell was brought in, saying that she hoped the wet weather would not prevent the badger watching, and that even if it did they were looking forward to seeing Mr. Mildmay at dinner on Friday, as arranged ; they had some new gramophone records which it might amuse him to hear.

Now was Mr. Mildmay's chance. He should have firmly replied that he much regretted an unforeseen rush of work which kept him chained to a desk and made him unable, after all, to accept Miss Shelling's kind invitation.

But he was not firm ; he fell. The opportunity of boasting about Hagaar to a group of young people was too much for him. He went ; he went through steady rain and dripping woods, spent a very pleasant evening, and returned more deeply embroiled than ever, and pledged to dine and watch badgers on the first fine evening which presented itself. He did make one or two feeble protests but they were authoritatively over-ruled by young Mr. Shelling, who, it seemed, had long been extremely interested in badgers, and quoted so fluently and flatteringly from Mr. Mildmay's own works that Mr. Mildmay felt it would be ungracious (and bad for his reputation of old-world, shy courtesy) if he held out any longer. So he agreed to their proposals.

But he was not at all pleased about it. It was more convenient for a writer on Nature to work by himself. When such a writer was alone, any deficiencies occurring in Nature's Pageant could be made up by a judicious use of imagination and the careful consultation of textbooks as to what should take place about that time of the year . . . and which, of course, did take place in other places on which one had not been lucky enough to hit. A glimpse of a hare while one was alone could be afterwards amplified into five pages of silver prose. Who knew what hares did, anyway ? and even if this particular hare did behave in an unorthodox manner, that made it all the better to write about : no one wanted to read about how Hares behaved : it was A Hare they were interested in, and what Mr. Mildmay thought about it. Fortunately.

But when someone else was with you, everything was so different.

" Can Punch come ? " Bell had asked eagerly, fondling the Alsatian's head. " He'll be so good ; he's a perfect lamb."

Mr. Mildmay had allowed a full frightful three seconds to elapse before he said gently, " My own dog, Lady, who has been with me for seven years, is not coming. I never take her on these excursions. Gentle though she is, trained to answer a look on my face, a shade of meaning in my voice, I never take her. I am afraid that *any* kind of dog is out of the question in such circumstances."

" Why ? " demanded Albert, who had a hazy and shocking idea that they were all going to hunt badgers, and knew that one took dogs when one went hunting.

" Badgers," explained Mr. Mildmay, " have a very keen sense of smell."

"Punch doesn't smell," said Bell indignantly (she was enjoying herself). "He's bathed once a fortnight. I do him myself."

"Nevertheless, a badger would scent him immediately," said Mr. Mildmay firmly. "A badger has dim sight, but keen hearing and sense of smell. We shall probably have to watch for a good hour before the time Brother Brock is likely to put in an appearance. We shall have to keep as still as stones; motionless, every nerve alert, for a very long time."

Now it was Mr. Mildmay's habit, on the few occasions when he had watched birds and hares and otters, to fall asleep. He never admitted, even to himself, that he fell asleep, but that, in vulgar English, was what usually happened. He was not really very interested in otters and birds; he was only interested in what he was going to write about them, and what words to arrange round the plain fact that an otter slipped off a projecting piece of bank into the water. He found that falling asleep made no difference to the lucid quality of his prose, so he was not really ashamed of himself. The Craft of The Word was what mattered.

Still, he hoped he would not begin to feel sleepy, and to yawn while he was watching badgers under the large eyes of Miss Bell Shelling.

"It *will* be fun," she sighed, with a lazy movement which sent her deeper into her chair.

It was with gloomy forebodings that Mr. Mildmay perceived unmistakable indications, at the end of the second week in July, that the weather was about to mend. The clouds cleared off, the glass rose steadily, Miss Baker reappeared in an orange voile dress, and the papers spoke of anti-cyclones.

In irritation and alarm, Mr. Mildmay awaited a

summons from Baines House ; and sure enough, at the
end of the first steadily fine day, it came. Queenie and
Punch walked over with a note to say that, if it was as
fine as this the following evening, they would all love
to go and watch badgers. They would meet Mr. Mildmay
in the car, at any point he liked, eat a picnic supper, and
go on to the sett after the meal (George was acquiring
a good badger-vocabulary, which he enjoyed airing).

"It will have to be early. Fully early," said Mr.
Mildmay. "As I believe I told Miss Shelling, we must
be at the sett a good hour before the badger is likely to
appear. In the summer months when the nights are
very short they come out before it is quite dark, in
the gloaming, to begin their hunting."

"Oh," said Queenie. "Well, shall I tell them half-
past seven ? And where ? "

"Half-past six would be better, I feel. Yes, much
better. I have two setts—or possible setts—in mind.
The most promising one is in a place which is rather
difficult to locate, so I think I had better be called for,
here, at half-past six. Of course, it may rain."

"Oh, I don't think it will," said Queenie confidently
looking up at the cloudless evening sky. "I think it
is going to be lovely." She smiled at him, and walked
off followed by Punch.

The evening's activities began badly because the
Shellings were late. Mr. Mildmay had been standing at
the gate of The Tower for nearly fifteen minutes, getting
crosser and crosser, when the car at last came round the
curve, with George driving and Bell next to him in an
old cotton dress, Miss Catton at the back and Albert in
the dickey.

"Terribly sorry," said George, stopping opposite
the silent Mr. Mildmay. "I was late getting back from

Reading and I had to change. Do hope you haven't been waiting long? Beastly hot, isn't it—do get in. Queenie, shift the basket along, will you—that's right. Now, where do we go from here?"

He sat slewed half-way round in the driver's seat, looking expectantly at Mr. Mildmay. He was pale with the heat and looked cross but ominously determined to find the expedition amusing.

" Straight down the road would be best, I think. Yes, straight down. The most likely sett is about five miles from here, on the edge of a little wood near Skirle. There is a pond at the bottom of a steep bank, and a large hole in the bank which I am convinced is a sett. Then, on the opposite side of the pond, there are a number of trees in front of which we can station ourselves."

" *Behind* which, you mean," said Miss Catton pertly.

" Don't you *remember*," said George, vigorously starting the car, " Mr. Mildmay telling us that badgers are less likely to see you in front of a tree than if you stand behind one and keep on peering round?" She did not reply, and occupied herself with moving the picnic basket along to make more room for Mr. Mildmay's feet.

Mr. Mildmay's ruffled feelings were not soothed by the incidents of the journey. Twice he directed George down wrong roads, and he hesitated at every crossroad; Mr. Mildmay was not very good at remembering how to get to places, and George, who was very good at it, got angrier and angrier. Bell never said a word; she looked half-asleep and even half-witted. Albert had to shout to make himself heard, and so did not trouble to talk, and Queenie, after a few timid questions of Mr. Mildmay about *Hagaar's Portion*, became silent, and sat watching the dark woods go past.

The air was so hot that the car's passage could not stir a cool wind; air poured into their faces like warm water and dust settled over their clothes and hair. The drive could scarcely have been more disagreeable, and everybody felt a gush of relief when Mr. Mildmay exclaimed "Ah! There is our fellow!" and pointed to a track going into the woods, on the left side of the road.

"Down there? It's very rutty—hellish for my tyres. I think we'd better park the car just inside—it'll be perfectly safe, if I lock it up—and walk in."

Everybody's spirits rose when they had once left the car and were walking into the woods. It was true that the excessive heat had produced more flies, of more variety in size, shape and colour, than anyone remembered seeing since their earliest years, and that most of these flies were the kind that likes to bite, but everybody lit cigarettes and made the best of it, and after all Mr. Mildmay had warned them that there would be flies, and that they were sure to get badly bitten: badger-watchers always did.

And as for ants, there were always ants in the woods in summer, and caterpillars; and a sort of little round beetley thing which ran very fast and was extremely tiny and of which there were billions, was only to be expected; and so were midges, and spiders and earwigs. Such things were part of a picnic; no one grumbled about such things, even if everyone used up a heap of nervous energy by refraining from grumbling. One just set the cloth on top of the ants, put out the food, and ignored the midges, the caterpillars and the little round beetley thing.

Mr. Mildmay had insisted on the picnic taking place at a good distance from the sett, because he said the badgers would hear them if they went trampling about overhead near the sett, and then they would not come out.

Badgers were passionately suspicious, terrifically obstinate, and had ears like microphones—or so George gathered, after listening to Mr. Mildmay—and they also hated other badgers, trusted no one, and could smell anything the wretched badger-watcher might smear on himself to keep off insects. In addition to the badger being able to hear anything two miles off, the entrance to a sett " collects and amplifies sound, like a reversed gramophone trumpet," and you had to approach it on the lee side, or the lurking badger smelt and heard you.

" I wonder anyone ever *does* see them," sighed Bell. " Do have some cucumber. What is the lee side, anyway ? Oh, god, there's a beetle on the ham."

" The side that blows away from you," said George. He was tempted to add that he wondered why anyone ever wanted to see them, but refrained. It seemed to him that the scales were loaded a bit too heavily in favour of the badger; in fact, he was suddenly more than a little bored with the whole expedition, for he and Bell had something more interesting to think about, which was revealed towards the end of that nightmare meal.

Mr. Mildmay insisted on their sinking their voices in case the badgers heard them talking and laughing, and though George thought that this was quite absurd he felt compelled to defer to Mr. Mildmay's superior knowledge of the devilish habits of badgers ; and there they all five sat, talking almost in whispers with their midge-bitten faces thrust forward in order to catch each others' remarks. Their legs ached because no one except Hindus can sit on the ground comfortably and not ache, and the food tasted beetley. It was excellent and even luxurious, as Shelling food always was, but somehow no one enjoyed it. The heat, they all supposed.

Albert, having exhausted Mr. Mildmay on the subject of badgers, had pigeon-holed the information thus obtained and took no more interest in badgers; he knew that he could now discuss them with an air of authority should the subject come up at a dinner party and that was all he cared about. He was at the picnic because Bell was there, and for no other reason.

He was excessively bored and wretched and longing to kiss Bell (which he was occasionally allowed to do and it was like kissing a bunch of cool feathery flowers) and had already confided gloomily to Queenie that he wished he was far away somewhere in a comfortable hotel. Silently, she almost agreed with him. Oh, what was happening to this hitherto exquisite summer?

In the last stages of the picnic Mr. Mildmay, shifting his position for the fourth time, suddenly observed with uncontrollable irritation that the heat was intolerable; it was an offence against civilised life, such heat, and added that, for his part, he was longing to be on the way to Derbyshire; he was spending September there; had Mr. Shelling decided where he was going yet? Or perhaps he was not going away?

"We're going to Sweden on the third," said George, not looking up.

Queenie's heart seemed to stop beating. "We?"

Oh, what did he mean? For a wild second she thought he meant that he was going to take her—or that she was going with them—but then she realised that he could only mean himself and Bell. He must have known for the last fortnight that they were going, yet he had not told her. He must have talked it over in secret with

Bell, looking at maps, laughing, making a hundred ridiculous plans, as she had seen him do when he was talking about going to Spain, earlier in the year.

He would not look at her. He was bending, with an obstinate expression on his pale face, over one of the vacuum flasks, which worked unsatisfactorily. She glanced at Bell. Bell's lids were lowered and she was chasing a daddylonglegs off the cloth with a spoon. She looked interested in the chase.

"Delightful," said Mr. Mildmay, who hated everywhere except England; he was the exact opposite of the Continental Travel Snob who knows little places in Provence where the truffles are gargantuan and the *vin ordinaire* superb. Mr. Mildmay specialized in buried Essex inns and almost extinct but incredibly potent brands of ale.

The third . . . that was less than a fortnight away. Why had he not told her? It was absurd; she would not have minded. Of course he must have a holiday, and didn't he always go with Bell, every year, and always abroad? She knew that she could not have gone with him to Sweden; she would not have made a fuss if he had told her about it. She was only hurt and frightened because he had shut her out of his plans, and when she thought of those laughing, secret conferences with Bell.

If we were engaged, she thought suddenly, I should have the right to be very angry about this : not that I would . . . but I'd have the right if I wanted to. But we are secret lovers, and so I can't say anything. I haven't any standing at all. I stand on love, and no one recognises love as a vantage point. It only makes one more helpless.

An exhausted, bored silence had fallen. She could not endure it ; she felt too miserable, hysterical with surprise and vague alarm, and pain. She said suddenly, in a shrill, impertinent voice, " Well, that *is* a surprise. I'd no idea you were going. Had you ? " to Albert.

" Yes," said Albert gloomily. " But I was told not to tell," and he looked across spitefully at Bell.

" . . . lovely for you," said Queenie, beginning to stack the plates neatly and to screw up greasy papers. " How long are you going for ? "

" About a month, I expect," said George, suddenly looking across at her. His expression was pleading, almost loving, all his ill-temper seemed to have gone. " You must forgive me : I can't help it. That's the way I'm made. I'm sorry " said his look.

" Bell wants to see Milles's fountains, and I want to see the City Hall at Stockholm. Besides, Sweden seems to be one of the few countries left in the world where they go on quietly making beautiful things—glass and pottery and metal work—and not having revolutions and making asses of themselves wearing black, brown or blue shirts. I long to go there. It sounds like a paradise to me ; it will be a marvellous experience. I'm looking forward to it immensely."

He spoke almost defiantly, as though trying to show her that she and her love were not necessary to his happiness.

" Well . . . bring me back a rose and a nightingale " she said lightly, meeting his look with a friendly, forgiving one. She was still so stunned by the pain of hearing that sentence " I was told not to tell " that she scarcely heard what George was saying. She could only dimly recall that Sweden was supposed to breed exquisite roses and to resound with the crying of nightingales, and she spun her poor little sally round that legend.

" I will," promised George eagerly. Thank goodness, he thought, she's not going to make a fuss. What a darling she is . . . a *darling*. Pure gold. I was right, of course : we ought to have told her at once. Bell doesn't understand her, that's the trouble. I do feel a brute . . . I wish she were coming too.

While they were repacking the basket he managed to cover her hand with his for a second and to murmur " Dear one." She smiled at him, and happiness flooded back into her heart. He'll write to me, she thought, and I can keep his letters. I've never had a letter from him. I shall be able to keep them for ever. . . . I hope he'll write often, so that I shall have lots of them. . . .

" I don't wish to *hurry* anybody," observed Mr. Mildmay, " but I think we should be at our posts by now. Indeed, we should have been there half an hour ago—we may have to wait hours before friend Brock shows himself. Now . . . this is the way, I think. *All* cigarettes out, please, and will *everybody* refrain from talking and laughing. As I think I explained before, the badger can hear sounds which occur a good hundred yards from the sett."

Through a stifling, fly-haunted twilight they wound along a narrow path between brambles which caught in the girls' skirts with a tearing noise and made Mr. Mildmay turn a warning face over his shoulder. The trees were chiefly ancient oaks and may which had been afflicted by the blight of caterpillars, then ravaging parts of Buckinghamshire and Hertfordshire, and overhead was a disagreeable canopy of pitted leaves and myriads of tiny insects swinging on webs. These fell into the girls' hair and down their necks.

" This is a beastly little wood," suddenly observed

Albert very loudly. "How I wish I had not come
here!"

This so entirely expressed what everyone else was
feeling that no one, not even Mr. Mildmay, had the
hypocrisy to rebuke him. Mr. Mildmay had at least
the gloomy satisfaction of seeing those who had come
to mock remaining to curse : he felt that they deserved
all the brambles and midges they got. But it was hard,
very hard, on himself.

When they had been going down the unpleasant
path for some eight minutes George found his admiration
for Mr. Mildmay's woodcraft was so strong that it
must be expressed in words. He was, in fact, amazed
that such an effete ass as Mr. Mildmay could ever have
located the sett through this nasty wilderness of bramble
and matted grass.

"How did you ever find the place?" he whispered
admiringly.

Smiling, with his finger on his lip, Mr. Mildmay
shrugged his shoulders. Was he not Mohican?

He had, in fact, paid an old farmhand ten shillings
to show him the two setts.

At last it became apparent, by increased caution in
the movements of Mr. Mildmay, that they were
approaching the sett. The ground became more
broken ; they were evidently climbing the lower slopes
of a large wooded hill. A thrill of anticipation refreshed
the company. Suddenly Mr. Mildmay paused, wheeled
about and faced his followers :

"Quiet—quiet, here," he mouthed. "You can
see the sett through the trees," and he pointed to the
left. There was the gleam of dark water, and on the
other side of the pool rose a steep bank. In the middle
of the bank was a large, black, exciting hole.

" The sett," muttered Albert, who up till now had disbelieved in the existence of this curiously named object. And there it was! He began to feel better.

A group of old may trees faced the pool, and the party with the greatest caution now advanced upon these. There was a tree for each person; most fortunate; and fortunately, too, the pool had shrunk during the summer months and left a narrow marge beneath the trees on which feet could be firmly planted. The marge sloped a little towards the pool, which made it rather uncomfortable to stand on, but they did not discover this disadvantage until twenty-five minutes later.

Each one had been told what to do and each one did it, placing him or herself in front of a tree and immediately becoming motionless. Everyone was careful to get into a comfortable position, because when once a badger-watcher is in a position he may not move out of it. If he does, he does not see any badgers. Badgers always know when people move.

Unfortunately for the watchers, the most comfortable position becomes fiendishly uncomfortable when you have been in it for fifteen minutes and know that you must not move from it for another forty-five or more. If man ever owned the art of staying still, he has lost it; it has followed his sense of direction and his sense of smell; and the five very highly civilised people under the may trees found it not only almost impossible to keep utterly still; they found it excruciatingly painful.

Albert and Queenie suffered least; Albert because he did everything with solemn and tremendous con- centration, and if keeping still was to be mastered, master it he would: and Queenie because she was suffering so much mental pain that she scarcely noticed cramp and monotony and midges.

Now she had time, and time enough, to feel the full force of that sentence " I was told not to tell." She tried to dismiss it from her mind; it would not go. It beat round and round in her head like a crazy tune. It meant that George had taken Bell into his confidence about her : he had said, perhaps, that she might make a scene if she knew about Sweden. And then Bell had told Albert that they were going—to hurt him, perhaps, or to see what he would say—and warned him not to tell Queenie . . . perhaps she had told him that Queenie was jealous, or perhaps George had told him—and then they had said " So don't tell her."

It was horribly cruel of them. She writhed at the thought that Albert knew she loved George. Oh, he must know, of course; he must guess about their week-end, and the long evenings they spent together in the woods, but she could not endure that he should discuss it with George and Bell. They had shut her out, like three laughing cruel conspirators.

How *could* George shut her out, when he was supposed to be her lover, her dear secret lover and friend? How could he bear to shut her out, after the things they had done and said, and after that moment when they had stood together at the window, on that night, and had slowly drawn the curtains which scarcely shut out the glimmering flowers, the silence and starlight of the garden?

She stole a look at him. He was leaning against his tree, looking amused, bored and angry, all at once. She wretchedly became aware that she ached all over, and that she was agonizingly sleepy. She wrestled with a yawn, rather unsuccessfully, and Mr. Mildmay warningly slid his eyes round at her, and frowned above a smile.

I

But cramp was nothing, sleepiness was nothing, to the insects.

The pool, which smelt, was peculiarly rich in insects, chiefly midges. Mr. Mildmay had told his party that they could not possibly find their vigil dull because they would be able to observe the nocturnal wild life all about them. Round this particular sett there was simply no nocturnal wild life at all except midges, and spiders (at least presumably they were spiders but no one dared to investigate) which ran busily down one's neck and scavenged about in one's spinal ridges, and the ubiquitous little round beetley things which ran happily all over one's shoes and ankles.

At first the midges simply could not believe that here were five things which they could bite and which would neither flap at them with coarse hairy tails nor slap at them with hard stinging palms. But they soon got used to it, and there then set in a refinement of torture so exquisite that Mr. Mildmay really began to feel quite frightened about what would happen when the vigil was over, and people could say what they thought about it. It was true that they had suggested coming with him and that he had not wanted them to come, but he was the originator of the plan, and had he not announced his intention of watching badgers, they would not be here.

Slowly, slowly, with the incredible slowness of an English summer evening, darkness crept into the wood. The last rays of the sun had gone an hour ago but a hot pale twilight lingered interminably; you could not say it was dusk yet; no, there was still plenty of light to read by if anyone had been able to think about anything but the frightful agony of their midge-bites, and still no one moved except to twitch hysterically their facial muscles, trying to dislodge a feasting midge, and still not a glimpse, not a whiff or a shadow of a badger.

No one whispered; no one even smiled. Everyone was sunk in a kind of sullen determined fury; see badgers they *would*, or die. Bell, whom the midges simply loved, because her skin was so fine and fair, felt that she probably would die, from blood-poisoning. She could feel huge bumps all over her forehead and they itched frantically, and still the midges came, and their sufferings from the heat and the smell of the pool and the frightful cramp were only interrupted by the sharp bites of the insects. It was too awful; it was not even funny; it was all grim and ghastly like a play by Strindberg.

They all felt they hated the absent, silent, gloating badgers like hell, and yet everyone was grimly determined to stay there and see the beastly things if they did not come out until four in the morning.

They are mad: my cousins are mad, thought Albert darkly and calmly. They are of the masochist type, which loves to endure agony, and yet they love to see others suffer, so they are also sadists. It is very interesting, but after this I shall never speak to them again. I shall go away to-morrow by an early train to Paris, and never return. I shall never see her again. She is a bad, sadist-masochist girl, my cousin Bell. God in Heaven, these mosquitoes!

George was so sleepy that it was torture to keep awake. He stared at the badger hole, which grew large and small and large again in front of his leaden-lidded eyes. If he dared to shut them, exquisitely, for three seconds, his feet began to slip and he nearly fell into the horrible pool. He felt that the absence of the badgers was insulting; it was a visible affront, like someone cocking a snook. It was more than just the absence of badgers ; it was a damned sneer at the whole party. He felt that the badgers knew about the midges and were glad.

He glanced across at Queenie. She was looking down at her toes, over which, as over everybody's toes, the little round beetley things were making hay, and she looked so sad ; she seemed apart from the miseries which consumed the rest of the party. He must explain to her about Sweden, and comfort her. It was too bad not to have told her . . . only he did so hate fuss and one never knew, with a girl, and she loved him so much.

Sometimes it gave him exquisite happiness to realise how much she loved him, and he bathed in the warm tenderness of the thought, but sometimes he was afraid ; he disliked the responsibility which her love placed on him. In short, he experienced almost every emotion except a simple delight in loving and being loved.

It was really dusk now. Surely . . . surely at any moment one of the blasted things would appear in the mouth of the sett ? What more did they want ? They were doing it on purpose——

" LOOK ! "

The shout shattered the heavens. It was a huge, sharp clap of sound and it startled everybody into hysterics.

" Where . . . what . . . god, what a dam-fool thing to do ! " stammered George, springing upright against his tree. " What's the matter, Albert, have you gone mad ? "

It was, of course, Albert. Probably no one else would have made the mistake. Albert, quivering with excitement and triumph, was pointing to a tangle of briars a little to the left of the sett and saying, over and over again "There he was! There he was! A badger—a badger!"

George crossed to Bell, who was standing with tears running down her face, dabbing at her midge-bites, and began to pet her. "You're a fool," he said shortly to Albert. And Mr. Mildmay added sombrely:

"I am afraid it was a rabbit. I had been observing it for some time before you er—spoke. It was a pity you did—a great pity. A few more moments and I believe our quest would have been achieved. Now all this tedious vigil has been wasted . . . and I am afraid Miss Shelling is in great pain."

"I'm all right, only I'm so bitten and miserable and hot," said Bell, crying comfortably into George's handkerchief. "And my legs ache. I'm so glad you shouted, Albert dear. If you hadn't, no one would have dared to, and we might have stayed here all night, and got bitten to death."

"I regret very much if I have spoiled the evening's pleasure," said Albert stiffly; he was glowing with happiness at being called "dear," but thought it due to his dignity to be stiff. "I was mistaken. I thought it was a badger. I see now that it was not. I apologise."

"I was never so glad in my life as I was when you let fly," confessed George. "I was nearly at the end of my tether, and I'm sure the rest of us were." Fervent murmurs from the girls; a smiling obstinate silence from Mr. Mildmay, who had been wildly planning a sham faint when Albert shouted. Mr. Mildmay's silence implied that *he* could have stayed there for another hour, and was sorry that the opportunity to do so was now lost.

"Oh well, the ruddy badgers must have heard *that*,

unless they're stone deaf," said George comfortably. " They probably won't come out at all to-night, and I don't care if they do ; I hope they fall into that stinking pool and get drowned. And now for god's sake let's get back to the car. I want some sherry and quarts of ammonia for these stings. Come on."

The party retreated by the route along which it had come, rubbing its stings, yawning, and hobbling on aching swollen feet. It was now nearly dark and the ease of the return journey was not increased by the dusk and the brambles. Long scratches were added to the company's wounds, and Mr. Mildmay barked his shins on a log.

From his hiding place in the tangled briars which grew above the bank where the sett was hollowed, a fine boar badger watched their retreat with some satisfaction.

# CHAPTER XXI

" You *will* write to me, won't you ? "

" Of course I will. I only wish you were coming too. But it's impossible, I'm afraid. Oh, I shall miss you, my sweet."

Both of them took it for granted that it was impossible, and so impossible it remained. Queenie hugged to herself his remark about missing her, and it was well that she had something to comfort herself with, for she hardly saw him alone during the ten days before they left ; he took Bell up to town every other day and brought her home in the evening laden with new clothes, maps, rucksacks, boots, books, and luxurious oddments in the way of thermos flasks and sandwich cases, and they crawled all over maps spread on the nursery floor planning a dozen routes and itineraries, which they afterwards threw over in favour of others.

George's new tweeds came home the day before the departure, and he rushed upstairs to try them on and came down again to display them to the other three, looking charming, and solemnly anxious over the colour, cut and fit. It hurt Queenie to see him so absorbed in his own affairs ; she told herself wretchedly that he needed a holiday so badly, and was looking forward to it so much ! that he was like a delightful schoolboy at the end of term, and that she did not want him to be unhappy because she could not go with him.

Yet she continued to be miserable. She sat in silence
while the others laughed over their plans; she was
unbearably jealous. Bell would have him to herself for
a whole month; she would see beautiful new places with
him and share silly little jokes and adventures.

Yet Queenie, in spite of her pain, never once thought
" It's not fair." She blamed herself: she was the
selfish one, who was possessive and over-earnest,
over-affectionate, wickedly jealous. She had no right
to be any of these things, she told herself roughly.
George had never given her any right to be. He and
she had made love a secret link between them; an
airy, swinging chain of beauty. Not a word had been
said seriously about loving one another for ever, or
being faithful, or not hurting each other.

Yet she thought that she would love him as long
as she lived; and for the first time the idea of the
future terrified her. I can't lose him, she thought,
lying awake and staring into the summer darkness.
I shall *die* if I lose him : I want him for ever, as long as
we both live. Oh, if only he would come home less
tired and nervous and more settled about things, and
say that we could get married! She suddenly thought
of him married to another woman. The idea was so
agonizing that it sent a pain through her breast, and
she thrust it violently from her ; I should die, she thought
in terror. I couldn't bear it.

But on the last day all these miseries and terrors
dwindled and seemed almost foolish when she remembered them. George seemed to realise that he would
not see her for a month, and was very loving ; he took
her for a long drive in the afternoon, alone, and when
she looked at him as he sat beside her, his young face
sad with the thought of their impending parting, she

was comforted. She regained some self-respect, because
he also was suffering; she had come to believe that
he would not miss her at all, during this last miserable
week.

" I'll miss you all the time," he said almost violently.
" No one's so restful as you are to be with, nor such
fun . . . I should enjoy it twice as much if you were
coming. We've had lovely times, haven't we ? "

She nodded, smoothing his cheek as it lay against
her shoulder. She used to remember, afterwards, how
many times she had comforted him when he was ill or
tired, and how unnatural it had felt to lie in his arms
and be comforted herself, on the one occasion when an
attack of pain had tempted her to do so. His very arms
had felt unused to their task, but he lay against her
breast as naturally as a child lies.

She could say hardly anything of what she was feeling ;
she felt too much. But one question was forced from
her against her will. Her jealousy had to find some
relief in speech.

" Shall you kiss many people while you are away ? "
she asked casually.

The casualness did not deceive George. He grinned
at her impishly, and peered under the brim of her hat,
as was his habit.

" I always know when you put on that prim little
voice that you're minding something very much. . . .
Probably I won't kiss anyone. I shan't promise. If
I promise not to, it will make me want to. But I
don't expect I shall . . . nor sleep with them, either.
If I do, I'll tell you."

She laughed. She thought he might perhaps kiss a
few people, and it was no use minding, though the
thought hurt her. The other possibility was

unthinkable. Both might joke about it, because it
was one of the things that could not happen.

The next morning at ten o'clock they left. By
the early post came an annoyed letter from Mrs. Shelling
asking them to postpone their departure until to-morrow,
as she was coming home to lunch and would like to see
them before they went, but of course no notice was taken
of that.

"What an old cow Ma is, grudging us our pleasures,"
said Bell, tossing down the letter. "Catch me missing
a whole day's holiday just for the joy of seeing her.
Isn't that just like her? Oh Punch my angel, shall you
miss your Aunt Bell?" Punch made a suitable response,
and the subject of the letter was dropped.

Bell had been charming to Queenie for the last week:
it was almost as though she knew how Queenie felt
and was regretting her suffering. She could afford to
be generous, and was. If she had put her mood into
words, they would have been "Poor little beast."
But her casual pity never for one second made her
swerve from a plan which she had made nearly four
months ago, and which looked like succeeding.

They went off in the car, George driving and the
gardener-chauffeur at the back; he was to bring the
car home. Queenie watched them go with a curious
feeling of gaiety; he would write, the time would
soon pass, and so on. But Albert was quite green
with misery; he looked so ill that the cook, who was
observing the departure from the rhododendron bushes
on her way back from picking currants in the kitchen-
garden, observed his pallor and commented sympathetically upon it to the housemaid.

The car had gone; the two who were left turned
slowly back to the quiet house, exchanging strained

little smiles. Each knew what the other was thinking,
and feeling, yet neither felt very sympathetic. Each
wished to be alone with misery; and Queenie, in
addition, was rather afraid that Albert would try to
kiss her the instant he was left alone with her; one
always felt, with Albert, that he would try to kiss one
quite automatically, without reference to time, place,
suitability or even preference; to try to kiss, with Albert,
was as natural as breathing is to everyone.

But Queenie did Albert an injustice. So far, the
thought of trying to kiss her had not entered his head,
though it soon would. Part of Albert's depression,
also, was because he would have to keep a weather
eye on the factory, and put in a certain amount of work
there while George was away; and he detested the
factory, though he intended to master the details of its
workings; and part of it was due to sympathy for
Queenie.

"Come on Punch, my lovely—walkey," muttered
Queenie, hoping Albert would not hear, and putting
her hand for an instant on the dog's head: George
had patted it in farewell, only five minutes ago. He
had only smiled at her. He could not kiss her, because
of the cook in the rhododendron bushes. She was
very much afraid that she was going to cry, and began
to go upstairs to get her outdoor clothes.

"I shall go to the factory," announced Albert. "It
is well to begin at once, otherwise they will suppose
that I do not mean to come, and they will begin to
idle."

"There's no 'bus until eleven o'clock."

"Oh . . . then I shall read *The Times* until that
time. I hope that you will have a pleasant walk.
Good-bye for the present."

But the walk was not at all pleasant.

When Mrs. Shelling returned about half-past one the next day, she looked tranquil and well ; but became cross on hearing that the children had gone and that Albert and Queenie had passed a night in the house with only the three servants. She said nothing about this breach of the proprieties, but Queenie knew that she disapproved, though she did not think that Mrs. Shelling was angry with her, or even with Albert ; her indignation concentrated on George, who was not only selfish, but had no right feelings.

Queenie was surprised to find how pleased she was to see Mrs. Shelling. It was more than a sentimental pleasure in having George's mother to talk to, and to serve. There was a queer comfort in feeling the reins of Baines House resumed by an elderly person. Unconsciously, Queenie felt that somebody aged fifty-nine must *know*, be established, their storms over, their wisdom reaped. She had been for too long with moody young people ; they were tiring, they gave one no rest.

But she hardly realised in what lay her pleasure at Mrs. Shelling's return ; she was, as usual, a little afraid of her, and when about four o'clock that afternoon Mrs. Shelling called to her through the open bedroom door, as she was passing " Come in, Miss Catton ! I wish to speak to you," her heart gave a horrible guilty leap. Oh God, she thought, what's the matter now ? Has she found out . . . ?

And she went in with a set, defiant face and a racing heart, but the face Mrs. Shelling turned to her was not angry, it was benevolent and even—how amazing !— a little shy. She was unpacking (I ought to have been here, helping, thought Queenie remorsefully) and

the bedroom was scattered with her clothes. She
pointed to one pile, saying :

"Those are to be sent to the cleaners, Miss Catton.
And these to the laundry; you must make a list, to
be ready when the van comes to-morrow. Well,
how has it all been, while I have been away? I have
not forgotten you. Look . . ." and she lifted something from the bed, "here is a little present I have
brought you from Innsbruck," and she held it out to
Queenie.

It was a white muslin blouse, thickly embroidered
with cross-stitch in charming gay colours. One sees
hundreds such, hanging in every second shop window
in Innsbruck. It was not a distinguished nor an
expensive present, yet at the sight of it such strong
feelings rushed into Queenie's heart that she could
only go on staring, and stammer: "Oh, Mrs.
Shelling . . . it's so kind of you . . . I love it . . ."
and then to her horror, hot tears rushed up into her
eyes, and she turned her head aside, biting her lips
helplessly in an effort to stop a storm of crying. She
could not run out of the room; she stood there shaking
with the thick tears spilling out of her eyes and rolling
down her cheeks, making strange little sounds.

"Ach . . . my dear child! Now what is the matter?"
demanded Mrs. Shelling, advancing upon her. "What
is all this? Why do you cry so? Are you unhappy
here?"

Queenie could only shake her head, muttering something about "the heat . . . I haven't been sleeping . . .
I'm so sorry . . . silly . . . I can't sleep in this hot
weather," she added more coherently, fumbling for the
handkerchief which she always carried childishly tucked
into the top of her stocking, "and I suppose it's nerves.

I'm *so* sorry, Mrs. Shelling. It's such a pretty jumper, and it was so kind of you to think of me . . ."

"Nonsense. It was not kind. I like to give presents," said Mrs. Shelling, looking at her keenly yet doubtfully, and sorrowfully, too, " only it is so difficult to know what to give, for everyone has everything they want. You should not cry when someone gives you a present; you should laugh."

" I will," said Queenie, blowing her nose, and trying to. " You must think I am mad . . ."

" Not so. But nerves . . . you are too young to have nerves. I had no nerves when I was a girl of your age, at home in Stuttgart; I was as strong and gay as a little horse. That is how a girl should be . . . strong and gay." She paused and came a little closer to Queenie, peering doubtfully at her averted face. " You are *sure*, Miss Catton, that you are happy here ? You do not wish to go home—to leave us ? "

That " us " nearly started the storm again, but it was quelled by terror at the thought of leaving.

" Oh no . . . please . . . I love being here," she cried uncontrollably. " *Please* don't send me away ! "

There was a pause, in which Queenie tidied her face with her handkerchief, and Mrs. Shelling suddenly turned away and began closing a suitcase.

" That is well, then," she said, with her back to Queenie, " I do not like to think of a young girl being unhappy here. If you ever become unhappy, you must tell me, and you shall go away. And now I think you shall make out this list of the laundry. Work is a good cure for these nerves," she ended, rather severely.

She said no more. She resumed her usual manner, and Queenie was grateful to her. And yet when she had finished the list and escaped to her room, she could not cry; she lay on the bed, longing for the relief of tears to wash away her misery at George's absence, and the uncertain future of their love, and the unbearable knowledge that she loved him more, so very much more, than he would ever love her.

But no tears would come. Dry-eyed in the August heat, languid and exhausted with misery and lack of sleep, she lay staring at the silk of the drawn curtains against which beat relentless sunlight, and wondered when there would be a letter.

Her wish for a pile of letters could not be gratified, simply because George could not write to her too often. If he did, his mother and the servants would suspect. He had told Queenie this, adding that he loathed the idea of people gossiping about his private affairs; it would be horrible, damnable, it would spoil everything; and besides, it would be bad for Queenie's reputation, in case she ever wanted to get another job. The last remark was another blow at her timid hopes; a man who thinks of marrying a girl does not talk of her getting another job as a companion-help. But she knew how the idea of being " bound down " infuriated and scared him, so she said nothing.

There were to be two letters sent direct to her, and as many enclosed in letters to Albert as could be managed. He would have to write to Albert about the factory fairly often, and he would always enclose a note for her.

" Don't write if you're tired, or anything."

" Dear one, I shall like writing to you; I shall want to tell you about everything."

So now there was nothing to do but wait for the first letter; she could pass the time in steadily rejecting some doubts which tried to torture her, and this she loyally did. Had not George, of his own accord, mentioned Albert's remark "I was told not to tell"? He had : he had explained that he was only reluctant to tell Queenie about the Swedish holiday because he feared the news would hurt and depress her.

She tried hard not to remember his expression as he said this ; a shamefaced, half-laughing expression, one that was also a little impatient.

She had seen this expression before, and it was the one which most humiliated and terrified her. Sometimes she could answer it with a smile and irony, and George liked that, but too often she was silent, and looked sorrowful, and then he was bored. He sometimes told her that she was too serious, too intense. Why did she always want love to be so solemn ?

She did not know.

Into this mood of misery and doubt came the first letter.

She came down to breakfast five days after they had gone, and there beside Albert's plate was a fat letter from George, upon which Albert immediately fell, and opened it. She was very afraid that he would look across at her with awful meaning or otherwise give the game away to Mrs. Shelling, but she misjudged him. His manner was perfect. He read his own letter aloud, having unobtrusively slipped a second folded sheet beneath the envelope, gave its correct messages to everyone, including Miss Catton, and paused to drink his coffee as though he were not hiding a letter from George to George's mistress.

She was in an agony to have her letter ; she could hardly wait until breakfast was over. Oh, would Albert be too cautious and go off to the factory without finding his opportunity ? Again she misjudged the peculiar Albert. Passing her in the hall with an expressionless face, he suddenly slipped the letter down the open neck of her dress.

She shrank from his hand, but was too happy to feel angry; the coarse, kind, familiar gesture revolted her but she could not stop to resent it . . . and she dare not offend him! She flew upstairs with her treasure and shut the door of her room.

It was short, but how divinely loving! He missed her, he loved her, there was never a moment of the day when he did not wish that she were with him to share everything, he was longing and longing to hold her again. He had not realised how much she meant to him. They had found this charming gay little pension, full of friendly Swedes and Germans; it was all great fun, but he missed her . . .

Oh, it was a lovely letter, it blew away all doubt and complex misery like a spring breeze. Why, it's absurd, she thought, I'm only twenty-three and he's twenty-five, we've got forty years, perhaps, to be together. Anything may happen in a year—in two years. I shan't worry any more. I *won't*. Lightly and steadily does it.

Albert benefited by this mood. She accepted with a feeling of gratitude his invitation to go for a walk that evening, and since Mrs. Shelling did not seem to mind, this walk was the first of many.

.     .     .     .     .     .

Presumably Mr. Mildmay succeeded in watching a badger or two after the fiasco with the Shellings, for it was not long after that event that he told Miss Baker and Miss Padsoe how sorry he was to be leaving The Tower; he had now enough material for his new book and was going back to London to write it.

"We shall look out for it," promised Miss Padsoe, glowing with interest, but Miss Baker promised nothing.

Miss Baker was rather disturbed about their joint finances; suppose no other boarder came after Mr. Mildmay left, how would they manage about money? She was not going to live on Miss Padsoe's money, not she, yet her own hoard was dwindling slowly but steadily and she had " nothing coming in," as the dreary phrase goes.

During the time Mr. Mildmay was paying his thrice-blessed two and a half guineas a week, they had reduced their joint contributions from thirty-five shillings a week to a pound each, and paid ten shillings to the seventeen-year-old maid out of Mr. Mildmay's money.    They had also thought it prudent to reduce the gardener's visits to one a week, and to make other small economies.

However, nothing could now get round the fact that, when Mr. Mildmay left, they would be living on capital and on an invested income which tended to grow a little less each quarter.    It was a black outlook.

Yet it was difficult to feel depressed on a summer evening in The Tower, with the windows open to the garden and the light peacefully fading.    Miss Padsoe had some embroidery to do, Miss Baker was supposed to be writing to Miss Worrall but kept on interrupting herself to talk to Miss Padsoe.    Both women looked content, and just enough worried about the small affairs of everyday life to make that life filled with interest. (How blessedly absorbing Providence has made everyday life, and how one sometimes pities poets, who are forced to burn out from it more than may be there !)

" I really don't *see*," Miss Padsoe was saying, carefully trying to thread her needle in the after-glow and failing, " why you should *mind* my . . . my . . . helping a little, later on, with what my dear father left me (dear

me, how dark it has got! We really must . . .) ₄ You
do *more* than your share here; you must *know* that."

"I've never been beholden to anybody," said Miss
Baker, who had been beholden to her family, Haddons'
Paper Patterns and the grocer uncle who had died and
left her the two hundred pounds, ever since she drew
her first breath, "and though it's kind of you, and you
mustn't think I'm ratty about it, I'm not going to
begin now. Now *he's* gone (and glad I am to see the
back of that nasty fat dog of his, eating us out of house
and home and sicking it up all over the place) I'll go
back to paying what I did before. I've still got a nice
little bit left; and p'raps next time we'll get two people
instead of one, or even three. You never know your
luck. After all, we never thought it'd turn out so
well as it has, did we? First time I saw this place, to
tell you the truth, I never thought I'd come here. Fair
put me clean off, it did. But now . . . well, it's really
like home."

Miss Padsoe was still peering closely at her needle,
holding it against the white material on her lap and
making ineffectual stabs at the hole with her damp silk.
"It's no use!" she said at last, letting her hands drop
into her lap. "I can't see a thing, and it's nearly
dark."

She sat in silence for a moment, looking out into the
garden and remembering it as she had known it forty
years ago, and thinking that she and the garden were
growing old together, a forgotten woman and a dearly
loved garden, about which no one ever thought
and no one would regret. Yet this thought did not
make her unhappy. She was a Christian, and the gift
of faith had been given to her; and faith atones for the
lack of everything which makes life, for most people

worth living. Her faith was natural to her as her quiet breath while she slept and her love of flowers.

She said suddenly :

" Have you any relatives living ? "

" Not a soul," said Miss Baker cheerfully " (drat, I can't finish this to-night. Lily'll have to whistle for it till the week-end). I did have a brother in New Zealand, but he died, five years ago. Me uncle wasn't married, and he was the only one. Me only uncle, I mean. He was an old dear ; I *was* fond of him, if you like."

In her turn, she let her hands fall in her lap and lie there, while she stared out into the garden. But Miss Padsoe was no longer looking out at the garden ; she had turned back to the slowly darkening room and her glance fell upon the portrait above the mantel-piece, the young woman in the white dress with roses in her hair and at the breast of her gown, who looked out serenely into the twilight.

Miss Baker had turned to break the silence with a remark about breakfast, but on seeing the direction of Miss Padsoe's gaze she became respectfully silent. She wove stories about this younger sister of Miss Padsoe's who was never mentioned, and she sometimes toyed with a supposition that anyone so pretty and about whom there hung so unbroken a silence might have gone to the bad ? This evening she felt encouraged by the twilight and the friendly nature of Miss Padsoe's remarks to do what she had never done before, and mention the rose girl. She cleared her throat, lowered her voice a few semitones, and said respectfully :

" Was it long ago ? "

Miss Padsoe started.

" I beg your pardon ? "

" Her, I mean. Was it long ago that your sister . . . ? "

Even after the explanation came, it took a little time to remove the shock which Miss Baker felt when Miss Padsoe laughed. But it was a cheerful laugh, and should have reproved the many people who contend that spinsters can never be happy.

" Oh . . . you mean the portrait! That is not a sister; I never had a sister. I wish I had. That is a portrait of myself by L'Estrange, the *great* L'Estrange. He was a friend of my dear father's, and he often used to stay here. He had such a pretty, fanciful name for that portrait (he was very fond of fun and nonsense). He called it ' Queen Rose.' You may have noticed that she carries a bunch of *moss rosebuds* in her right hand . . . and the quotation comes, of course from *Maud*, ' Queen rose of the rosebud garden of girls.' But that was all a very long time ago."

She picked up her work again, but it was too dark to see the needle, and Miss Baker, exclaiming " Don't . . . you'll ruin your eyes. Let's have a little light on the subject, shall we ? " got up and darted across to the switch. The room leapt into soft colour ; suddenly the garden looked strange and unreal and nearly dark.

Miss Baker paused an instant before the portrait on her journey back to her seat, and stood gazing up at it. Divinely confident, the happy young eyes looked out at life. Their story struck Miss Baker as being a sad one, but whether it really was so, it would take a far wiser person than Miss Baker to decide.

. . . . . .

" *Everybody* doesn't want to get married. You always think that's all everybody thinks about. It's so absurd. I know dozens of people who are quite happy being unmarried."

" I, too, know many who are happy so. This Bassett is full of such people. And it is not true to say that I think every person wishes to marry ; I do not think so. But I think that every person wishes to have some romance in their life . . . some passion, and all people except a few believe that one only feels passion about another person, and so everyone wishes to love, and to love is (almost all over the world) to wish to marry with, to be with for ever. But that is a great mistake, to think so. Some persons, many persons, do not need another person to love."

" ' Some people ' is better than ' some persons '— you don't mind my telling you ? "

" No, my dear child, I wish you to tell me, as I have said. Some *people* can have their passion over work, over music, over pictures, or working in the garden. (Oh! I think it is offal, this working in the garden. Everywhere I am in England I see people working in the garden.) Miss Padsoe has her passion over the garden ; she does not want a man at all."

" Perhaps," suggested Queenie, " she wanted to marry when she was younger ? She must be nearly sixty, I should think."

" I do not think she has ever wanted to love. Nor has that little woman who lives with her. I wonder," mused Albert, " I wonder very much what *her* passion is ? "

Miss Baker herself could not have begun to tell him that her passion was suspecting sauce, tracking it down, and uprooting it.

" And Mr. Mildmay . . . what was his passion ? " pursued Queenie, longing and yet dreading that the next few sentences should bring another name into the discussion.

"Oh, he is his own passion. He seems to love his writing but he truly loves only himself. And my Aunt Minna—I am not sure what her passion is. No, I do not know at all about my Aunt Minna ; she is a queer sort of a woman. It is plain that she did not wish to be married at all."

"Then why did she, do you think ? "

"I cannot say," said Albert, whose face had already altered its expression a little at the thought of Bell, who also did not wish to be married at all, nor, apparently, to lose her virginity ; Albert was in a position to know both these facts about his cousin. An awkward silence was beginning, into which Queenie dashed with a half-defiant, half-nervous question :

"And what about me ? "

"Ah, you . . ." he turned the force of his calm, impudent stare upon her lifted face, yet his expression was also kind. "There will always be a large battle going on in your body and your spirit."

"That will be fun for me," said Queenie, turning her confusion into flippancy in the Shelling style.

"I do not know what you mean . . . fun. You will be very unhappy. You have strong passions, you have a large power to love. You are good, too. You are a good girl ; always I am telling Aunt Minna you are such a good girl. But you are also very loving. You are a *marryer* ; you must mix your spirit and body with the spirit and body of another person or you will feel you will die  But your love must be a good love, as well, and end properly in children. So what will you do if you cannot find a loving person who is also a marryer ? "

"Die, I suppose," she said hardly, flicking the parched grass heads with her stick, as they walked slowly across the fields.

"No, you will not die. You will turn your love away to a cause, perhaps, as good-loving women do who cannot find a good-loving man. You and me are the only marryers in this village, Queenie."

"Mercy, I shouldn't have thought *you* wanted to marry anyone. And it's you and I, not you and me."

"You and *I*; I thank you. Aunt Minna, Miss *Chose*, Mr. Mildmay, Miss Padsoe and . . . and most others in this Bassett are all non-marryers—spinsters, you call them. But you and I are marryers. I shall marry one day, and mix my body and my spirit with another body and spirit. This village is full of persons who are not marryers, Queenie. People who love working in the garden, or playing at bridge or writing books or . . . music . . . but do not wish to mix. They will all stay here being happy with their passions and waiting to die. No one here will ever have any babies or put their spirits and bodies into the river of life, except you and me. And yet," added Albert, magnificently, pausing in his march, and gazing down at Queenie, "yet I love them all. I think well of them; I do not wish any of them to die. What use are they all, except you and me? and yet I love them. I shall be so sorry to leave here; I shall be most miserable."

"I'm glad you like us," she said, divided between laughter and pain. Was it true? Was George a non-marryer? She glanced at Albert, whose face still looked fat with feeling. She said steadily:

"How about your cousins?"

How repulsive his face became when he was spiteful!

He said with a sort of gross widening of his voice and accent :

" Oh, they will die as well. They do not wish to become a man and a woman, it seems. They are like the *Cherubini*, they have no bottoms. They are charming now. But when they are forty—fifty—sixty, will they not be horrible ? "

" I don't know, and I don't think you ought to say beastly things about them. Anyway, I'm sick of talking about marryers and non-marryers. Come on, Punch, let's run."

He called after her, watching her slim ankles tossing from side to side as she went down the path in a stumbling run—

" You asked me to speak of them. Also you know that what I said is true."

She ran on over the brown grass, through the sickening heat. She could bear no more. No letter for ten days, no respite from the beating heat, the breathless nights that were filled with silence and dim exhausted stars, every hedge and wood full of millions of flies and mysterious floating webs, and the pale coarse flowers of summer's end. The beeches had layers of leaves thickened to a gross dark-green, almost black, by the heat, the chestnuts were all over curled rags of bronze leaves, the sky was drained of colour and the stacks and sheaves were burnished and dry as silk.

Oh, if rain would come, sheets of pouring silver rain, and a letter, only a word, only a word to say that he still loved her !

There had been two longish letters after the first one, filled by amusing descriptions of the places to which they had been and the little margin-drawings he did so badly and always liked to make, and at the end of each letter a sprinkle of tender words. But neither letter was so loving as the first one had been, and neither told her that he still missed her.

He's having too good a time, she thought sensibly at first, to miss me very much. He will come back so well and looking beautiful with sunburn and be so much better that he will probably love me more than he's ever done. Everything will be all right. . . .

But how could it? she began to think, as the time lengthened and no letter came. What did " everything will be all right " mean? Only that he would come back still loving her, and then the wretched secrecies, the moods, her pitiful efforts to be tranquil and intelligently interested in music and surgical instruments and poetry would begin all over again. The desperate trying not to be jealous of Bell, the fear of the servants suspecting his visits to her bedroom, the torturing suspense about the future, they would all be resumed.

How *can* I possibly be tranquil, she thought? It's a terrible position for me; he's got everything and I've got nothing—no money, no talent to earn money with, a home I'm ashamed of (wicked, but still I am), no real job, no place in the world. I can't even devote myself to him; he doesn't want me to. I've just got to keep this up for three years, perhaps, and then, if only I'm tranquil and intelligent and non-possessive enough, he *may* want to marry me at the end of them.

I can't do it. I want to be married now—*now*. I need most *desperately* to be married and allowed to show the world that I love him. I want to give him a child; I want to make a home, and live in it with him. It isn't greedy—I can't help it. I'm made like that—*and he's made in quite another way*, and I haven't got the courage to try to change him. It would take too long—I'm not

old enough—I shouldn't know how to begin and then,
if I did try, he would feel I was trying to make him
different and he'd be furious—he *hates* people who try
to change him. He told me so. Oh, God, what has
happened to me? I used to be so sensible, I was so sure
I could manage this affair, and now I'm wretched,
I wish I could die. Oh, if only a letter would come,
or it would rain.

No letter came, and the sucking, burnishing heat
remained unbroken. It wanted only a week to the
end of the month, when the two were expected home,
and Mrs. Shelling began a grumbling saga about their
vagueness, their idleness, their failure to write. Each
day Queenie suffered, as Charlotte Brontë suffered, the
agony of post time, and each night passed in tossing,
broken sleep and in heat without a waft of relieving air.

# CHAPTER XXII

"HERE they are! George—Isabella—oh—you bad children! Why did you not wire? How brown you are—Elsa, take Mr. George's case—but why did you not write? We have been so worried, we thought perhaps you were ill—have you had some tea? Isabella, you would like some tea, yes? Elsa, we will have tea in the drawing-room in half an hour, please. Albert is out, at the factory; he has been such a good boy, George; how I shall miss him! Well, have you had a good time, a really pleasant holiday, now?"

"Marvellous. That was why we didn't write—we were having too good a time. Ma, what do you think— a Turk fell in love with Bell! a frightful little tick staying in the pension! He asked her to marry him, too. Oh, his intentions were quite honourable. What would you have said if we'd brought you home a Turkish son-in-law?"

"George, how foolish you are! But a Turk, really a Turk? How imprudent of Isabella to encourage him. . . ."

"*Encourage* him? I was nearly sick every time he looked at me. He got no encouragement out of me, I assure you."

"She was a swine to him, and he ate it and asked for more. He was a beastly little masochist. Bell swaggered about in her shirts and boots and he crawled round after

274

her, buying her more and more presents. It was all too morbid and sinister, if you ask me."

The ringing voices came nearer and nearer up the stairs; mother and children were mounting slowly, gossiping as they came. Queenie sat on her bed, with her hands clenched and her heart banging. Oh, love—oh my darling—I can't face you yet! But she longed to fly out of the door and into his arms. She had seen the taxi come round the curve of the drive, and darted away from the window at the first glimpse of the two brown faces. Presently she would hear him say "How's Queenie—where is she?"

Or perhaps he would come quietly to her door, and tap, and she would open it to see him standing there, looking brown and unfamiliar after a month's absence, and smiling mischievously down at her in silence.

But the voices grew fainter down the passage and she did not hear her own name. They were still shouting over Bell's Turk.

She heard them go into their rooms, and presently a bath began running for Bell, who always got as black as a sweep on the shortest railway journey and she heard Mrs. Shelling go downstairs.

I'm a fool. I ought to have gone down the second I heard they were here; that would have been the natural thing to do and it wouldn't have annoyed him. Now I shall have to go in when they're all at tea, which will be awful. . . .

She slipped off the bed and stood for a few seconds trying to sober her heartbeats. I must see him, before they go down. I *must* see him . . . after all it's my right to see him; I am his lover and his wife. She opened her door and went quickly along the passage to George's room, and knocked at the door without giving herself any more time to think.

He did not call " Come in," but she heard him cross the room.

The door opened. He looked down at her and she smiled up at him. She saw, under the curve of his arm, someone sitting on the bed wrapped in his dressing-gown ; it was Bell.

She looked up at a stranger. He was smiling, friendly, but he was a stranger, and with terror she saw Bell slowly lift her head from the book at which she was glancing and look across at her, also smiling.

" Hullo," said Bell. " There you are ! How've you been getting on with the nasty little Albert ? "

" Do come in," said George, moving aside to let her pass. " We're just unpacking. I've brought you something nice from Paris. Wait a bit ; it's at the bottom of my big case. Do sit on the bed ; Bell, budge up, can't you ? Isn't your ruddy bath ready yet ? It ought to be, god knows."

" I want a lovely deep one. Well, how *is* Albert ? Did he try to sleep with you ? "

" I'll bet he did," said George, going on with his unpacking. " The minute our backs were turned I'll bet he tried."

" He didn't," said Queenie in a low voice (I *will not* cry—I will not. I *will* get through this without crying in front of her). " He's been very decent, really. . . ."

" Very decent, has he ? Didn't he even try to kiss you ? Not once ? He must be getting impotent or something. Just as well. Oh, here's your present. Like it ? "

It was a smart little white silk evening bag, sewn with sequins ; a characterless, vulgar, prettyish thing. It looked as though its buyer had chosen it with scarcely a second glance.

"It's lovely. Thank you very much."

Her hand closed over the little bag, which he handed across without looking at her. *He's afraid. He's afraid to look at me. He knows he's behaving cruelly and he's afraid. Oh, why can't she go?*

"Did you have a good time?"

"*Wunderbar!* We could hardly bear to come home. Dancing every night and all sorts of insane parties—god, I've been tight every night for the last week—out in the air all day and tight all night. It was undoubtedly the life."

"Did you see the City Hall?"

"He saw two!" giggled his sister, rolling over on the bed. "He gave a crowd of us a lecture on it at three in the morning. There was a marvellous girl there called Pretyman. Well, he bet Pretyman he'd . . ."

"Do shut up, Bell. Queenie isn't interested in your revelations; she wants to hear about the Milles fountains. Say your piece."

"Oh, the fountains were so *satisfying*," said Bell, screwing up her eyes. This was evidently a quotation, for they both began to laugh. "I'm sure you would have *loved* them."

"And did nobody wear coloured shirts?" *She must go on brightly asking questions, in order to assert her right to be there, in George's room.*

"How do you mean—coloured shirts? There were the usual tourists and young men in coloured shirts."

"Oh . . . I only meant . . . don't you remember, before you went away, you said Sweden was the only place where people weren't making fools of themselves wearing coloured shirts?"

" Did I ? "

Silence. Miserably in her mind she finished the sentence for him "—but then, I said so many things before I went away." She seemed to hear the words sounding hard and ominous in the embarrassed silence.

" Bell, your bath *must* be ready ; off you go, and you too, Queenie. I'm sorry to turn you two young women out, but I've got to change."

Still smiling, he shepherded them out. His door closed. Bell went singing to her bath and Queenie walked downstairs and straight out into the garden. A huge lump ached in her throat but she was too angry to cry.

Real rage, a choking rush of blood to her heart and brain, had almost driven away her misery.

While George was away he had been slowly growing as remote to her as a young god, and she had felt more and more humble with each letterless day. She had crawled about, flayed with misery and humble jealousy of unknown rivals. But now he had come home and she had seen him, he had suddenly become a man again ; one whom she had seen in some undignified and funny, if lovable, circumstances. One literally cannot grovel before a young man whom one has seen wearing nothing but a shirt, although one could easily grovel before a young man whom one had only seen naked.

She felt about him once more as a wife sometimes feels ; he was an irritating, lovable joke. She would have liked to box his ears and then kiss him tenderly and laugh all the unhappiness away.

So she walked round the garden fighting the hysterical aching lump in her throat and whipping her good rage to a mood which should last all the evening.

She went in to tea with a flush and sparkling eyes

and when she spoke her voice rang. It had lost its murmuring drowsy love-sound. She did not speak loudly nor irritably but the ring was there; Mrs. Shelling told the children three times that they looked very well, and added kindly that Miss Catton looked well also. Only Albert, said Mrs. Shelling, looked pale. Was he tired, poor boy? Perhaps he felt the heat?

Albert was pale because he had had a brief but frightful quarrel with Bell in the nursery. She found him there before dinner; he had hidden himself, and was writing to his father. He at once tried to kiss her. She permitted this, but while in his arms murmured that in Sweden she had yielded to the supplications of a Turk who was staying in their *pension.*

"Jesu-Maria!" cried poor Albert, flinging her from him like a snake. "But no—" hastily—"I do not believe it! Oh, *Isabella,* and I shall never know whether it is true! You are . . . a virginal wicked bitch!"

Bell crowed with delighted laughter (she was practically uninsultable except by George, who knew where to flick her feelings) but became very angry when the tortured Albert tried to kiss her with indelicate violence. They struggled, whispering angrily, for a few seconds and at last she broke away from him and ran to her room. She too came down to dinner flushed under her tan, stimulated and sparkling, and malicious, offsetting Albert's pallor and sulks. The air of the dining-room crackled with ugly under-currents of feeling, and Mrs. Shelling sat dispensing salmon and smiling because her flock was so flushed, vivacious and talkative.

George could see that Queenie was in a rage. He seemed glad. He talked at her, arguing, looking straight into her eyes with mockery and hardness in his own. He ceased to feel guilty when he could feel angry with her;

K

and she was so impertinent and dogmatic, and contra-
dicted him so often with such an ill-bred coquetry that
his anger (a stranger to them both would have sworn)
was justified.

After dinner he was in excellent form.  He imitated
Bell's Turk and the marvellous Pretyman, good-naturedly
brought a sheaf of postcards and souvenirs down to
show his mother, and traced their wanderings on
a map for Albert (who was not interested but who liked
sitting in a position whence he could peep down Bell's
neck and smell her scent).

Queenie, silent at last, sat apart.

She was still burning with rage but under the rage
the awful misery was beginning to creep back.  She
knew what would happen ; it had happened to her
before, over more trivial pains and shocks.  She would
go to sleep in a state of hard calm grief which numbed
the pain ; and then she would suddenly awake, a few
hours later, and lie drowned, annihilated with anguish
which made her body ache as though it had been beaten,
and she would cry for an hour or more until the waves
of pain ebbed, and she fell asleep.

Her burning wish was to talk to George alone ; to
have matters out with him.  She knew he loathed having
matters out ; he would never talk about anything, but
he was going (she swore sullenly to herself) to talk
about this.

So when everybody began to trail up to bed about
eleven, she deliberately, under the surprised glance of
Mrs. Shelling, stopped a moment behind the others and
stood by George's side where he was winding the
hall clock.

"I've got to talk to you," she said in a low voice.
"When can I see you ? "

"I'll take you for a drive to-morrow evening. I want to talk as much as you do. You don't suppose I'm *enjoying* this, do you?"

He looked so fine-drawn under his sunburn and so nervous and wretched as he spoke, that she felt impersonal pity for him. He can't help it, she thought. He didn't *want* to stop loving me, I suppose. . . .

"All right. Good-night."

But he did not answer.

A secret, so sad that it was almost terrible, trembled between them; it floated from her eyes to his as she stood looking up at him. He had said, before he went away, that on the first night of his return he would come to her room; and every night for a month she had gone to sleep imagining his arms wrapped round her, his whispers of tenderness falling mysteriously out of the darkness and silence and the soft strong pressure of his mouth; and he, too, had imagined this first night of his return and longed for her softness and tender silence.

They looked at one another for a few seconds in miserable silence, until neither could bear the look in the other's eyes; and then she turned away and went upstairs alone.

. . . . . . .

When the engine of the car stopped, silence came. It was nearly dark and the wood was brimmed with soft twilight, warm, dark-rosy, suiting the leaves darkened by days of sunlight. The trees looked greenish-black in this light, deep and still, with not a leaf moving, and the trunks were only a darker grey. There were no sounds. Snow sounds, May sounds, both were over and the earth seemed too near harvest and too exhausted to make autumnal sighings.

He had driven in silence and she had not spoken. She was not thinking about anything, only wishing, as she had wished once before on a night in May, that there was no need for them ever to speak. She felt so sorry for him.

They sat quietly for a little while, she looking down at her hands, and he staring heavily into the calm darkening glades of the wood.

At last he said :

" There isn't anything to say, except that I'm sorry, and I feel such a swine."

" That's all right," she said faintly. " What is it ? What's happened ? Is it just that you don't love me any more ? "

After a long pause—

" I'm afraid so. I was afraid this would happen, Queenie. You remember . . . I *did* tell you, didn't I ? that it might. You see I know myself so well. I did love you more than I've ever loved anyone, and then you were so different; you didn't pretend to love me at once, like all the others did, and it was all so new, and I wanted the experience . . . I wanted so much to be in love. And I was . . . I loved you very much. You do believe that, don't you ? "

" I *can't*," she said, her voice and mouth beginning to tremble. " I can't believe you did—if you can stop so suddenly, without any reason, like this. How *can* you ? If one *really* loves someone, one can't stop like this, just in a month. Are you *sure* you don't, George ? You get these awful dead moods you know, don't you ? Are you sure it isn't just that I'm getting on your nerves for the time being ? Let's leave things for a bit, and perhaps they'll get right. I can feel I'm getting on your nerves. I'll try not to."

She stopped and put her hand up to her throat, swallowing angrily.

" Is it anything I've *done* ? "

" Oh, heavens, no," he said, moving impatiently. " It isn't you at all. It's just me. I can't help it. God ! you don't think I *want* to feel like this, do you, when I remember. . . ."

" *Don't !* "

" I feel such a swine."

A wretched silence fell. She said at last, crying openly, the tears running down her face :

" Is there anyone else ? "

" No . . . nor likely to be. The fact is . . . I don't think I need love very much. I want it, or did want it, because I'd never had it and I felt I was missing something wonderful, a marvellous experience that other people had and I hadn't. But I don't really *need* it. I can get along without it ; I'm not like you."

" You said once . . . You seemed to think we might marry . . . later on."

" That was when I loved you. That was quite true, Queenie ; I did seriously think about marrying you at one time. But I can see now, it would never have done."

" It might have, if only we'd been together for long enough and really got to know each other. People do change. . . ."

" There you are—that's just it ! You want me to *change*. You want to make me into your kind of person, not let me stay as I am. I *always* felt that ; you wanted me to change, and settle down and give up my freedom, and marry you."

" How could I help that, after the things you said— all the things you said ? " She was rocking herself to and fro, crying bitterly.

"Queenie, dear one, don't. I'm so sorry. I feel such an utter swine. Don't cry. We can still be friends. I want to be. We've enjoyed so many things together, music and poetry and the country, and I should miss you so much if I lost you as a friend. Please don't cry, my very dear one."

"I can't be friends with you. How can I?"

She sat up, drying her eyes, and turned to look at his unhappy face in the twilight; it looked so young, so lost in shame and embarrassment that she smiled through her tears and put out her hand—

"Poor George! Such a fuss, isn't it?"

He took the hand and held it, covering it with his own in the old way.

"You are a brick. No one but you would have said that. I believe I do love you a little, still, you know. I've got the most tremendous respect for you, anyway."

"You'll have more before the battle's over," she said, the ring coming back into her voice.

"Why? That sounds very alarming?"

"Because," vigorously, "I'm not going to let you go. I believe you do still love me, only you think you don't. It's just a mood, that's all, and I won't let it part us. I bet you'll be back in a week!"

"You'll lose your money," he said a little angrily. The arrogance, the sudden vitality in her voice, irritated him. "I don't like women who try to get men back; I like to do my own pursuing, thanks."

"I shan't pursue you," she said steadily, though she writhed at his tone. "I'm just not going to give up, that's all, when I *know* its best for both of us that we go on. You admit we're friends. Well, friendship is the best basis for marriage."

"Thanks, I don't want to marry Bell or Bertie, and they're my most intimate friends. I shall want something else, when I marry."

"What?"

"I don't know yet. But as I don't intend to marry anyone for quite ten years, it doesn't matter much. I've got plenty of time to find out."

Silence fell again. His mood had changed and he was angry and his nerves were jarred. She was on the crest of a wave of hysterical confidence; she felt almost happy. It was to be a fight! and she loved a fight. She felt as though, in some strange way, he and she were allies and enemies too. I *will* get him back, she thought. He's like a child; he only wants managing.

But he was not like a child at all; he was a very nervous, complex and over-civilized young man, moody as a cat, knowing next to nothing about his own deeper motives, living by impulse and by a daily ritual which soothed his nerves and which his deepest instincts were against breaking. Work—music—Bell—Bassett. This was the pattern. It was a net, too, and a drug, and a frame—it was everything from which escape is difficult, and trebly difficult when the prisoner wants to stay in prison.

He moved back in his seat, at last, and said to the silent figure at his side:

"We'd better be getting back, I think."

"Yes. It would never do to be mixed up in a scandal, would it?"

The wood was dark; a rather sad, starless night had come. As they drove silently home through it he said suddenly:

"I've got that line of Shelley's going round and

round in my head ' I could lie down like a tired child '—
you remember."

Silently she slipped her hand through his arm, and
drew closer to him. She leant her head against his
shoulder, and closed her eyes against the beam of white
light thrown out on the road. He was comforted by
the kind pressure of the little hand and, with his friend
by his side, forgot love and drove less unhappily through
the night.

Most of the charm of a forlorn hope lies in the fact
that it succeeds; if it fails, it was merely forlorn, and
does not merit admiration.

Bell could have told Queenie just how forlorn her
hope was, but Bell was scarcely interested in the Queenie
affair any more; it was going so well, and so according
to plan and so true to type, that it might be left to destroy
itself. Bell hoped George would not mope and feel
guilty after Queenie had gone, but beyond this and
beyond sardonically observing how Queenie murdered
what chances she had, Bell took little interest in the last
stages of the boring business.

Albert saw: the prawnish eyes of Albert sorrowfully
observed, for three hellish days, Queenie growing
steadily brighter and more archly irritating, and George
growing more nervous, more furiously jealous of his
privacies and his attitude to life, and less and less likely
to want Queenie back. But Albert said nothing. He
was more sensitive and kind than he seemed to be, and
he knew how Queenie would suffer if he advised her to
change her tactics, and ask Mrs. Shelling if she might
take her fortnight's holiday now, instead of in October.
Besides—tactics! When lovers (thought Albert despondently) adopt tactics towards one another, the charm
of love has gone. He had been forced to adopt tactics

ever since he was fourteen, because he was so plain. Hence his yearning for candour, spontaneity, a fresh bloom in love.

And Bertie Barranger, who came down one evening to dinner and to stay the night, saw the battle too. He had seen many such battles between George and girls but none had made him feel as this one did.

George, who loved music and silence, for three days seemed to hear nothing but Queenie discussing music, clearly and amateurishly. He was told at dinner, that he did not know his own mind ("That is quite true, Miss Catton. Now what do you say to *that*, George ? " cried Mrs. Shelling). He was what the older school of novelists call " unmercifully chaffed " in a high, impertinent little voice which he resented more angrily because he heard behind its shrillness the fear and love which he had brought into its owner's heart. He was constantly besought, with increasing hysteria and terror, to join in a game which was beginning to bore and disgust him.

It was no use. He would have to stop her. The pathos and embarrassment were beginning to rub his nerves ; he was already feeling less well than when he came back from Sweden, and this infuriated him : he was not strong at any time, and he had hoped that Sweden and a quiet autumn would keep him free from nervous attacks through the winter.

But this guilty feeling, mixed with irritation and embarrassment and pity—it was hell. It rasped his nerves like a torn fingernail on silk. The muscles round his eyes were beginning to contract, as they always did when he was tired and worried, and his eyes felt as though they were set in hot caves. He felt taut, unrelaxed, and all this was Queenie's fault. Curious ways women had of loving one !

K*

So on the third morning, when she came up to him in the hall after breakfast as he was getting ready to leave for London, and said in a low mischievous voice: "Are love's labours going to be lost George?" he turned on her suddenly and said loudly and very brutally, "Oh, for god's sake shut up!" and turning away, went quickly out to the car.

She started back as though she had been hit. Her look, her parted lips and the quick, warding-off movement of her hand, stayed in his memory all day: and indeed, for some years afterwards. As it happened, it was the last thing he said to her and the last time he ever saw her.

She went into the morning-room, and closed the door.

She heard the car start, and go rapidly down the drive, and the sound of the engine die into the still morning. Leaves were falling calmly from the tall aspens outside the window, golden leaves spinning lightly on the windless air.

She sat down at the table and put her head on her arms and remained still. She knew that she ought to go upstairs at once to find Mrs. Shelling, who wanted her to help check linen, but she could not move. She could not. His look, the words, the tone, went grinding on in her mind and in her memory's eyes and she knew that she had lost the battle; he would never come back to her. Never. Never. She said the word, but it meant nothing.

Extreme pain made her silent, she could not even cry. She rolled her head a little from side to side and made a faint moaning sound, but she could not cry. Then she stayed quiet for a long time, clenching her hands as memory broke over her in awful waves; long, relentless waves of splendid memories, receding in beauty and tenderness, remorselessly withdrawing and leaving agony.

Eleven o'clock struck : and a few moments later the door opened very quietly. Someone crossed the room to her side, and stood there ; a hand was laid gently upon her shoulder. It made a little patting movement, timid yet tender, and she looked up, in a second's wild hope.

Mrs. Shelling stood there.

She said, looking sorrowfully down at Queenie :

" My dear, I think it will be happier for all of us if you go home to-day. I do not mean to be unkind ; stay if you wish, but I think you must see that it can only end in a great unhappiness for you. I do not know what has happened, and I do not ask you to tell me, but I think you had best go. Really, my dear child, my poor girl, I think you had better go to-day."

Queenie said, after a little pause :

" You're quite right, of course. I . . . yes, I will. I'm so sorry . . . so sorry. . . ." Her voice began to break and flutter oddly ; she strained her head away from Mrs. Shelling's glance, closing her eyes.

" Now, now, my dear. It is bad, but it will pass. All things pass. I am old, and I say so ; you are so young (one feels so bad, when one is so young as you) and so you do not believe me, but it is true. All this unhappiness, it will go away. Now I think you should go and pack your box, and I will perhaps telephone your parents that you are coming, yes ? I have sent Isabella to Reading in the little car to buy new plants for the greenhouse, so she will not know you are going. . . ."

" Thank you,"—a whisper.

" . . . and I will say good-bye to her for you, and to Albert. Poor Albert, he will be so sorry; always he is telling me how fond he is of you and how good you are. Now you go to pack your box, like a good child. We will see to everything, yes."

And when she had once been dismissed, she wanted above all other things to go: it was the only desirable thing left in the world, to creep back to her family, who loved her, and stay quietly with them, lying still until this terrible wound should get better. Suddenly she longed to be gone; she wanted to rush out of the house that very instant.

She followed Mrs. Shelling out of the room, pressing her fingers to her head because she found it difficult to think properly; and packed her little trunk and her suitcase in half an hour. Mrs. Shelling, watching her a little uneasily as she packed quickly and in silence, came in and out of the room, once to promise her references, once to give her a starkly white envelope, with a cheque in it, and once to look at the little trunk and murmur that she would have it sent off by an afternoon train as soon as the car came back from Reading.

" And I have told your mother," she said, sitting on the bed and looking sadly at Queenie, " that I am sending you back for your holiday now, because you are a little run down. She seemed quite to understand, your mother, and is so pleased to hear you are coming to-day, and she said ' Give her my love, bless her. I will soon take care of her. . . .' Then, you see, you just need not come back."

Queenie drew another queer little fluttering breath; it gave her a strange frightening feeling; it was like having a living bird inside her breast. This must be sobbing, she thought.

"So that is well," said Mrs. Shelling. "Is your case heavy? Not so—I can lift it easily. Now, my dear child, there is a train at half-past one. I think it best that you catch the twelve o'clock 'bus and go now. I have made a little lunch for you," she held out a neat packet, "so you will not be hungry. So. Now, good-bye. I seem unkind. Perhaps you think that I should say to you, stay, and perhaps all will come right in the end. But I do not say so, because I am sure, I know in my heart, that all will not come right in the end unless you go away, and never come to Bassett again."

Never come to Bassett again.

"Yes, I want to go. Thank you very much for being . . . for being so kind. I'm sorry—you know—I'm so sorry because I—because I——"

"Sh—sh. There. Now try not to cry any more. Hush. Be quiet a minute, and try to stop crying, because you must go in the bus and you will not want all those common people to see that you are unhappy. Now good-bye."

They had stopped at the hall door, which was open to the lovely cool morning. The house was quiet.

Mrs. Shelling kissed Queenie, and gave her a gentle push, as if to start her on a journey which she had not strength to begin of her own will. Queenie muttered "Thank you" again, and went slowly across the terrace and down the three steps. But she began to move more quickly, and soon, very soon, she was out of sight. She vanished round the curve of the drive, walking rapidly between the fading trees.

.        .        .        .        .        .

Mrs. Shelling, fifteen minutes later, went irritably to the telephone.

"This is Bassett 7. Ach, it is you, Bertie. Now what do you want? You know well that it is George's day to go to town with Albert, and Isabella has gone into Reading. What is it?"

"Oh, I say, I'm fearfully sorry—I just wanted to speak to Miss Catton, if it's not too much trouble or anything."

"Miss Catton has left us."

"Left? Oh, I say. Not for good I hope?"

"Certainly for good."

"Oh, well, look here, would you awfully mind giving me her address and 'phone number if she's got one?"

"I will get it. Stay there, Bertie."

Bertie stayed, and in a moment Mrs. Shelling came back with her address-book and told him what he wanted to know.

"Thanks most awfully, Mrs. Shelling. Awfully sorry to have bothered you. The fact is, I've got the use of a Press pass for the Proms: and I wondered if she'd care to come one evening when she was up seeing her people. That's all. Now she's left, it'll be easier for her to come, perhaps. I say, are you quite fit and all that? I do hope you had a good holiday?"

"I am very well, thank you. How is your poor father?"

"Oh, fit as a flea—I mean, flourishing, thanks. Well, I must blow off and do a spot of daily-breading. Good-bye, and thanks awfully."

"Will you leave a message for the children?"

She thought that he had heard, but the answer was the click of the receiver.

Mrs. Shelling's expression was a little less troubled as

she put back her own receiver.   She disliked Bertie, but she, like old Mr. Barranger, was an old-fashioned person, and she could not give the address of a young girl to a young man without a feeling of satisfaction.

# CHAPTER XXIII

QUEENIE got home at three o'clock, the most languid hour of the day and the saddest. Her journey had passed in a daze. She remembered standing up in the bus to try and see, above the hedge and the fields between, the shape of the big holly under which he and she had met on that happy morning, but she could not distinguish it; a woman rose to get out of the bus, and when she had pushed past Queenie, the bus started again and the chance had gone.

The train was almost empty. She got a carriage to herself and surrendered to crying. All the way to London she cried, now hysterically, now quietly, now in sobbing gasps, now with ugly moaning sounds. She felt the movement of the train, carrying her away from Bassett, as though the train were alive, a wicked animal or a demon. She seemed to be straining backwards, trying to resist the forward rush of the train; she could feel the miles being put between herself and the place she loved, and it was agony to her. She felt helpless, a tiny object in the arms of a mighty monster.

London smelt of stale air, breathed and breathed again. Millions of roofs, as far as the horizon on either side, huddled under the sad hot sky, pale with lifeless heat. It looked filthy, hideous, hopeless. She opened her purse and saw that she had plenty of money, by Islington's standards, apart from Mrs. Shelling's cheque, so she took a taxi. It would only cost about six shillings at the

very most and she felt too sick and exhausted with
crying to face the Tube or the bus. It was extravagant,
of course, but she did so long for solitude and coolness.
It would be her last extravagance in the Shelling manner.

There was no one at home, except the tiny maid
Cissie. Mr. Catton was down at St. Saviour's Hospital;
it was his clinic day. Mrs. Catton was out at a meeting.
There was a note for Miss Queen. Cissie saw Miss
Queen turn aside while she read the note, and missed
nothing of her swollen face and red eyes and her faint
tired voice, and wondered passionately what was up,
but she also felt sorry.

She admired Miss Queen, whose attic bedroom was
next to her own, who spoke so clear and pretty. She
and Miss Queen kept up a pretence that neither noticed
the other's shabby nightgowns. They ignored the
noises each made in her bedroom. There was just
five years' difference between them. Cissie never
thought about any of these things; she just liked
Miss Queen and burned to know what was up.

DEARIE,
I've had to go to a meeting this afternoon but will
be back about 6.30. Have a good tea; there's an
egg if you're hungry. Bless you, love.
MUMMY.

"All right, Cissie. How are you? How's your
sister?"

"All right thank you Miss Queen. 'Asn't it been
hot. Was it hot where you was?"

"Awful. Too hot to breathe."

She went slowly upstairs.

Her room smelled of stale sunlight and dust, but
the window was open, and someone had put a bunch

of marigolds on her dressing table—that was probably Mummy. She felt ashamed of herself suddenly; Mummy was so kind, so fond of her, and she did so little !

She went to the window and drew the curtains against the afternoon sun. Roofs and pigeons again ! There were the acres of old roofs and humble attic windows like her own, and the pigeons kept by the policeman in Pelier Street going up in a cloud, as usual, from his flat roof. There, miles away on the horizon, were the heights and trees of Highgate.

She drew the curtains, and in the hot dusk, began to unpack.

While she had things to do, she could fend off thought and pain.

She put her things away carefully, setting aside in two heaps (as Mrs. Shelling used to do) those which must be washed and those which must be mended, put her few clean clothes away in the empty drawers, took out her books from their box under the bed, and put them back on their shelf, went downstairs and fetched a duster and a broom and pan and swept the room out, clipped the stems of the marigolds and was going to arrange them less stiffly but remembered that her mother had put them so, and let them stay.

But at last all these things were done and still it was only four o'clock.

Only four o'clock, and the sun still riding high and the pain was beginning to sweep back and the tears were coming and the frightening fluttering in her breast. Biting her lip, she sat down at her little table, and resolutely drew towards her a German grammar. She had begun to learn German, while George was away, with Albert's help, and she thought she would go on

with it and work very hard; it would keep the misery
at bay to use her brain.

She sat upright, her chin sunk in her cupped hands,
reading by the blinding rays which crept through the
swaying curtains and pierced the hot twilight. She read,
but saw nothing. Still she sat there, fighting with agony,
biting her lip and forcing the thoughts back.

It's only six hours since I saw him. Only six hours,
and I feel like this! I shall never be able to stand
months of it—perhaps years—no one could—something
will break. I don't believe anyone *could* go on feeling
like this—and loving so much—and knowing I shall
*never*, I shall *never*, be with him again. I can't—I can't.
I must write or telephone—I can't *live* like this. It's
frightful—think of days, weeks, months of it, this awful
endless pain. I know the days he comes up to town,
and what he does when he's at home, every hour of the
day. How can I ever get better? How can I ever forget
or be cured?

Shivering, she sat with her head in her hands, her
eyes closed. Half-past four struck somewhere. The
fierce sun still beat on the roofs, the streets far below
hummed and shuddered with noise.

She repeated grammatical rules to herself, over and
over again, trying to drive them into her head, fighting
the pain with them, but the pain won.

I haven't *done* anything to deserve this. I did nothing.
I only loved him—and he made me. I didn't love him
at first; he made me. I don't hate him or feel bitter.
I can't. But *why*, *why* make me love him and then—
suddenly—everything gone—as though nothing had
been, and nothing left. He *must* feel sorry; perhaps
he'll write or telephone to-night, Mrs. Shelling's got the
number. Perhaps he'll come . . .

But she knew that he would not come.

The fit of passion passed, and she slowly lifted her face from her clenched hands; they ached, and her eyes stung with crying. It was half-past five; in an hour her mother would come, and she must answer questions—but not so many as in most families, thank goodness, because her family was too wrapped up in its own affairs to be very inquisitive or to suspect horrors where none were. But there was horror enough; months of pain to come.

She dipped a handkerchief in the water jug and slowly bathed her eyes and went languidly back to the table and her books.

I *must* get some work of some kind. Real work, not just running away from ugliness or work to earn money; I want to work to help people. I *must* help people. I've always wanted to, and now I'm quite alone, everything gone, and I can. It won't be the best kind of helping, because it will be partly to stop me feeling so ghastly, but perhaps that doesn't matter, so long as the people are helped. I might do that social service course mother wanted me to, if they can afford it. And *really* work. I shall suffocate or die if I can't get all this feeling away from me, and make it into work. I'll try to talk to them about starting a course, to-morrow . . . oh love, my love, how can I ever forget you, and the little may trees, and that night by the river?

She heard steps coming up the stairs.

" Mummy ? " she called, and got up.

There was a tap at the door.

" Dearie—are you there ? "

She opened the door. Her mother stood there, thin, shabby, looking at her anxiously but seeing little, for all her keen look.

" Well, my lovey, what's the matter with you ? Want a holiday ? " With a blessed sense of peace and familiarity she kissed her mother, and drew a little fluttering breath.

" I'm all right, darling. Only very tired : I want some iron, I think, and I hate this awful heat. I don't think I—think I shall go back——"

She stopped, and went on quickly :

" Go back there. It's all right. Don't worry, will you ? "

" I don't worry, dear, if you're really only tired. I'm so glad to have you back. It isn't like home without you. We'll have a nice autumn, won't we ? "

There was a pause, in which she looked lovingly, timidly at her daughter. They were good friends because she had learned never to ask her children questions. Then her face changed :

" Queen—I'm so sorry to bother you when you're feeling seedy—but could you give a hand with supper ? Ger wants hers sharp at seven—it's her choir evening— and Cissie's out."

" Of course, Mummy. I'll come now."

She went over to the window and pulled the curtains back. The royal light rushed in, gold, triumphant ; the pigeons went up in a fluttering cloud.

" There's a breeze now . . . lovely."

They went downstairs together, and as they reached the landing Queenie said steadily, " I'm glad to be home."

.        .        .        .        .        .        .

George could not sleep that night. He came home to find his mother shut in her room ; she had left a message that he was to go to her immediately he got back. Bell knew nothing, except that Queenie had gone during her absence in Reading, and Ma was livid

furious, angrier than Bell ever remembered seeing her.
And she had been crying.

George went straight to his mother. He hardly
believed Bell's tale; if it was true, Queenie must have
been sneaking to his mother. · But that was impossible :
he knew her, she would never sneak or complain.
You might half-murder her; she would stay loyal.
No; Ma must have guessed.

He never forgot that row, which lasted all the evening,
without pause for dinner, until after eleven at night.
He had never seen his mother really angry. Now the
miserable affair with Queenie had brought her
smouldering anger with him into the open, and he saw
her furious, white and choked with sobbing, ashamed
and terribly lonely, with every tender feeling and
honourable instinct which she possessed stained and
hurt.

Old grievances of resented selfishness and callousness
were thrown up in her storm of anger. He heard how
useless he was as a son, how casual, how vilely rude and
cold, how he and Bell were like strangers in the house
who were only polite to their mother when it suited
their convenience; shutting her out from their lives as
though they hated her.

She would not listen to him when he grew as angry
as she was and flung on her the blame for his elegant
empty life; - the black agonizing discontent which
sometimes made him suicidal came boiling to the surface
of his spirit and he rounded on his mother in cold fury.
She chained him to the cursed factory; his life was
mapped until the day he died, he had never had a normal
youth nor known real freedom of choice. If she was
disappointed in him, it was her fault.

He would not answer her accusations about Queenie :

he felt too guilty and miserable. When he heard of her sobbing and packing her poor little possessions he felt as though he had hit a child in anger; he was sick with shame. She had gone; he would never see her again, and they had so loved each other: their love had been like a May morning. He longed for her to be there, to take his part and make him feel safe again.

But deeper than his rage with his mother and deeper than his shame when he thought of Queenie, was another instinct, the strongest in his nature. It was an instinct to end this scene, to stop having violent feelings, and to retreat into his inner life, where he protected himself from the assaults of reality.

He could not stand reality: he was not strong enough. When violent love or violent feelings of any kind came near him, he was afraid, because he knew his body and spirit were weak. So he shrank from anger as he had shrunk from Queenie's full, warm love: he could not meet it and embrace it; his job was to hoard his vitality, and get himself safely through life.

It was unfortunate that much charm of personality and beauty of body should be allied to this secret weakness, but that was not George's fault. When he said to an unhappy girl, as he had so often said—" I can't help it; that's the way I'm made," he spoke the truth.

That was the way he was made, and he could not help it.

The passions can drive men down to the water of life, but sometimes the passions cannot make them drink. An older, colder passion holds them back, and will not let them take a full draught of the life-water: the passion of self-preservation.

So George suddenly thought about eleven o'clock " God, I can't stand another second of this. It bores

me—god, how it bores me," and said "I can't stick
any more of this, Ma ; I'm sorry. Good-night." He
lingered for a second or two, but his mother said nothing ;
she was sitting huddled in her chair, leaning forward
and staring into the fire. She looked an old woman,
and a pitiful one, but George could feel no more that
night : he was too tired. Without another glance
at her, he went out of the room, closing the door behind
him.

But he could not sleep.

Sad dim golden moonlight, spread by a huge waning
moon which was going down behind the elms, beat
against the curtains of his room and disturbed him ;
the smell of the turning year floated in from the fields
through the window. There was a feeling of sadness
in the night, and loneliness. He lay with his eyes closed,
on his side, but could not sleep. His brain was bruised
with too many thoughts, and his nerves with too much
feeling.

One o'clock struck. Angrily he flung himself up,
put on a dressing-gown, and went along to Bell's
room. He tapped at the door and half-opened it.

"Hullo—are you awake ? "

"Oh it's you—I thought you'd probably come.
Well, was it very awful ? What hours and hours you
were at it ! "

Already soothed by the soft voice coming out of
the room sunk in dim moon-twilight, he went over
to the bed, sat on the foot and put up his legs, with a
sigh, and leaned his back comfortably against the rail.
Silence fell.

Gradually he could make out the shape of his sister,
lying very straight and still to the extreme left of the
bed, in order to make room for his legs and feet. A

thick dark line went up from the top of her head across
the pillow and over its edge : that was her nightly pigtail.
The clothes were drawn up to her chin.

" You look like a crusader."

" How original of me. What was it all about ?
Poor lamb, you must be starving. We waited dinner
half-an-hour, only Albert got so hungry he retched,
so I thought we'd better have it. He is disgusting.
Fancy retching with hunger ! "

" I'm not hungry, thanks. I'm too tired. Oh . . .
it was about you and me and how awful we are and
how rude and how we treat Ma like a stranger and all
the rest of it. The old stuff, only more so. And she
seems very upset about Queenie . . ."

Silence again.

" Bell, are you *sure* Queenie didn't say anything before
she went—didn't you see her *at all* before you went into
Reading ? "

" My dear, I told you I never saw her. I came
back to lunch at half-past one as usual, and Ma simply
said she'd gone. I wish I had seen her. It's all most
mysterious. Oh !—*George*—you don't think . . . ? "

" Good god, no ; I'm not that particular sort of
a fool," he said roughly. " Besides Ma would have
told me. Bound to, if there'd been anything like that."

" That's all right, then."

Silence.

" But it isn't all right," he said slowly, at last. " I
feel very bad about Queenie, Ding-Dong. I wish
there was something we could do. . . . I ought to
write, or 'phone or something. Don't you think
so ? I can't bear to think of her so miserable ; and
going back to that awful family, and I never said good-bye
to her . . ."

" Write if you like, but I don't advise you to. It'll only start the whole thing all over again. She won't have stopped being in love with you, my good boy, in twelve hours. You feel sorry now, because Ma's been at you and you're tired out, and the last thing you heard of her was how she was crying, and all the rest of it (I expect Ma piled it on anyway). But, honestly, now didn't you find her a bit irritating, these last three days ? "

" She was miserable. People often are irritating when they're unhappy."

" Well, you don't like miserable females, do you ? If you write or 'phone, George, you'll just start the whole business over again. Believe me, you will. She won't be content with anything except *marriage*. She's the type. Do you *want* to marry her ? "

" I . . . don't . . . believe . . . I really want to marry anybody, ever. Not for years and years, anyway."

" I'm very sure I don't. I have too good a time as I am. It would be awful if either of us married ; it would spoil everything. You know how amusing it was in Sweden, just the two of us. Well, there's no reason why we shouldn't do that for the rest of our lives, if you like. Only if you keep on getting entangled with serious hags who want to marry you, we can't, can we ? Sleep around as much as you like, of course . . ."

" I don't seem to care about sleeping around as much as most males do."

" All the better ; don't sleep around, then. I can't see much fun in it, myself : I intend to preserve my virginity for good. It doesn't worry me the way it seems to worry most people. But we'll have lots of fun. Think how many years we've got to be amused in, and listen to music, and go for country walks ! "

" And in the end," said George, staring as if hypnotized at the dark blur of her head and shoulders against the dim pillow, " what'll happen to us in the end ? Worms will eat us."

" They'll eat everybody. Besides, they won't eat me because I shall be cremated. So sucks to the worms."

" And after the worms ? " he persisted. It gave him a strange pleasure to put aweful questions to the dark head on the pillow, and be lightly, mockingly reassured ; it was like consulting an obedient oracle.

" Endlessly hearing Beethoven quartets on a summer evening, under a may tree ! "

" That's your idea of heaven, is it ? And what's your idea of hell ? "

" Being married to Albert," she said without hesitation.

They both laughed. George felt better ; his limbs were relaxed and he had yawned once or twice. In the valley, where the elm leaves fell slowly in the windless darkness, the clock in Bassett church struck the quarter. The broad ghostly moon was almost sunk behind the hills.

" I must go and get some sleep. Well, thanks for the buggy-ride : you've cheered me up. 'Praps you're right about Queenie, too. Poor Queenie ! I still feel a swine, but I think it would be kindest to let things go on as they are."

" I'm sure it would. Like me to come and tuck you up ? "

" I can tuck myself up, thanks. Good-night."

He bent over her as she lay there still and slender, and dropped one of his light, rare kisses on her nose.

"Bless you. Good-night."

He went, closing her door carefully.

She lay still for a few moments, smiling in the tender, moon-haunted dusk. Who could have dreamed, four months ago, that the whole affair would end so calmly and so easily?

All done by patience, by holding one's hand, by demonstrating how pleasantly a sister could make the time pass in Sweden, by never showing jealousy, by never making a brother, nervous to the point of disease, realise his own delicacy and the extent to which he relied upon oneself. . . .

Slowly, with relaxed easy muscles, she turned upon her side, slid a long arm under the pillow, and closed her eyes. She opened them once, a few moments later, and saw behind the thin summer curtains the broad half-shield of the moon, strangely lonely and ghastly, dropping, falling in seas of misty light behind the hills.

The church clock in the valley chimed the half-hour, but Bell was asleep, and did not hear.

.        .        .        .        .

Two years later, in the month of May, Miss Padsoe's cousin from Newcastle made a long-discussed tour of the south of England by car, accompanied by her son: and shortly after her return to Newcastle, called upon an intimate friend to drink tea and discuss her visit.

"And of course you saw Eleanor?"

"Poor Eleanor! Yes, of course I did. Bassett was one of the first places we went to, wasn't it, Dennis?"

"Is it a pretty place?"

"Oh, *very* pretty; quite charming. Very secluded, of course; not much going on there, I should say, but the duckiest place. Oh, we quite fell in love with Bassett, didn't we, Dennis?"

" Oh rather, mater. Ripping place."

" One of the prettiest things we saw there were the dwarf may trees; quite fifty of them, I should say, shouldn't you, Dennis—all growing up a big hill. Quite a sight it was, really. I did so wish I had had a film in the camera, but we had just run out, that very morning."

" And how was Eleanor ? "

" Oh, very well. Very well indeed. Yes, I must say the whole unfortunate business has turned out not *quite* so badly as one might have expected. Of course it is *bad enough.* When I think of what poor Uncle Edward would say to The Tower being turned into a boarding house (for *really*, that *is* what it is, isn't it, Dennis ?)—well! But I must say *Eleanor* looks well enough on it."

" But surely they cannot make it *pay* ? "

" Well, apparently they *do.* They have six boarders (doesn't it sound dreadful!) now, you know; four part-time students at Reading University, and two Indians. Research students, I believe they are called."

" *Indians ? Blacks ? * "

" Well, they are very high-caste, of course. Not like negroes, were they, Dennis ? "

" Oh, I don't know, mater. They were a bit thick, I thought. Bounders. Always grinning at nothing and trying to get you to play tennis. So likely ! "

" But they seem to pay quite well. The Tower looks most flourishing; and they have had the tennis-court laid out again."

" And the little creature—Miss Baker ? Did you see her at all ? What is she like ? "

" Oh, my dear—too dreadful ! You will hardly believe it . . . we got there about tea time (Dennis was driving) and the first thing we saw was the *Indians* rolling the lawn in the front garden and laughing all the time at nothing, that I could see. The hall door was *wide* open; and when I rang the bell (I had to ring it twice) up bounded a fat, dark, vulgar little woman with a slice of bread and jam in one hand, and her mouth full. I looked at her. Very quietly. I just *looked* at her for perhaps half a minute, and then I said, quite politely " Is Miss Padsoe at home ? I am her cousin, Mrs. Elmslie, from Newcastle." And then, my dear, the little creature bounced to the foot of the staircase, and she called up the stairs with her mouth full ' Nellie ! Where are you, Nell ? There's someone to see you.' ' Nell,' indeed ! Did you ever hear of such a thing ! "

**THE END**